The Outer Edge of Heaven

A Love Story

What readers are saying about Jaclyn's books

"Jaclyn Hawkes' book has a touch of humor that will appeal to many readers." Jennie Hansen-Meridian Magazine

"Hard to put down." Squeaky Clean Reads.

" A romantic romp. Exactly the type of book to read in a bubble bath." Marsha Ward

"I recommend her book to anyone who roots for the good guy, cries for the injured, and wants to see love conquer all." Cheryl Christensen-A Good Day to Read

"The romantic tension between her characters was riveting." Rebecca Blevins

"Enjoyable and uplifting." Janet Kay Jensen- Fiction for the Thinking Woman

Be sure to read Jaclyn's first published book
Journey of Honor A love story
An entertaining historical romance set in 1848 in the American West.

The Outer Edge of Heaven

A Love Story

by

Jaclyn M. Hawkes

The Outer Edge of Heaven

By Jaclyn M. Hawkes

Copyright © July 2011 Jaclyn M. Hawkes

All rights reserved.

Published and distributed by Spirit Dance Books. 855-648-5559

Spiritdancebooks.com

Cover design by Thomas Gasu

Printed in USA

First Printing July 2011

ISBN: 0615517773

ISBN-13: 978-0615517773

Dedication

This book is dedicated to my good husband, who knows exactly when to let me run and when to kindly rein me in. He is gentle yet strong, incredibly patient, and has been known to kiss in the pantry. I love him dearly.

Chapter 1

Charlie Evans made it all the way from an appointment in downtown Salt Lake City to the eighth north exit in Orem before her silver 1994 Honda Civic hatchback started making the noise. Knowing that she only had a few minutes before the ancient car she'd affectionately named the Taco Rocket would stall, she took the next exit, opting to be stranded on a surface street instead of the freeway.

She actually made it to within three blocks of her apartment complex near the stadium before the fickle import finally quit and she coasted to the curb. It was almost a mile further than she'd expected and she gave the car a half hearted pat as she dragged her backpack off the passenger seat and set off at a brisk walk in the early May sunshine.

Inside her apartment, she dropped her books, glanced at her e-mail in box and grabbed a bag of baby carrots out of the fridge. On second thought, she snagged half a package of Oreos off her shelf in the pantry. She might have to resort to bribery this afternoon.

"I'm at Fo's." Calling down the hall to whoever might be home, she headed back out the door and across the parking lot.

Half way there, she heard a familiar voice and

looked up at a third story window. "Bring milk. I'm out." She laughed as his neat blonde head disappeared back inside the window and she retraced her steps to procure the requested milk. They'd been friends since the third grade and could all but read each other's minds by now. Four minutes later, she blew a stray curl out of her eyes and knocked before she automatically opened the door to his apartment and let herself in.

Forest Eldridge sat on the floor in front of the TV with his laptop beside him and a clutter of textbooks and papers spread out nearby. Charlie turned off the TV as she went past and sprawled into the overstuffed chair beside him. "How goes the battle?" She dug into the bag of carrots on her lap and crunched into one.

Glancing up at her loud munching, he grumbled. "Don't tell me that you only brought healthy stuff. C'mon, Chuck. This is a chemistry final. I gotta have a Twinkie or something!"

He reached for the grocery bag beside her, but she moved it. "I brought Oreos, but they're for a reward." She held the bag out of his reach. "Unuh, chemistry first."

Letting out a sigh, he said, "You're brutal. How was the drive?"

Standing up, she put a leg underneath her and plopped back down. "Good. The Taco Rocket made it all the way with only one stall, and I only had to walk three blocks."

He laughed. "That probably means it won't run all day tomorrow. You had better plan to take the bus to classes. It'd be a shame to flunk out of college the last week because of car trouble."

"Not a chance! That car has carried me safely through and wouldn't dare let me down now."

He looked up at her and rolled his eyes. "Charlie, we've had to do something to that car an average of five times a week for what, six years now? It's time for a proper burial. Hey, we could grind off the VIN number and fly it off Guardsman's pass!"

She put a hand to her chest in mock hurt. "That is so rude! Okay, so I'll plan to ride the bus to finals. Did you finish your project?"

He groaned. "Done and turned in. Why do you think I need Twinkies?"

"Really? Dang, Fo! You're good! You'd better have an Oreo." She tossed him a cookie and automatically got up to go and bring cups for milk.

With the whole cookie in his mouth, he asked her a question that was wholly unintelligible and she laughed and said, "One more time."

Pausing to chew, he tried again. "Did you call your parents?"

"Heck no!" With a sigh, she returned to the living room and continued. "I love them Fo. I do. I swear it. But I just can't face them for the whole three months. They've gotten positively militant about law school all the sudden. They've always been pretty high pressure, but at least I've typically felt loved. Lately I feel like I'm in the German army or something. I thought I could handle going home for the summer, but now that it's here, I think I'm getting an ulcer."

"I've been trying to tell you. Just come with me to Montana, Charlie. You can work for my uncle on the ranch or come find something at the hospital with me. I'm telling you, the ranch is a huge place. They have like twenty employees. You might not make much, but it'd be a great summer and law school next fall is paid for anyway. You might even meet some handsome, debonair Montanan and decide to put a stop to this law school asininity."

"Can you just imagine my mother if I try to tell her I'm going to Montana to work on a ranch for the summer?

She'll have a coronary! She thinks Ohio is the outer edge of civilization."

"Better her with a coronary than you with an ulcer." He nudged her with his shoulder. "Make a decision, Chuck. You've got three more days of class, and then I'm out of here." He picked up his cell phone. "Say the word and I'll call my uncle. Montana is actually the outer edge of heaven. You have nothing to lose. If you don't like it, you can go home to Connecticut and play the power game."

"That's actually why I came over. Now that it's here, I can't face Connecticut. But what will I do in Montana? I'm not exactly ranch hand material."

"It is a huge ranch, but they also have an orchard and an herb farm, and they have household help and office help. If none of that sounds good, you could come into Kalispell with me and apply at the hospital or somewhere else. Kalispell is a real town, you know."

"There's a real town in Montana? I had no idea."

"Brat. Do you want me to call? Or are you going home to Elroy and the all-powerfuls?"

She groaned again and picked up her own phone. "Give me the number. I'll call for myself. His name is Christopher Elroy by the way. Not just Elroy. I'm surprised he doesn't go by Christopher. I'm sure he's a nice guy, but who marries a divorce lawyer? Who does that? The whole idea is bizarre."

"Who names their child Elroy? And who lets their mother try to talk them into who they should marry?" He scrolled down for the number. "I take that back. Your mother is the toughest bird I know. I'd probably be just as worried as you. My Uncle's name is Richard Langston. He, on the other hand, is the nicest guy in the world. Too nice actually. Here's the number."

After punching it in, she turned back to him. "You just called my mother a tough bird." Someone must have picked up on the other end. "No, excuse me. I was speaking to someone else. Is Richard Langston available please? Thank you." She put her hand over the phone and whispered to Fo, "They heard me say that."

He laughed at her. "Nice job interview intro, Chuck. Sorry about your mother."

Still whispering, she asked, "Sorry you said that or sorry that she's a tough bird?"

He took one of her carrots and bit into it. "Take it any way you want. Just come to Montana. I need someone to keep me on task."

Thirty minutes later, she had arranged to work in Montana and they had made plans for him to leave on Thursday, towing her worthless car behind his SUV. She would fly to Kalispell after she walked to get her diploma that weekend.

Knowing it had to be done sometime, she placed the call to Connecticut to notify her parents. Mercifully, she reached their answering machine and simply said that she had received a job offer from a large corporation in Montana for the summer, and had opted to go there to be near Fo. She didn't offer the fact that the large corporation was a ranch and hoped later they wouldn't ask.

****

At six o'clock Sunday evening, when she finally made it through security at the Salt Lake International Airport, she wished she had booked her flight for immediately after receiving her diploma as Fo had suggested. It would have been so much simpler than trying to visit with her parents for a couple of days, but she had thought it was too disrespectful. After all, they had come clear to Utah to see her graduate and be with her. They loved her dearly and she knew that. They just expected such different things from her than she truly wanted.

Because she didn't want to fight with her parents, she had gone ahead and gotten the bachelors degree in business administration they'd expected so that she could attend law school and become a powerful force in the world like the rest of her family. It had only been a few extra classes and hadn't hurt anything, and had saved her a lot of being lectured. But she had also gotten a teaching certificate in elementary education, which was what she truly wanted. She hadn't realized it would be printed right on her diploma and her mother had been horrified. A rather interesting conversation had ensued, and Charlie had been the object of no less than three lengthy discussions about choosing respectable careers that would make the right impression on society in her future.

By the time she kissed her parents goodbye, she had been sweetly, but very firmly reminded that even though she was their baby, they expected her to follow her siblings into career fields such as medicine and engineering and law. Her father was the patriarch of the bunch as an orthopedic surgeon, and her mother was the queen as a CPA who owned her own large and prestigious firm.

Their pressure lately made her want to do anything but capitulate, if she was honest. It brought out a rebel spirit in her that she struggled to quell because she knew it would only make her want to act immaturely.

Quite frankly, by the time she got on her plane, she was tired and more than a tad discouraged. The fact that she'd just graduated from BYU with top academic honors didn't even seem to register with her parents. What was it with them, anyway? At least she wouldn't need to deal with them too terribly much for the next three months while she was working in Montana.

After sleeping on the plane, she ran her fingers through the curls that hung past her shoulders, pulled them up into a loose knot at the back of her head and stuck a pencil through it to hold it. She picked up her carry on and walked off the plane, glad that Fo didn't demand anything more than an honest opinion and that she play coed softball without throwing like a girl.

He met her in the terminal with a smile and she put her mortar board cap on to wear out to his SUV, knowing he'd acknowledge that she had just graduated from college and give her that little pat on the back that she could admit she wanted. Their friendship was unconditional, and if she'd have dropped out, he'd have still supported her, but he knew her well enough to know that, occasionally, after being around her family she needed a bit of an emotional lift.

As they walked down the concourse, they had to walk around a couple that was wrapped in an ardent kiss. They were all over each other and Charlie commented on their rather public display of far too much affection.

Fo shrugged and said, "Uh, well. You'll come to find out there are worse things than where you display that kind of affection, I'm afraid."

"What does that mean?"

"I'd actually rather give you a little time to adjust to Montana, but you'll find out sooner or later. That woman is my uncle's wife."

Charlie's eyes grew wide. "Are you telling me that man was not your uncle?"

Matter-of-factly he admitted, "That man was not my uncle. His wife is a flight attendant who doesn't have a great deal of scruples concerning fidelity." He looked apologetic, but tried to laugh and said, "Welcome to Montana."

She felt a bit shell-shocked. "Is the whole family like that?"

"Oh heavens no! They're wonderful. You'll love them. Well, you'll love most of them."

"Would you care to enlarge on that last?"

"Nope, that would ruin all your fun."

From the airport they drove for twenty minutes through beautiful mountains and lush green valleys. Finally, Fo pulled through a huge log gateway and down a gravel road between two rows of log buck rail fence that seemed to go for miles. After a few more minutes, they rumbled across a river bridge and into a ranch yard that consisted of a number of barns and outbuildings, sprawled around a large ranch house that sat on a hill and backed up to a grove of dark pine trees.

It reminded Charlie of an old western television series she had seen a couple of times on cable. The buildings were of squared off logs with real chinking, and except for the slew of pickups and farm machinery, the whole setting could have come right out of a western movie. She qualified that thought when she realized there was a tennis court and swimming pool between the house and a large indoor arena. Cowboy movies didn't usually include those.

Fo pulled up in front of the house and, leaving her bags in his SUV, they went inside and he began to introduce her to his uncle's family who was at that moment sitting down to Sunday dinner. His forty-five-ish year old uncle Richard indeed seemed to be a nice man and was sharper than she expected given what she had just seen of his wife. Dark haired, he had a little boy in his arms who looked liked his miniature.

Smiling, Richard said, "Ah, Charlie. It's good to meet you in person. Let me introduce you to my family. This is Jamie. He's two." He nodded at the boy he held. "And these two lovely, dark haired, young ladies on either side of me are Evie and Elsa. They're four and five." He nodded next at a blonde teen with hair just a touch out of control and a cheerful smile. "That's Tuckett. Our resident court jester at fourteen and our wonderful housekeeper, Madge, there on the end. We'd die without her." Charlie took in a woman who reminded her distinctly of the housekeeper on the old Doris Day movie, *With Six You Get Egg Roll*. Madge smiled sweetly and waved.

"And that one grinning there at the other side of the table is Chase. He's my oldest son." She followed down the table to notice that Chase appeared to be in his mid twenties and incredibly full of himself. He had light brown hair and wore a golf shirt that was tightly stretched over his body builder's torso. He looked up at Charlie with a supremely confident smile.

Richard went on, "And somewhere I have another son, Luke. He's a year younger than Chase here. He didn't show up for dinner, but I imagine he's around. And my wife, Angela, is just due home from work. She's a flight attendant and should be here shortly. And that's the family. There are any number of hands around here who you'll meet eventually. It's good to have you with us. Welcome to Montana. Are you hungry? Pull up a chair."

She smiled and shook her head as Chase asked Fo, "Charlie is a girl? All these years, your friend Charlie is a girl? Why didn't you tell us she was a girl?"

Fo laughed and put an arm around Charlie's shoulders. "You're a girl?" He looked at Chase and shrugged. "I had no idea she was a girl. She plays a great game of baseball, and she kicks at Guitar Hero. She can't be a girl."

Everyone at the table laughed and Richard teased Fo, "As pretty as she is, if you never noticed, Fo, that doesn't say much for your eyesight."

Fo nodded at Chase. "Maybe I was just keeping her a secret from old Romeo here."

Chase gave Charlie another come on look. "Well, the secret is out, cuz. I have just fallen deeply in love."

Sweetly, Charlie asked, "As masculine as you are, Chase, I'm sure that would make me like the hundred and forty-sixth love. Am I right?"

Chase smiled suggestively. "Maybe."

Just as sweetly, Charlie replied, "Then I'd really rather just die an old maid, but thank you anyway." The adults around the table laughed uproariously, and even the little kids joined in as Charlie said, "It was nice to meet you all."

Fo pulled her back toward the front door, but Richard stopped them. "Fo, you'll take her to the south guest house, won't you?" Fo nodded. "Let Madge know if there's anything you need and check with Luke when he comes in to find out where she wants to work." He turned back to Charlie. "It's so good to finally meet you, Charlie. Fo has talked about you for years. I'm sure you'll love it here. Make yourself at home."

As they went back out to the drive, Fo said, "See? I told you my Uncle is the nicest guy in the world. He truly is that cool all the time."

She shook her head. "How did he end up with such a wife?"

"She's actually the third one. Chase and Luke's mom died of cancer when they were about eight and nine. She was a wonderful, sweet, kind, smart, strong woman. Then he married Tuckett's mom and didn't do so hot on the second one. She took off somewhere and then he married this third one. She's very pretty, but he would be the first to admit he made a terrible mistake. Still, he does the best he can to be a good dad. Sometimes he's just in way over his head with the ranch and Tuckett and the little ones and especially Chase. I imagine Chase gives Uncle Richard more trouble than all the rest of them put together. It's just a good thing he has Luke to hold everything together."

"Then Luke isn't like Chase?"

Fo chuckled. "No. Luke is nothing like Chase. Come on. I'll take you to your house."

"I'm to have a whole guest house? I thought I'd have a room or something."

"You get the whole house, but it's pretty small. It's actually an eighteen eighties homestead cabin that's been renovated. You'll love it. You'll feel like you're in True Grit or something. And around this crazy place, you'll be grateful for the privacy and peace sometimes. It's on the very edge of the compound and no one will bother you."

"Where do you live?"

He nodded at a set of long log buildings off to one side as he drove past. "I live in the left bunk house with Luke. The other bunkhouse has a handful of guys and then there are a couple of houses down the road a ways where some more guys live. The married hands live in houses of their own over east of here."

"Where does Madge stay? And Chase?"

They both live right in the main house."

"Why is Luke in the bunkhouse and Chase in the main house?"

"I'm not sure. My guess would be because Uncle Richard wants to know what Chase is up to as much as possible, but I don't know. At any rate, I'll bet Chase drives Luke crazy and he moved out here to preserve his sanity. He's pretty quiet living."

"And Chase isn't?"

Fo turned to Charlie. "Chase is pretty self explanatory. I'm sure you've figured that out. They're all supposedly members of the Church, but Chase never went on a mission and you've already seen what kind of a saint

Angela is. Although, over time she does grow on you a little. She's smart. Amazingly smart. And she has a pretty laugh.

"I won't say anything about Chase except to say he's ridiculously concerned with Chase and only Chase. His life's work is body building and then sharing that physique with women at a part time job in at a health spa in Whitefish. And honestly, I think he does that just so that my uncle doesn't boot his fanny out of here."

He gave her an apologetic smile and continued, "For the most part, the Langstons are wonderful people and I think we'll have a good experience here. Just don't believe everything Chase tells you. He's been known to tell people what they want to hear."

"And Luke?"

"Luke is as easy to figure out as Chase or even more so. He's just the other side of the spectrum. He served a mission to France. He's absolutely bulletproof, selfless, and works the ranch like a machine. I'd trust him with my life."

Fo pulled up to a small cabin that was maybe twenty four by twenty four with a porch than ran the length of the front and a view all the way across the valley to the south. Charlie loved it on sight.

She was pleasantly surprised when she got inside to realize that quaint though it was, it was furnished luxuriously and had every modern convenience hidden away within its rustic ambience. It consisted of a bedroom, bathroom and combined living room and kitchen, with a loft over the bedroom half. The kitchen cabinets and appliances were all faced with barn wood and the counters were some kind of dull gray green stone that just fit the rustic tone of the room.

She smiled as she touched the little button that dispensed crushed ice from the refrigerator door. What would the pioneer women have done for something like that in the eighteen eighties? A fieldstone fireplace and hearth filled one end of the room, and a hook hung down from the inside with a small cast iron cauldron suspended from it as if waiting for her to start making a homesteader's dinner at any moment. She felt as if she should be wearing a prairie dress and high button boots as she stood there.

The Taco Rocket was already parked out front beside Fo's SUV, and he'd brought her other bags in and set them neatly beside the queen size antique bed covered with a handmade patchwork quilt. She wandered into the bathroom and found the most unusual fixtures she'd ever seen. The sink was an old-fashioned enamel washbasin, and she wasn't sure, but the bathtub appeared to be a galvanized water trough like she'd seen in the corrals at historic museums. On closer inspection, she realized it contained a luxurious tub fitted with whirlpool jets and the barn wood cupboard next to it housed a towel warmer.

She turned to Fo. "Check this out. It's like the Ritz Carlton gone pioneer. This is incredible! Who came up with all this, do you suppose?"

"I don't know, but whoever did it went to a lot of trouble to make it luxurious without ruining the feel of the original cabin."

The log ladder drew her and she climbed up far enough to poke her head over the rim of the loft and look around. It had a simple barn wood floor over log joists and contained only a set of handcrafted twin beds, a bedside table and a single rocking chair under the window. The beds were covered in the same patchwork quilts as the bed below, and she was willing to bet the rain on the tin roof would sound just as it had a hundred and thirty years ago. She let out a contented sigh as she climbed back down. This little log cabin had a peace about it that was like a thick down comforter to her soul. She mentally compared it to her parents' huge brick Tudor that stood on its perfectly manicured estate lawn back in Waterbury, Connecticut.

Fo laughed and seemed to know exactly what she was thinking. "It's slightly different from the Dr. Evans' estate back east, huh?"

Shaking her head, she said, "Just a little. It's day and night from your parents' estate as well. How did your family and your Uncle's family end up so opposite?"

"My mother couldn't wait to get out of Montana when she was a teenager. She left the second she graduated from high school and has never looked back. She still can't understand why I like to come out here all the time. She thinks Montana is positively still in the Dark Ages."

Looking around, Charlie mused quietly, "Sometimes there's a lot to be said for the Dark Ages. I've only been here for half an hour and my ulcer is healing by the minute." She set a suitcase up on the antique farmhouse table and began to sort through it and unpack. "What do you suppose Luke will want me to do around here?"

Blandly, Fo replied, "I suggested roping and branding cows at four-thirty in the morning, but he looked a bit skeptical. He'll probably ask you to help in the office or the herb farm office. It's a girl thing, you know. Keep your hands clean."

Charlie cracked right up, and Fo had the wherewithal to look sheepish as he said, "All right, all right. So I'm the clean-handed one of the two of us. That's why I'm interning at the hospital, thank you very much, and you're the ranch hand. Still, I know you. You're going to love it here."

"I already do. Thank you for talking me into coming here instead of going home. I would have been positively miserable." She put out a hand to clarify. "But I do love my parents. I swear I do. Don't get me wrong. This is just much more comfortable." She pulled her hair back up into its knot and resecured it with the pencil. "Go rope and brand something while I unpack and I'll come find you in a while when I'm done."

He answered her with a ridiculously deep, "Yes, Ma'am.", doffed an invisible Stetson and disappeared out the heavy plank door. With another contented sigh, Charlie sat down in the wooden rocker beside the fireplace and absentmindedly pushed it lazily with one foot. This was going to be a great summer. She could feel it in her bones.

Chapter 2

Luken Langston pulled his pick up truck into the parking spot in front of the bunkhouse and shut off the engine in the lavender gray light of dusk. Opening the door and stepping out, he stretched his tired back and reached back in for his leather work gloves and the rope that lay coiled on the seat. He slapped the rope against his dusty pant legs and boots and breathed deeply of the evening smell of river bottom and beef cows. To some that may have been a questionable smell, but to him it was home in its purest essence and he loved it.

His stomach growled and he wondered if there was any real food in the bunkhouse fridge, or if he'd have to either settle for junk, or head back up to the main house before crashing tonight. He'd been up since four thirty that morning and was too tired to go for food, even though he'd skipped dinner. Maybe there was some fruit left, or some milk. Fo lived on milk, so there should be some. Or maybe that was backward. His boots sounded loud on the wooden porch boards as he mounted the two steps.

He tossed the rope onto one of the hooks inside the door of the bunkhouse, threw the gloves onto the shelf above it and reached to unbuckle his chaps. Hanging them beside the rope on the hooks, he pulled his shirt off over his head in one single motion. He dumped it into the laundry hamper next to his bunk as he kicked out of his boots and spurs, grabbed clean clothes from a drawer and headed for the shower. Thirty seconds later, he decided a hot shower was the greatest invention known to man and resolved to sleep right there under the pounding, steamy spray. This had to be the purest form of heaven.

The need to sleep there cooled with the last of the hot water and he got out, dried off, and wrapped the towel around his hips as he stood at the sink to shave. The aftershave he slapped on helped to wake him up enough that he decided he would go in search of real food, even if he had to go up to the house. It had been a grueling evening. He usually let the hands have Sundays off except for the barest minimum of feeding chores, but this afternoon he'd had a whole herd of heifers go through a break in the fence and get into a grain field. It had been a pain rounding them all back up, moving them alone, and then repairing the fence. The field would never been the same, at least not this year.

Slipping on a clean pair of jeans, he walked out of the bathroom, shirtless and bare footed. He was half way to the fridge when there came a light knock and then the bunkhouse door opened. A beautiful stranger with blonde curls and long legs stepped inside and called out for Fo. She didn't see Luke there in the half-light and came in several more steps, calling as she came and then abruptly pulled up when she finally saw him. Both of them were speechless for a second and then she stammered, "Oh, I'm so sorry. I didn't know there was anyone else in here. Please forgive me." She turned toward the door and he stopped her.

"No. You're fine. I just didn't expect company. I'm sure Fo is around here somewhere." He glanced down at his bare chest. "Excuse me, would you? I'll just go get dressed while you find him." He grabbed shirt and headed back into the recently vacated bathroom while she stood there looking at him without making a sound.

He shut the door behind him and stared into the steamy mirror for just a second, stunned. Who in the world was the heart stopping beauty who had just walked into the bunkhouse? Fo hadn't mentioned any girls stopping by that he could remember. Luke had never seen her before and even as tired as he was, she had jolted him like a bolt of lightning. He had to take a second and remind himself that he was engaged to be married and that she was with Fo anyway.

Pulling on his shirt, he was almost hesitant to go back out. Hearing Fo's voice outside the bathroom door helped. Luke went back out and headed for his bunk, but got sidetracked by the plate Fo carried and the marvelous smells emanating from it. Food was the only thing right now that could make him partially forget the stunning woman who had just walked in on him.

Fo brought the plate over to him. "I saw your truck and assumed you hadn't had any dinner. Are you hungry?"

"Ravenous. You're a saint. Thank you. There was just a girl in here looking for you." Luke put the plate on the table and turned back to get a fork.

"She found me. I guess you two have met then."

Luke looked around and saw that the girl was now seated on the cowhide couch across the room. "Uh, sort of. I'm Luke. Luke Langston." He stepped over to shake her hand. "And you are?"

"You haven't met then?" Fo glanced back and forth between them for a minute.

Slightly embarrassed, the girl admitted, "I actually walked in just as he was getting out of the shower. I sort of walked in on him half dressed unintentionally." She turned to Luke. "Sorry about that. I'm Charlie. Fo's friend from Connecticut, and school. I flew in this evening from Utah."

Luke turned to Fo in surprise. "Charlie is a girl? Your friend Charlie for all these years is a girl?"

Fo laughed at him. "Does she look like a girl to you? I would think it would be obvious, but maybe I'm just more discerning. Where have you been? Has your ox been in the mire this evening?"

Running a hand through his damp hair, Luke sat at the table while Fo sprawled onto the other end of the couch. "More like heifers in the spring wheat. A whole herd of them went on vacation tonight."

"Will it make them sick?"

He shook his head, "We'll know that in about three hours. I'm hoping not, but we'll see. Anthony's going to check on them. Thanks for dinner." He glanced up. "I still can't believe Charlie is a girl. You've been friends since you were like two haven't you?"

"I think we were seven. Well, I was seven. She was eight. She's way older than me, but we were in the same grade."

"Six months is not way older, thank you, Forest Eldridge. Plus, you've needed wisdom all these years. My superior maturity has kept you out of a lot of trouble."

Luke looked from one to the other of them as Fo retorted, "You have it backwards, Chuck. My superior immaturity has kept you entertained all this time."

She laughed. "That is probably true. You saved me from always being squished by the tough old bird. What kind of thing is superior immaturity? That sounds markedly suspect to me."

"I didn't call her old. I just said tough. Don't make it worse than it was."

Charlie laughed again. "If I'm ever mad at you, I'm going to tell her you said that. You will be banished from her perpetual worship forever!"

"No way. She adores me because I've taken such good care of you all these years."

Luke just sat quietly eating his dinner as they bantered back and forth. Finally, he asked, "Who did you call a tough old bird, Fo?"

Fo looked guilty and Charlie giggled as he admitted, "Her mother. It wasn't as bad as it sounds, I promise. And she is tough. The toughest. It's a good thing she does adore me. I've had to save Charlie her whole life. Momma Evans is a touch militant."

"A touch?" Charlie laughed again. "That has to be the understatement of the century." She turned to Luke. "My mother is a wonderful, Christian woman. Just a very strong one. Very in-charge. She's positively driven. I'm kind of a wimp about dealing with her sometimes. That's why I'm in Montana instead of Connecticut right now. Speaking of being here, your dad told me to ask you where you wanted me to go to work tomorrow."

He shook his head. "You're a girl."

She smiled. "I know that. I've been this way for twenty three years now."

Fo whacked her teasingly. "Quit being a smart aleck. He's tired. He's been getting the oxen out of the spring wheat mire all night. Give him a break."

Luke smiled quietly and then said, "No, I just expected a guy. A wimpy, city slicker guy like Fo. I've been trying to figure out where I needed a wimp and now I have to find a place for a girl." He smiled again.

"Careful Luke, she's practically engaged to an attorney named Elroy. You could be sued for sexist comments like that."

Luke gave her that same mellow smile. "Elroy? You're marrying a guy named Elroy?"

Fo laughed and teased, "Elroy the divorce litigator. Who marries a divorce attorney? That's gotta be the stupidest thing ever."

Luke looked surprised. "You're marrying a divorce attorney?

Charlie gave Fo a disgusted look. "No! I am not marrying an attorney of any kind. Stop it, Forest. He's going to think I'm a nut." She turned back to Luke. "Is finding a place for a girl going to be a problem? Because I can look somewhere else if it is."

He shook his head. "No. It's not a problem. I just don't dare put you into a bunch of guys. Work would come to a grinding halt I expect. We don't typically have ranch hands that look like you."

Charlie sat upright. "I don't know the first thing about being a ranch hand Luke, but I've certainly never been accused of not doing my fair share of the work."

Fo laughed. "I don't think that's what he's inferring, Charlie. It's the other guys who would quit working to see a pretty girl. I think he was giving you a compliment in a round about way."

"Oh." She made a perfect circle with her lips. "Well. I really doubt I would have enough of an effect on men to be a problem, Luke. But I'll be happy to do whatever you'd like me to try."

Luke sighed. "What I truly need around here right now is hard to hire. What I really need is a mother for my little brothers and sisters. Angela doesn't do motherly, and Dad and I aren't cutting it I'm afraid."

"What do you mean? What do you need that's hard to hire?"

He hesitated for a minute, lost in thought. "You know all the things moms do? From Band-Aids to making you practice piano and teaching you how to make pie crusts. These kids have stuff, and they have a clean house and they're loved, but that mother factor is entirely missing except for what Madge manages."

Charlie nodded in understanding. "Unfortunately, I was raised by a tough old bird, but the good part of that is I know exactly what you mean. Norma didn't do motherly either. If that's what you truly need, I'll give it a shot. I may have to learn as I go, but I know what I wished I'd had as a child. I can do that. But what will your dad think?"

He smiled tiredly. "My dad is the first person who will tell you there's a problem. He tries, but this is a pretty big operation. Even with me taking over a lot of the load, there's something missing. He'd love some help with the kids. All of the kids. I'm sorry to admit to you that you'll have to spend a portion of your time dodging Chase."

Fo chuckled. "She already knows that. She told him this afternoon, as soon as she met him that she'd rather die an old maid than be his true love. It was great!"

Luke turned to look at her with a laugh. "You told him that? Right up front?" He laughed again. "I wish I'd been there to see that. Good for you." More seriously, he said, "Hopefully, he'll behave himself. If not, let me know."

He finished his dinner and went to the sink and rinsed his plate. Then he dug in a cupboard, produced a package of Oreos and brought milk out of the fridge. He put the cookies and milk on the coffee table and turned back to go get glasses. "Anyone for an Oreo?" Before he had even asked, Fo had one stuffed in his mouth. Luke laughed when he turned to look at them. "I'll take that as a yes. What about you, Charlie?"

"Yes, please. I'd love one. They are the fifth food group, you know." He handed her a glass of milk and she asked, "So what should I do tomorrow?"

Luke sat on the rug in front of the couch near the coffee table and stretched his legs out. "Just go up to the house in the morning at breakfast and ask Madge what to do. Tell her what I have in mind and ask for her ideas. She'll know where to start. She'll probably be forever grateful. She spends half her time trying to do just what I'm asking."

"What's Angela going to think about this?"

Luke shrugged. "She probably won't even notice. She's only here about two days a week, and when she is here, she's usually shopping and having her nails and hair done in Whitefish. She probably won't even realize you're here for a while." He paused and then asked, "Is your name really Charlie?"

"No, but my real name is awful, so don't even ask what it is. I never use it."

"Shoot!" Fo interrupted their discussion, "I lost my Oreo down in my milk. I hate that!" He tried to fish it out with his fingers and overflowed the milk in the glass. "Dang it. I do that every time!"

Charlie laughed. "You'd think you'd learn, Fo. You gotta hold on like this." She demonstrated how to hold the cookie with just her pointer and tall man. As she went to dip the cookie, she lost hers too and they all laughed. "Okay, so maybe not. When I grow up, I'm going to design the perfect Oreo dipping cup. It'll be wide and short."

She drained her glass and then tapped on it to get the soggy cookie to come out, which it promptly did and plopped onto her face. "Aahh!" She tried to catch the remnants before they dripped onto the cowhide couch as Fo jumped up and grabbed a paper towel. When he helped her wipe her face, he smeared mushy Oreo all over her cheek and they both laughed while Luke looked on placidly.

Getting to her feet, she sniffed tentatively. "I now have Oreo in my right sinus. I think that means I should call it a night."

She took her glass to the sink and just as she made it to the paper towel roll, she gave a dainty sneeze and a small scream. She wiped her face with a paper towel as she headed for the door with Fo laughing and Luke wondering what was up with these two. At the door, she turned and waved. "It was nice to meet you, Luke. Night, Fo." She went out the door and the screen slammed behind her in the quiet Montana night.

Fo chuckled and Luke got up to put the cookies and milk away. "You two act more like brother and sister than friends. I still can't believe Charlie is a girl. What's her real name?"

"Charlene, but don't you dare tell her I told you. She's always hated it, but then several years ago when that song came out about the guy who wrote "Billy Bob loves Charlene" on the water tower in John Deere Green, she was thoroughly disgusted and now she hates it even more."

Luke laughed. "That is a pretty deep, thought provoking song. How did I miss the fact that she was a girl all these years though?"

"She's not just a girl. She's a machine. You'll find that out. Your family will never be the same. In a good way. You'll see. Even Chase will wonder what happened."

****

Charlie woke up that first morning to the birds just beginning to sing in the dark before dawn and felt alive on a whole new level. She paused for a second to breathe in deeply of the breeze coming in her bedroom window. The air smelled of the woods and river and a farm, and was a smell she was sure she would always remember as the aroma of Montana.

As she stretched like a kitten she thought about the man she'd met last night in the bunkhouse. When she'd finally realized there was someone standing there when she'd been looking for Fo, she'd been almost star struck at the vision in front of her. The sight had been fairly breathtaking honestly.

Luke definitely had the physique of the ultimate male. She still wasn't sure if he had black hair or just dark brown because the lights in the bunkhouse had been low, but she knew he had quietly topped Chase's proudly displayed muscles without even trying. Luke's mellow, understated demeanor had been far more intriguing than Chase's obnoxious and pushy self-superiority. Luke had a discrete but powerful sense of self that left no doubt that he was incredibly competent, not to mention incredibly good looking.

Suddenly working here in the mountains of Montana felt a whole lot more like an adventure.

After lying there for a few minutes, she read her scriptures and prayed and then hopped out of bed. Changing into a pair of running tights and shoes, she quietly slipped out of her little cabin and began to stretch on the porch in the first light before heading out for a morning run. It was brisk in Montana and she went back inside and dug out a jacket before heading out into the early morning crispness.

It was wonderful to be able to run here without feeling the slightest bit guilty. Her mother hadn't felt that athletics were a positive use of her time. Charlie had actually become an NCAA champion cross-country athlete, but had never dared to even mention it to anyone in her family.

She had no idea where she was headed and simply went up the gravel road and across the bridge for a couple miles before turning and heading back to her cabin to shower and dress for the day. It was her first day and although she had no idea what she would be doing for sure, she felt really good about being here. The indecision of a week ago that had been stressing her out was marked in its absence. She donned a pair of jeans and a knit shirt and headed up to the main house.

She hadn't gotten any groceries for her little cabin yet and hoped she could beg some breakfast before starting her workday. As she headed up the drive, she texted Fo good morning and asked him if he would bring her some basic groceries for her new little home on his way from town tonight. Then she focused on trying to remember all the people she'd been introduced to the evening before at the dinner table. The Langstons were quite a family.

Upon hesitantly entering the house, she was nearly knocked over by the two little girls and a handful of dogs of all sizes. She followed the herd through the great room toward the kitchen, noticing they left a veritable swathe in their wake of muddy footprints. Madge met them at the door of the laundry room and before Madge even started swatting, the dogs knew they were in trouble and headed back out the way they had come. Evie and Elsa didn't seem to take notice and simply wondered what was for breakfast as Madge fussed.

Jamie went past in his underwear, and Tuckett breezed in in a baseball cap and with three inches of his underwear showing above the waistline of his pants and below his T-shirt. Charlie stood looking around for a moment, wondering if breakfast was always this wild and if she was right in her assumption that these were the kinds of issues that Luke said needed some mothering influence. It certainly couldn't hurt. But how in the world did a complete stranger to this family start to go about calming and organizing?

Just then, Richard came to the door of the kitchen carrying a platter of sausage and pancakes and a pancake turner in his other hand. The dogs went past him on the run and only Charlie's quick reflexes saved the entire platter from flying across the room like a Frisbee. When the platter was securely sitting on the table, she closed her eyes, took a deep breathe and dug in. She pulled Tuckett's ball cap off and tossed it toward the mudroom. "No hats at the table, Tuck. Would you do me a favor and bring me a pair of shorts for Jamie? And a T-shirt?" She ruffled his wild hair and smiled her best smile at him. "Please."

Next, she snagged Jamie where he was trying to climb into his high chair by himself and helped him in as she spoke to the girls. "Evie and Elsa, would you two go put all those dogs out, and then wash your hands and come in for breakfast?" She turned to Richard. "If you'll point me toward dishes, I'll set the table."

He gave her a huge smile. "Charlie, something tells me this family has needed you for a long, long time. Dishes are in the first set of cupboards this side of the dishwasher."

The table was set and she was mixing a can of orange juice when the dogs came racing back through again. Charlie looked at the little girls. Elsa shrugged her shoulders and said, "We put 'em out. They just let themselves back in."

Charlie smiled at them. "Okay, girls. The goal was to get the dogs out of the house. So if they can let themselves back in, maybe you'd better lock the door behind them until we can fix the door so it's dog proof. Try again please." Obediently the two girls began to herd the unruly canines out again. Tuckett came back in and was helping Jamie to dress himself before putting him back into his highchair. Charlie set the orange juice on the table and then turned and gave Tuckett's pants a big tug to cover up his underwear. He looked up at her in surprise and she said, "Sorry. Get used to it, Tuck. Nice people don't show up to dine with their unmentionables hanging out." She turned back to the kitchen and Tuckett looked to Richard.

He shrugged and said, "She's right, son. Can you see the prophet or the president showing up with their underwear showing?"

"Dad! I'm not exactly the president."

"You might be someday. Would you bring the butter and syrup in? And then help Madge and Charlie with their chairs."

The girls came back and while Richard helped them, Tuckett did indeed help Madge and Charlie be seated. Luke came in from outside just as Chase showed up shirtless and yawning from the back hallway. Immediately upon seeing Luke, Jamie started to squeal with his arms outstretched, "Lukey, Lukey!" Luke went to his highchair and tickled him and hugged him for a minute before he sat down. Tuckett looked at Charlie. She could tell that he was wondering what she was going to say about Chase's lack of apparel.

Not sure what to do, she ducked into the nearby laundry room and grabbed a shirt that looked to be about the right size and headed back in to the table. She draped it over Chase shoulders and then sat back down and bowed her head to pray. Chase looked around bewildered for a second as everyone stared at him, then slipped the shirt on and began to button it, smiling at Charlie. Richard bowed his head and said the prayer himself and they all began to eat. Charlie said a prayer of her own that things would continue to go smoothly as she tried to help this nice family get a handle on things.

Looking up, Luke caught her eye. He gave her a smile of encouragement before hurriedly eating his breakfast, squeezing the three little ones and high fiving Tuckett before heading back outside to get busy again. When the rest finished, Charlie and Madge began to clear the table and Richard talked to Tuckett about working with him that day. Charlie came back in with a wet cloth and wiped Jamie's hands and face and then set him to wiping down his own high chair tray, which he thought was just great. Next, she took Evie and Elsa and went in search of cleaning supplies. She got rags, cleaning spray, and a mop and sent the little girls to clean up the dog tracks as she and Madge cleaned up the last of the breakfast dishes.

When that was done, she found out the little ones had swimming lessons in town and she got directions for how to get there and then set out with the three of them for Kalispell. They were almost late because she insisted they round up a car seat and boosters so the kids would be properly buckled in before she headed out.

By the time they got back, Jamie was asleep and both girls were looking decidedly blinky in their own seats. She took them all inside, fed them lunch and then put Jamie down for a nap while she read a story to the other two in their own beds. When they were asleep too, she went in search of Madge. Charlie finally told her what Luke had suggested and they discussed a list of duties and ideas for Charlie to look into for the future. She spent the balance of the afternoon doing various things around the house while becoming better and better friends with the three little Langstons.

Angela showed up for dinner. Seeing her without her lips all over another man, she truly was an exceptional beauty, and Fo was right. She had a wonderful laugh that made you join in. It made Richard's decision to marry her slightly more plausible. Charlie did her best to keep an open mind until Angela caught her alone in the kitchen later and in a positively venomous voice braced her. "You might be working here for the time being, but if you even think about getting near my husband that'll end in a way that definitely won't be pretty. Do you understand me?" Charlie looked at her in utter disbelief. This woman had a lot of gall. A whole lot of gall!

When Charlie could finally close her mouth, she assured Angela in her most diplomatic tone, "Of course, Mrs. Langston. I would never dream of such a thing. You can be sure."

The dark haired beauty gave her a brittle smile. "Good. See to it that it stays that way." She turned on her heel and left Charlie to finish putting the rest of the dinner things away in complete amazement.

She must have still looked shell shocked when she met up with Fo that night because he asked, "Are you okay? You look a little weird. Has something happened?"

Charlie recounted what Angela had said in the kitchen and Fo tried to reassure her, "Try not to let it bother you. She's just paranoid because of her own lifestyle. Just don't be too floored when she even hits on her stepsons when she's been drinking. It can be fairly shocking."

"Sheesh, I can imagine. Poor Richard. He's a genuinely nice guy, too."

That night, before she went to bed, she sat down and tried to brainstorm about what kinds of things a good LDS mother would encourage in this household. The kinds of things she had wished for as a child who had all manner of worldly things, but not a lot of hands on mother time, and ended up with a whole long list. She decided to start by checking with Richard the next day about dance lessons for the girls and planting a vegetable garden with the children.

He agreed wholeheartedly and told her to make whatever arrangements she wanted for the lessons and said he'd see about having someone get a garden plot ready to plant as soon as possible. Charlie took the kids with her to the nearby farm and ranch supply and let them pick out their own seed packets to grow their favorite vegetables. She had never done this before and she prayed before buying her own seeds that they'd have at least moderate success to encourage the kids to do as the prophet had asked again in the future.

Luke himself saw to the plowing and then tilling of the little garden and he smiled his mellow smile at her as he went past once they got started with their planting. Charlie had them singing the Primary song about gardening as they worked to make the rows the way she had researched on the Internet.

She remembered his comment that first night about teaching the kids to make piecrust and she put that on her mental list for the next day. When they were through planting their little garden, she let them all change back into their swimsuits and took them out to the pool for an hour to cool off after their work. After they swam, they had lunch again and Jamie napped while Charlie and the girls sorted through their closets and pulled out the clothes they'd grown out of and packed them up to go to the Good Will.

That afternoon, the three kids took Charlie for a walk to show her around the ranch. They explored for more than two hours and Charlie exclaimed about how it all reminded her of Charlotte's Web. The three of them just looked at her as if she was slightly nuts and she put renting the movie on her list as well. Every child should see Charlotte's Web, shouldn't they?

By the end of the first week, she believed that she had finally met all of the people that worked somewhere on the Langston holdings and she was a little bit mind boggled at the scope of their operation. Fo had been right that they had everything from a housekeeper, to multiple ranch hands, one of whom made her frankly nervous when he looked at her, to a full time grounds maintenance man. This was a huge enterprise.

She had almost succeeded in teaching the dog herd to stay out of the house and Chase to wear a shirt when he came to meals. She had more success by far with the dogs actually, but Chase had made some improvement. When he was home, he fairly haunted Charlie as she worked around the house with the children. She had yet to see him actually do anything around the ranch, but she hoped that was just because she hadn't been right there where he was working.

He would walk around the house posing like a body builder in front of various mirrors or windows until Charlie finally asked him one day, "Did you earn those muscles fair and square working this ranch, Chase? Or are you the Soloflex poster boy?"

Chase seemed to think she was complimenting his physique when he answered proudly as he patted his own bicep, "I earned these babies by working hours and hours a day down in the exercise room. That's the only way to get a body like mine. You don't get ripped like this just being lazy you know."

Charlie thought to herself that he had it all backwards. To her, spending hours and hours a day working on your muscles was lazy and she had to differ with him expressly over the fact that you could get ripped by working. She remembered Luke's build that night when she had inadvertently walked in on him in only his jeans. His physique was far better than Chase's ever hoped to be, and she had no doubts he came by it honorably. He was working from before it got light in the morning until late, late at nights sometimes. There were even nights he drove a tractor all night for some reason or another.

She and Fo and Luke had developed a habit of hanging out in the bunkhouse late in the evenings or else on Charlie's front porch rockers. Luke never said much, but that hadn't stopped Charlie from developing a healthy schoolgirl's crush on him within the first week of her stay there. She felt positively ridiculous about it and then was completely floored one day when she found out he was engaged to be married. It came as a complete surprise to her because she had never even seen him with a girl, let alone act as if he was in love with someone.

Charlie had wondered aloud one morning if the girls knew how to ride well enough to go out on horses with her, and Richard had shaken his head. "I've been meaning to spend more time teaching them, but for now I don't think they're safe without someone riding with them."

Madge had suggested that maybe Lindie could begin to give them riding lessons and Richard had thought that was a great idea. Charlie had no idea who Lindie was and finally the next day Luke took her out to the indoor arena and calmly introduced her to a pretty, dark haired girl. "This is Lindie Snyder. Her dad is our main horse trainer, and she's very good with horses. And she's my fiancée'. She'll help teach the girls everything they need to know." Charlie was so surprised by this announcement that she was his fiancée' that she almost missed the rest of the introduction. She looked blankly from one to the other of them. They hadn't so much as touched, let alone acted in love and what's more, Lindie looked distinctly like she was expecting a baby.

Charlie was floored. She would never have pegged Luke as a guy who would be intimate before marriage. And especially not act so casual about it after. She did the best she could to act nonchalant about it all, but that night she had to ask Fo about it. Luke was out somewhere still working and she got right to the point. "Did you know Luke is engaged?"

Fo nodded, but he looked uncomfortable. "He mentioned it when I arrived." She wondered if it would be gossiping to ask if the girl really was pregnant or just had an unusual figure. She decided it would be and didn't ask, but the next day Madge put some light on the subject.

Madge and Charlie had become fast friends as they worked together to keep an organized and happy home. Madge had told Charlie somewhat self-consciously about an on-line romance she had going. It seemed Madge had a virtual boyfriend over in Missoula somewhere. "I know, I know. These on-line flings don't ever amount to much, and I'd never actually think about getting remarried after losing Burt or anything, but a little friendship never hurt anyone, did it?"

Charlie smiled at her and hugged her around the shoulders. "As long as you're careful not to get scammed Madge, I think it's wonderful. The world needs more romance." They talked back and forth about romance and somehow Charlie voiced her surprise at finding out Luke was engaged.

Madge had pursed her lips and made a sad sound. "It's a bad deal all around, I say. I know Luke's trying to help that girl, but I think it's all going to blow up in his face eventually." Charlie had no idea what she was talking about and she didn't know how to answer that, so she didn't say anything and Madge went on, "To be honest with you, Charlie, I don't believe that baby is Luke's." She shook her head sadly. "No, not for a minute I don't."

Charlie looked at her and said, "I'm sorry. I don't know anything about it or a baby."

Shaking her head again, Madge replied, "Well, poor Lindie is expecting a baby and I think that's the reason Luke has asked her to marry him. I don't think he's in love with her or her him, but he has this sense of honor that's going to have them married in spite of that." She continued peeling vegetables for their dinner. "I suppose a baby does need a family, but I hate to see young folks marry when they aren't truly in love. Marriage is too important and hard enough without going into it without being head over heels for each other. I mean it's wonderful and fun and all, but even the best marriage can be hard at times."

Charlie still had no idea how to respond to that. She shook her head and said, "I've never been married or in love either one, so I wouldn't know, Madge. But either way, it's a sad situation."

"Well, Luke is trying to be selfless about this, but I don't think he's stopped to consider how Lindie's going to feel someday when she realizes she's stuck in a marriage to someone she doesn't love. At that point she may not think Luke's idea was all that great, baby or no."

The next day Charlie took the three little ones out to the arena at the prearranged time and began to help Lindie give the girls lessons. She didn't realize that Lindie intended for her to ride as well, but she was enthused about it when she found out. Lindie put Evie and Elsa and Charlie up on their horses and then she took Jamie on her own horse with her. Charlie had assumed you weren't supposed to ride when you're pregnant, so she was a bit surprised when Lindie climbed on, but she didn't say anything, although later Lindie herself admitted that Luke wouldn't be very happy about her riding if he caught her. Still not sure what was going on, Charlie came right out and asked her, "Why wouldn't he want you to ride?"

Lindie gave Charlie a sweet, sad smile. "I'm five months pregnant, Charlie. Riding isn't too great of an idea. I wouldn't do it at all except I've had this horse my whole life and I trust him completely, no matter what. That's why I'm taking Jamie too. I know he isn't going to want to be left out. I'm just not sure Luke will agree with my decision. He's kind of protective of me right now."

Unsure of what to answer, Charlie settled for. "There're not enough men that are protective of women in this world, Lindie. Enjoy it when you can." She continued. "I've always wanted riding lessons. I'm so excited for this. Thank you for teaching me."

They had been riding for most of an hour when Luke showed up. He looked at Lindie up on her old horse, but didn't comment on it. He watched for several minutes quietly and then asked, "Why isn't Charlie wearing a helmet like the little ones?"

Charlie hurried to spare Lindie any blame and replied, "I'm afraid my head is too big for any of the helmets, Luke. I'll get one before the next lesson, I promise." He nodded and after a few more minutes he went back to whatever it was he had been doing.

Chapter 3

Over these couple of weeks, Charlie had come to understand that while Richard was the owner and the big boss, he rarely overrode the decisions Luke made as the second in command. And in fact, he often deferred to Luke's judgment. Because of this, she was surprised when one afternoon Chase was making snide comments about Luke's college education. "Luke is going off to college during the winters to become a big CPA. Doesn't that just sound fun? I think I'd rather die than be stuck messing with a bunch of numbers all day everyday."

The idea that Chase would do anything all day everyday was a bit preposterous, but Charlie didn't mention that.

Luke going off to college didn't surprise her, but his choice of accounting did. She was very familiar with CPAs because of her mother's firm and he definitely didn't seem like the type. She asked him about it that night in the bunkhouse, "Are you really an accounting major at school?"

He nodded quietly. "Yes. Why?"

She shrugged. "You just don't seem like the type to me."

He smiled. "What is the type?"

"My mother has a huge CPA firm. You're not like any of the accountants. You're much more... I don't know, -different than they are."

He gave her a sad smile. "I don't have a burning need to calculate tax returns, if that's what you're asking, but it'll pay the bills when I'm gone from here. That's all."

Both she and Fo were shocked and she had to ask, "When you're gone from here? Why in the world would you be gone from here? You love it here and this place would disintegrate without you!"

Sounding incredibly resigned, he explained, "This place has been in my family for almost a hundred and seventy years, Charlie. It's always been handed down to the oldest son. They haven't split it up because it would eventually be too small to be viable. There's no way I can stay here after it's handed to Chase. I can't do it. He'll run it into the ground. It would kill me." He shook his head. "When that happens, I'll go somewhere and be an accountant. It'll pay the bills."

She simply looked at him for the longest time. Would Richard really leave the whole place to Chase? It seemed preposterous. But then so did the thought of Richard marrying Angela. Richard seemed so sharp and responsible usually, but sometimes his judgment was a little skewed.

****

That Saturday afternoon, she and Fo and the kids were making sugar cookies and had flour and cookie cutters strewn clear across the kitchen counters. Chase came in shirtless again and after popping a few more obvious flexes, he leaned across the counter almost in her apron pocket to steal a pinch of dough. She turned to him and said sweetly, "Dude, your abdominals are in our cookies. Move 'em."

Chase grinned his ever suggestive grin, "They are right in the mix of things aren't they? I tend to like it that way."

She calmly slapped him across the stomach with the pancake turner she was moving cookies with. "Move it, Chase. We're working here. Aren't we kids?" Evie and Elsa responded enthusiastically, but Jamie was too busy creating to bother answering.

When Chase was gone, and the kids were washing their hands, Fo asked her, "Why do you encourage him? You've been here for a couple of weeks and he's still strutting around you like one of those birds on the Discovery Channel. Just tell him to leave you alone. Even he ought to get the message sooner or later."

She shook her head. "What would Jesus do, Fo? Not only that, but the goal is to help make a happier, more stable home. Remember? Fighting with Chase isn't going to help that. Plus, you know me. I'd ten times rather deal with him than fight with him. I'm too much of a marshmallow."

"You're not a marshmallow. And you need to back him off, Charlie, or Luke is gonna tear into him. Which is what he needs, but it won't be a happy home moment. It wouldn't take much to make Richard insist Chase leave. He doesn't help and causes problems. And he's such a flake with women as it is. Don't encourage it." He took another bite of dough. "Just don't put up with any of his garbage. He isn't all that trustworthy and Luke would kill him if he pulled something on you."

Nodding quietly, Charlie agreed. "Okay."

Later, they all watched Charlotte's Web together. It had taken her a while to find a copy, but they finally got to see the classic farm show Charlie had loved as a certified city child. The little ones thought it was great except that Elsa cried when Charlotte died. Charlie was careful to make it perfectly clear that the animals that came into Charlotte's house were only allowed because it was a movie.

The next morning Charlie wondered if she'd opened a can of worms when Jamie wanted to go out first thing and find out if they had any pigs anywhere. She was trying to placate him as she helped him into his highchair for breakfast when Luke came in.

When he understood what Jamie was asking he assured the little guy, "Yes, we do indeed have pigs out in one of the sheds." He gave Charlie a shake of his head as he cautioned, "But pigs can sometimes be really mean and bite little boys. You can't just go out there." Charlie ended up promising the three little ones that if Luke said it was okay, then they'd go for a walk and see the pigs some time soon.

When they did, she planned to take Luke along to discourage his ranch hand who tended to watch Charlie too closely for comfort.

****

Church in Montana was as much of an adventure as the rest of this life had proven. She had been surprised to learn Richard was a high councilman, so Charlie, Luke, Fo and Madge were left to the task of dealing with the kids for the meetings. Jamie was still wondering if he actually liked going to the nursery, and Evie and Elsa seemed to believe church was a unique cross between the Junior Prom and preschool class. They were far more caught up with their beautiful dresses and coloring books than listening. Tuckett did reasonably well considering and Chase spent a good portion of the time sitting outside in his truck listening to the radio. At least he made a show of attending which was frankly more than Charlie had expected.

Luke was the ward financial clerk and spent hours in the clerk's office and Charlie had to wonder just how things had gone before she and Fo arrived on the scene.

Sunday dinner that afternoon was singularly satisfying. Everyone showed up dressed appropriately, and no dogs did show up at all, which was wonderful. Angela didn't show up either and her absence was so comfortable that Charlie felt guilty. Even the little kids pitched in to help get it on the table. When it went more smoothly and serenely than any meal yet, Charlie felt that she had made a positive impact here at least a little bit. As they cleaned up, Chase totally baled, and Jamie accidentally knocked a whole jug of milk off the counter, but all in all, it felt like a success.

Fo and Charlie and then Luke ended up on the porch rockers late that afternoon at Charlie's house and she was amazed at how smoothly Luke fit into the friendship she and Fo had spent a lifetime forging. Time with Luke with them was every bit as comfortable as it had been before they'd come here. She still had a crush on him, but she tried to ignore it and simply enjoy her high country summer. She'd still never seen him spend any time with Lindie or show any affection to her and she had to wonder about that, but it truly wasn't any of her business.

As they sat and lazily rocked, she asked Fo about a certain nurse at the hospital she knew he had an interest in and when he gave her a goofy grin she perked right up. Apparently he liked this girl more than he'd let on at first. She turned to him and said, "Out with it Fo. What have I been missing?"

He chuckled. "You haven't been missing anything. I just happen to have found out when and where she takes her lunch and we've been eating together for three days now."

"And?" He smiled and didn't say anything and she had to repeat her question. "And? Have you asked her out yet?"

"Of course not! That would require far more bravery than I have and you know it!" She groaned and he laughed. "Give it a rest, Chuck. She'll ask me sometime hopefully and then I won't have to get out of my comfort zone."

"Geez you're a wimp, Fo! It's just a lucky thing the good Lord made you gorgeous or you'd never even go on a date. Do you know how many years I've been praying for you to finally find the right girl? Like three! Since about the second you got home from Brazil to be exact. At the rate we're going here, you're going to be seventy before you even get a gut to ask someone out!"

At this Luke sat up and turned and looked at the two of them. Stared at them really. Both of them met his gaze and finally he said, "What's going on? Why are you hassling him to go out? Are you two not, um, like together? I thought you two were an item."

Fo laughed and Charlie looked at Luke blankly and asked, "Like an item item? Fo and me?" Luke nodded and then Charlie laughed too. "Oh heavens no! That would be like dating my brother. Ick! No offense Fo. Sorry. You truly are adorable, but... Well, you know."

Luke continued to look at them as if he didn't know whether to believe them. "You're kidding, right?"

Fo leaned up and slapped him on the knee. "Dude, she's Charlie. I couldn't date Charlie. Get serious."

Still looking from one to the other of them, Luke couldn't hide his skepticism. "Is there a problem with Charlie? You two have been practically inseparable for years. Why could you not date her?"

"Of course there's a problem with Charlie. She's Charlie."

At this she had to interrupt. "Now you're not sounding all that complimentary, Forest Eldridge." She turned to Luke. "There's not really anything wrong with me, I promise, but I'm just... We're only... We could never date. That's all. We're too good of friends."

"I thought you were supposed to marry your best friend. How can you be too good of friends?"

Charlie simply shrugged looking at him wishing she could ask him about him and Lindie, but she didn't dare. She was watching his eyes and he seemed to get almost a bit wary and Charlie said, "Fo and I really are just like a brother and sister. We always have been. But I do wish he'd get a little more driven about finding his princess charming."

Fo interrupted their look. "You have no room to talk, Charlie. You're not any closer to finding the prince."

Charlie went back to lazily rocking. "I have an excuse. I have to get through my stupid law school. So there's no hurry for me. You're all but done."

"You don't have to go to law school, Charlie. You could find that gut you were talking about and tell your parents you don't want to be an attorney."

She sighed. "It's not a gut thing. It's an effort thing. I honestly think it's going to be easier to make it through law school than to convince my parents I don't need be an attorney. I'm sure they know I have no interest in it."

Luke was staring at her again. She looked back at him and he finally cracked a smile and returned to rocking. "You two are putting me on. So are you joking about both law school and being an item, or just about going to law school?"

She stopped rocking and turned to him as Fo chuckled. "You deserved that Charlie. It really is ridiculous beyond ridiculous. This is going to take years and years of your life. At some point you need to grow up and quit being such a wuss. Your prince is going to give up on you and marry a waitress."

Charlie busted up laughing. "Holy brutal, Fo! A waitress? Oh my! You're forgetting that theoretically there are some single, eligible men in law school." She turned to Luke. "See. You can't be an item when you're that painfully honest. A girlfriend would kill you."

Luke smiled. "I guess I see what you mean."

Chapter 4

The funny thing was Charlie and Lindie were becoming truly good friends. Even though Lindie was nineteen and Charlie was twenty-three, their friendship came incredibly easy. Lindie must have understood that Charlie wasn't judgmental of her in the slightest because they hit it right off, in spite of Lindie's naturally quiet personality. One evening Charlie needed to go shopping and Fo had actually finally asked his nurse friend out, so Charlie called Lindie and together they took the Taco Rocket and headed into Kalispell.

Lindie was soft spoken, but she had a nutty sense of humor and they laughed the whole time they looked through the mall there. They'd almost made it back to the ranch compound when the Taco Rocket began making the noise. Charlie tried to warn Lindie that they were going to end up walking, but even that cracked the two of them up and they laughed all the last mile of the gravel lane as they walked carrying their packages. Before turning off toward her house, Lindie told Charlie, "You should get Luke to look at your car. He can fix anything."

The next day when the computer in the kitchen went on the fritz, Evie said the same thing to Charlie. And indeed, when Luke came in for dinner and she mentioned it to him, he had it working in no time before he headed back out for evening chores.

Before riding lessons the next afternoon, Charlie took the Taco Rocket in search of a new helmet at the farm and ranch supply and ended up walking the last ways in again. She told Lindie what had happened during their lesson and the two of them laughed together again as they rode. Luke came in during the lesson and seemed pleased about the helmet, but he asked Charlie what was up with her car out on the gravel road. She told him, "Sometimes it stalls. It'll be fine again when I go get it this evening, don't worry." He simply looked at her and shook his head as he headed back out of the arena. She and Lindie laughed at him this time.

Charlie finally got up the guts to ask Lindie when she and Luke were getting married. They were riding side by side around the arena watching the girls ride and Lindie looked at her and admitted, "Actually, I'm trying to talk him out of getting married, but he's pretty hard to convince." She glanced down at Jamie asleep on the horse in front of her. "We're not really in love with each other."

She dropped her eyes self consciously. "I made some pretty stupid decisions a while back. One of them was to trust Chase. Please don't tell anyone, but this is Chase's baby not Luke's. Luke just felt like he needed to marry me to make up for Chase not staying with me. I appreciate what Luke is trying to do, but I think it might be a better idea to give the baby up for adoption rather than make Luke feel he has to marry me out of responsibility. Someday he may end up hating me for it.

"I know that sounds cold hearted to give it up." She hesitated, "But honestly, I had a lot of hopes and dreams before this happened. And much as I do love Luke, I mean we've practically grown up together. Much as I love him, it's more like a brother than a husband. Does that make sense?"

"It does. I know exactly what you mean. Fo and I are that way. And I don't think putting your baby up for adoption sounds cold hearted. I think it means you love your baby enough to want it to have a happy, stable home where the parents do love each other and the baby will be desperately wanted. As opposed to being an oops."

She paused and then continued. "I think it's okay to have hopes and dreams for yourself Lindie. I've never been married, but I would imagine it's hard enough without trying to make a go of it without being in love. It's not truly any of my business, but if you feel strongly about it, you'd better keep trying to talk to Luke. His sense of duty is strong, but he also obviously cares a great deal for you."

Lindie nodded. "He does. He's a wonderful man. The best. But he's also pretty stubborn when he thinks he's right."

"I can only imagine. How come you don't wear an engagement ring?"

"Oh, he tried to get me to go shopping with him several times, but I'm not really a ring kind of a girl. It would always be in my way. And it's not like it would symbolize some eternal, true love anyway."

This last comment sounded almost bitter and it broke Charlie's heart. She reached over and patted Lindie's arm. "Hang in there. Everything will work out however it's supposed to, in the end."

****

Thinking back on that conversation that night as she laid down to go to sleep, Charlie decided she truly believed that. When the people involved were honestly trying to do their best, God had a way of ironing out the wrinkles. She tried to keep an objective point of view in spite of her lingering crush on Luke. She genuinely liked Lindie and wanted the best for both her and her baby. It was too bad Chase had so few scruples. And that Lindie hadn't kept stronger morals and been wiser.

****

Things had been going well at the Langstons, but that all seemed to come to a grinding halt one afternoon when Richard happened to be out of town at a bull auction. To start with, when Charlie and Madge were trying to figure out why the printer was caput, Evie cut Elsa's hair while at the same time Elsa cut Jamie's. They were all sitting in a row like a miniature assembly line. Evie had a lovely neat handful of two dark braids and Jamie looked as if he'd been caught in the lawn mower.

That same day, Charlie wondered if she was smelling cigarette smoke on Tuckett. He had been spending a lot of time hanging around with the ranch hand that watched Charlie and gave her the creeps. She knew the ranch hand smoked. She hoped Tuckett had just been around the smoke and not actually smoking.

And then Angela came in from the airport in a bad mood for some reason. Her bad mood escalated rapidly when she saw the new haircuts Charlie hadn't had time to remedy yet, and then from somewhere Angela produced a bottle of wine and she started drinking. Charlie was shocked and immediately took the four kids to the swimming pool to get them away from her and her influence. Charlie thought she had things relatively under control by the time Luke showed up a little later to join them. All three of the little ones started to squeal his name and even Tuckett said, "Hey, Luke."

Charlie was just trying to discretely explain what was going on up at the house when a pretty blonde girl she had never seen before showed up. Luke didn't look very happy about her appearance, but he introduced her politely enough. "Charlie, this is our neighbor, Summer Harmon. Her dad is another rancher up the road and she comes sometimes and swims or uses the tennis courts. Summer, this is Charlie Evans from Connecticut. She's staying with us this summer and helping out with the kids for us before heading off to law school this fall."

Summer had given Charlie a halfhearted smile and then turned abruptly away to begin to all but hang on Luke. She was so obviously here to see him that Charlie looked around, wondering how in the world this girl had known Luke was taking some down time with the kids and was in the pool for once. It was the only time he'd been here with them since Charlie had gotten here and she wondered if somehow the other girl had been spying on him. She gave that thought up because of the sheer distances here and then just for a second, wondered if Luke had invited her. Almost immediately she rejected that thought, knowing without a doubt he would never encourage another woman when he was engaged to Lindie.

Charlie had no idea how Summer had known Luke was here, but Summer certainly wasn't wasting her time about nearly drooling all over him. She was hounding him so hard that Charlie wasn't the least bit surprised when he abruptly got out and went back to the bunkhouse, and then left again in his pickup truck. The fact that Summer wasn't far behind him in leaving came as little surprise.

Once she was gone, Tuckett looked after her car heading down the gravel lane with disgust. "Poor Luke. She's like a blood sucking leech or something. Always stuck to him when she's around. It drives him crazy. He can't even take an afternoon off for once."

Charlie tried to look for the positive. "At least she didn't stay long."

Tuckett laughed. "No. Not after Luke left. She's not in love with any of the rest of us, I guess. It's too bad she doesn't have a thing for Chase. He has all the time in the world to spend with her." He changed the subject. "Come on Charlie. I'll have you a cannon ball competition."

For the next half hour they had a cannonball competition. Fo showed up in the middle of it and then won. It probably wasn't very fair because he was so much bigger than everyone else, but the little kids laughed and cheered for his gigantic splashes anyway.

Eventually Charlie hauled them all out and up to the house for dinner, and then did her best to remedy the hair situation. When she was through, Evie and Elsa no longer looked like twins which was probably a good thing since they weren't. Evie still had her long, silken tresses but Elsa now sported a wispy, short pixie that was actually adorable and just fit her. Jamie was now the proud owner of a crew cut, and though Charlie was sad to see his little, endearing curls go, he could never be anything but darling. Charlie did the best she could under the circumstances and hoped Richard wasn't as upset as Angela when he got home.

Once the little ones were safely down in bed asleep, Charlie left them with Madge and took Tuckett with her to go out with Fo and Luke on the bunkhouse porch to keep him away from Angela again. Her drinking had picked up steam. An hour later, Charlie heard her musical laugh and was horrified to realize Angela actually had a male friend with her in the swimming pool right here at Richard's own house. Luke and Fo realized the same thing at about that same second and the four of them abruptly picked up and went inside the bunkhouse.

She was sure they'd all been hoping Tuckett hadn't seen what they'd seen, but she could tell from his expression that he had as well. Deciding to deal with it head on she said, "I'm sorry you have to deal with something like this at your own house, Tuck. Some people have zero respect or character. At least you can be aware that some people can't be trusted and can try to avoid this kind of thing in your own family when you grow up, huh?"

In a voice full of disgust and sadness, he replied, "Yeah, I guess so. I don't know why Dad doesn't boot her. He ought to. I don't think he even really loves her anymore."

Luke dropped a big hand to his shoulder. "He doesn't want to teach us that marriage is disposable is all, bud. He knows he's made a huge mistake. He just wants us to know that when you get married, you stay married."

Bitterly, Tuckett looked up, "Yeah, I only hope he doesn't get some terrible disease from her because of all the other men." His answer about ripped Charlie's heart right out of her chest. What an awful thing for a fourteen year old kid to have to worry about. The worst of it was he was right. Richard probably was at risk for something like that.

They ended up just keeping Tuckett out there and putting him to bed in one of the other bunks and then calling Madge to let her know that. Once he was asleep, Luke turned on the stereo low and came back to Charlie and Fo on the couch with a long, sad sigh. "Between Angela and Chase and Summer, this has been a long day."

Charlie didn't know what Chase had pulled and she didn't want to, so instead of asking, she teased, "What you need Luke, is a screen writer. Look on the bright side. There's a lot of money in film. You could call it something about putting the fun in dysfunctional. So you might have an X rating, but it'd be riveting entertainment."

"That's not very funny, Charlie."

She laughed and said, "Oh, it was too! You have to admit that was one of my cleverest of the day. C'mon"

Fo laughed at her and Luke finally cracked a smile and shook his head. He glanced over at Fo. "Has she always been this much of a nut?"

"Or worse. You should have known her in that awkward, giggly training bra stage. She was awful!"

Charlie elbowed him. "You're not supposed to use the words training bra in mixed company. Nice people don't do that. Not to mention that that is the all time hardest part of life in this universe. A fact that the entire male population doesn't even come close to understanding. It's not very fair."

"Oh, quit whining. You survived beautifully and turned out gorgeous and brilliant. We guys had to survive way worse stuff. And we couldn't bawl about it like you could."

"Hey, I didn't know bawling was allowed. Why didn't you tell me? It would have come in very handy sometimes." She was thoughtful for a minute. "What could be worse than a training bra anyway?"

He chuckled. "We can only divulge that on threat of death."

"Ah." She waved a hand. "I'm too tired tonight to threaten anyone." She got up and gave them both a high five as she went by. "I gotta go to bed. Watching infidelity is exhausting. See you guys in the morning." She stopped and put a gentle hand on Tuckett's head and whispered, "'Night Tuck."

****

The next day went better, thank heavens. Surprisingly, without even being asked, Chase helped out more while they were short handed from Richard's absence. And Angela got up and left for the airport almost immediately, in spite of the fact that she was miserably hung over. Charlie was surprised, but she had to respect Angela for it.

A few hours after she left, Richard got home. Charlie wondered all afternoon if she should try to talk to him about what happened. Finally, after dinner when Luke said he had a surprise for the three little ones and they all headed outside to see what it was, she pulled him aside. "Luke, should we tell your dad what went on here last night?"

"I already did, but it's not like he doesn't know she's doing it. He was pretty crushed when I told him what Tuckett worries about. The only thing is if they get divorced he'd have to let the kids go with her sometimes and then he'd have no way of making sure they're okay. He said he'd talk to Tuckett about it."

"Oh, good. It's none of my business, but I feel guilty hiding it from him. I saw her with another guy at the airport the very first night when I came in."

He shook his head in disgust. "Man, nothing like breaking you right in. I'm surprised you even decided to stay after that. I think she's been this way from not long after they were married. Dad says she was raised that way."

"Why did she even marry him?"

Luke gave her a lopsided grin. "Some of us think he's pretty loveable."

"He is. I'm sorry. But you know what I mean. Why get married and narrow the field?"

"I think it had a lot to do with the fact that he's kind of well-to-do. She wanted a chunk of Montana real estate to her name."

Charlie looked all around at the glorious mountains and valley, brilliant green in the late evening sunshine. Quietly, she said, "It is amazingly beautiful here. I can hardly blame her except that that's an awful reason to get married."

"Not if you're a mercenary."

"If she's that mercenary, he could offer her a tidy little sum to grant him irrevocable full custody." She nodded at the three children skipping ahead. "It's not like they're her life's passion."

"No. But he'd rather put up with Angela's stunts than have them feel like they are disposable to their own mother, at least this young. He knows from wife number two what kind of scars a mom walking out can leave on a very small child. I'm sure he'll dump her once they're older and can understand better. Otherwise, he'd just be teaching them that her escapades are acceptable. As it is, I'm pretty sure she won't be entertaining any more men in our own pool, or drink around here either. He threatened to cut off her funds."

"Good for him."

They caught up with the children and Luke asked, "Aren't you even going to ask where we're going?"

"Nope. It doesn't matter. It's all joy."

"There's a new litter of pigs."

"Really? Cool! That's a wonderful change of subject! Now I'm excited!"

"Just plan to be careful. The mother would eat these guys if she could. Literally." He nodded at the children. "Don't ever let them come out here by themselves."

"She truly would? That's horrible!"

He scooped Jamie up and lifted him to his shoulders. "The babies are cute, but pigs aren't pretty. They're big and mean and dangerous."

She took both of the little girls by the hand as they entered the barn. The smell was every bit as big and mean as Luke claimed the mother pig was, but when they got a glimpse of the babies they forgot all about the pungent odor. Luke was right. The babies were adorable and Charlie could see why Charlotte had been so enamored in the movie.

Luke tossed some feed into the trough and then leaned in and scooped up one of the babies. He handed it squealing to Charlie and then leaned in and snagged another one. They helped the little ones hold the piglets for several minutes and then put them back in and watched from outside the pen for a while longer. There were ten of them and they were fascinating as they rooted around their mother.

Just like in Charlotte's Web, there was one that was smaller than the rest. Charlie looked up at Luke. "Will that little one be okay? Will it be able to compete with the others?"

He hesitated. "We'll simply have to see. I can't do anything about it if it doesn't do well. There's no way I could take on an orphan piglet right now. Reality isn't like the cartoons, you know."

"No. I suppose not. We'll have to pray for it, -that the momma will be able to take care of it just fine."

He smiled down at her. "Pray away Charlie. God loves baby pigs."

****

She ended up on her front porch rockers again that night with Fo and Luke. She wondered out loud why he never brought Lindie with him when they hung out like this. He was somewhat hesitant when he replied, "The baby makes her really tired. By this time of night she's pretty beat."

Charlie decided to level with him. "Lindie told me the baby was Chase's."

57

There was no hiding his bitterness when Luke replied into the dark, "Chase told her he'd always loved her. She trusted him and made some poor choices she'll have to live with forever now."

"He's twenty-seven years old, Luke. You can't change him unless he wants to change. He's another one that all we can do is pray over."

"I know that. Although, there have been a few times that I've done a lot more to him than just pray for him. There's no way I can stand by and watch him disrespect women, or Dad without doing something about it. Still, I can't help being thoroughly disgusted that he can hurt people so deeply without a second thought about it. Until the day I die, I'll never be able to understand the way he thinks."

"Be grateful for that. It's a good thing. A truly good thing."

****

The next morning, before they'd even eaten breakfast the three little ones wanted to head straight out to the pig pen again. Charlie was having a time convincing them that they should eat first until Luke showed up. He quietly said they had to eat first or no pigs and the kids didn't even try to argue with him.

When they were through and it was cleaned up, he came with them to see the babies again. By the time they made it to the pig shed, Evie was getting a piggy back from him, Elsa was on his shoulders and Jamie wouldn't rest until he was seated right on top of Luke's head.

Charlie took pity on him and made jokes about getting piggy back rides to see the piggies and insisted Jamie get down and she'd give him a piggy back instead.

Luke handed him to her with a grateful sigh. "Thanks, they're all getting so big they're gonna kill me."

"They kind of like you, apparently."

He reached up and tickled Elsa. "I kind of like them too. Don't I?" Elsa squealed and began to wiggle until he nearly dropped them both before they made it to the door of the barn.

Inside it didn't take long to notice that the littlest pig wasn't holding its own all that well. It was still active, but its little sides were sunken in and it rooted around hungrily while the others were fat and lazily nursing. Charlie looked up at Luke with concern, but he only shook his head in resignation.

On the way back up to the house when the kids ran ahead, she turned to him and asked, "Will it make it?"

Again he shook his head. "Probably not. It'll probably do okay for a day or two until the others get so big and strong that it can't compete at all. Then it'll starve."

Charlie was quiet for a minute and then asked, "Is there nothing that can be done? Can it really not be bottle fed?"

"Charlie, you'd have to feed it like every two hours and it'd probably still struggle. Not to mention that pigs aren't the sweetest smelling little beasts. It's not like you could keep it in a box in the house."

As they walked, Charlie had a thought. "What if we left it in there with its momma and supplemented it with a bottle? Would that work?"

He looked at her with a slow smile and a shake of his head. "It might. It would depend on how it took the bottle I guess. You could give it a try."

That morning she went to the farm and ranch supply once again and came back armed with piglet survival gear. She had two glass bottles with black rubber nipples and twenty five pounds of milk replacer. The kids thought it was a grand idea and they rushed out to the pig barn with the warm bottle with enthusiasm. They were so excited that Charlie worried about what would happen if her idea didn't work and the runt died after all. As they went, she prayed silently and then when the little pig began to suck hungrily on the bottle almost instantly she prayed again to say thank you.

Their little pig became the highlight of their day and Charlie had to admit Luke had been right. Caring for it was a time consuming project. Every few hours during the day they would take it a bottle and then just before she went to bed and first thing in the morning before her run, Charlie would take it one as well. She didn't give it one in the middle of the night, but it seemed to be doing fine anyway. As it got stronger it was able to compete better with its siblings and sometimes when they were out there she was glad to notice it nursed its mother as well.

They'd only been at it a couple of days when Charlie realized the children had begun to share the bottle with any of the little pigs that cared to stick their noses through the fence and try to reach the bottle. She smiled when eventually there was a whole group of little piglets trying to reach for the bottle at once.

The mother pig began to try to reach the bottle as well and Charlie was concerned with how aggressive she was to the children. The next morning Charlie brought a pair of wire cutters with them and carefully cut a neat hole in the fence that was barely big enough for the piglets to get out of. It worked beautifully and the little pigs could get clear out and away from the fence. Charlie no longer worried one of the children would be bitten by the mother during their bottle feeding sessions.

When they were through bottle feeding, the babies climbed back through the hole to their momma as if they'd been trained, and Charlie wedged a piece of wood into the hole to keep them in until they came back to feed again. Watching the littlest pig eat and grow alongside the three children so happily was very fulfilling actually, and she walked back up to the main house feeling as if things here were truly going well.

Mid afternoon of that day, Charlie was in the kitchen when she heard Tuckett in the great room grumbling about something and then she heard him swear. For a few moments, she debated whether to let it go and then decided that no, swearing wasn't what a priesthood holder should be doing with a motherly influence around. At least not on her watch.

When she walked into the room with the bottle of dish soap, he knew he was in trouble and made a dash for the door with her right behind him. He had quite a head start, so she wasn't able to catch him until he'd nearly reached the indoor arena. But she finally ran him down and tackled him, laughing in the grass. Several messy minutes later they were both covered in dish soap, but there was a good chance Tuckett would never swear again in his life.

He got up gagging and spitting and she knew he wanted to cuss her, but he still laughed again anyway when he saw that she was as soapy as he was. He went to the water trough and began to rinse his mouth with the hose, and said, "Okay. I'll stop swearing. Just don't ever do that again. That stuff is nasty!" He accidentally blew a bubble and they both laughed some more.

Heading back to the house with her bottle of soap, Charlie looked up and saw Richard and Luke sitting their horses near the door of the indoor arena. They had watched the whole thing. She waved, wondering if they would think she was out of line, and then decided she had done her best and had to be okay with that. Still, at dinner that evening, she was a little bit tentative around Richard and was glad when he pulled her aside and gave her a one armed hug and thanked her for going to the trouble to wash Tuckett's mouth out with soap.

****

Things *were* going well for her here in Montana. Her folks hadn't found out she was working on a ranch, but they still weren't thrilled that she was "fooling around out west". She tried not to let her parents' disapproval over her decision to come here bother her and she was having the time of her life.

Angela and Chase were a pain, but she'd learned to deal with them. There were times when Chase would come up behind her and try to hug her that she got feisty and learned to throw an elbow with expert precision, but all in all, he was mostly only a nuisance.

One day in the great room after just having knocked the wind out of him soundly, she tore into him. "Chase, how was it your parents knew to name you that when you were only a newborn baby? Would you please just leave me alone?" She shoved him as she walked past while he was still bent over sucking air. "Keep your hands off me, or I'm going to let you have it every single time!"

She picked up the basket of folded laundry she'd been carrying and was headed for the stairs when Luke poked his head out of the office to see what was going on. His face wasn't happy and she tried to down play things as she rolled her eyes as she went past him. "He'll grow up and figure it out sometime."

Chase was relatively harmless and was only a nuisance to her. There was another guy there that actually scared her just a little. There was a ranch hand named Tyree something or other who lived in the other bunkhouse and had decided he had a thing for her. The very first time he'd paid extra attention to her, he had made the skin on the back of her neck prickle. There was something about him that flat out gave her the willies.

Fo had picked right up on her discomfort and tried to protect her from having to be around the guy, but it was a pretty small place when it came to that. She had to walk right past both bunkhouses on her way from the main house to her little cabin, and it had begun to feel a bit like running the gauntlet the last few days. She'd finally taken to following a circuitous route clear around the perimeter of the compound where Tyree wouldn't see her, but she felt foolish for letting him intimidate her like that. It wasn't like her to back away from much, but he truly bothered her for some reason.

She was determined not to let this new issue of the ranch hand interfere with her intentions to have a fabulous experience here this summer. Although she tried to stay away from him, she went on about doing what she could to be a mothering influence to the children as planned. Their garden was coming along beautifully, and she and the little ones spent some time every couple of days weeding and watering it with care. The little girls had started their dance lessons, and they had been practically living in their leotards and little dance skirts from the very first day.

Weeding and dancing and feeding the piglet were a bit of a deadly combination and the dancing clothes would probably never be the same, but the girls didn't seem to comprehend this. Charlie had worried the first time she caught Evie bottle feeding the pig and doing twirls at the same time, but the piglet appeared relatively durable and seemed to be able to handle it without throwing up its breakfast.

In the middle of the night that night Charlie woke up with the terrible thought that maybe piglets couldn't throw up and that it hadn't been able to even show it if it was motion sick. At breakfast the next morning she asked Luke if pigs could be sick if they needed to. He looked at her as if she'd grown an extra head. At that point, she decided she would let the pig be at risk rather than have Luke think she was crazy.

One day as she came in from helping Tuckett with a cow that had kicked the scraper he was using, she met Luke in the great room and had to laugh out loud when he smiled and said, "You stink like a farm girl."

Smiling sweetly in return, she replied, "That would be because I have bottle fed a piglet, taken a riding lesson, weeded a garden and helped Tuckett keep a cow from bleeding to death." Luke had sounded just like Fo for a second.

He raised his eyebrows and shook his head. "That explains it. How did you help Tuckett?"

"I held pressure on the bleeder while he did his darnedest to keep the cow snubbed tight to a post until the vet showed up."

She had to laugh again when he mimicked Fo as he said, "Dang, Chuck! I'm impressed! Your aroma is completely warranted."

She shook her head and grinned. "Well, if it's all the same to you, as soon as I check on the kids I'm going to go shower anyway, although it made Chase keep his distance, for once."

As he went into the office, Luke said, "Maybe you should wear that scent more often, for Chase's sake."

"It might even be worth it, but Fo would tease me mercilessly."

"Tell me if Chase gets over the top and I'll make him stop. And I promise I won't tell Fo anything about you smelling."

Charlie shrugged cheerfully. "He brought me here, knowing I could handle it."

Much as she tried to ignore the fact that she liked Luke too much, it was nearly impossible. There was a lot to like about Luken Langston. He was involved in everything around the ranch, and was in and out as he oversaw all the different crews and operations. A good portion of his time he spent in the ranch office there in the main house, and he took an active interest in how the kids were doing that was nothing short of admirable. He truly loved them dearly and they all knew it and adored him back.

Charlie tried, but the more she got to know him, the more respect she had for him and the way he lived his life. Every time she rode with Lindie, and especially as they became fast friends, Charlie felt guilty about her feelings for Luke.

The riding lessons were one of her favorite things about the whole summer. She had always loved horses, but had never had much opportunity to ride consistently. She was enjoying the whole experience enough that she felt silly about being paid for the chance to be here. After a week or two of riding in the arena, Lindie took them outside and they began to takes long trail rides. They would all come home tired but happy, and their skill and confidence with the horses were impressive for the short time they'd been at it.

Chapter 5

By the time she'd been at the ranch a month, about the only thing she could recognize from her old life was the ever undependable Taco Rocket. One afternoon it quit on the way home from town again. This time it didn't make the noise and then stall. This time she was only about a half mile from the ranch compound when it made a horrendous boom that nearly gave her a heart attack and shuddered as it belched a white cloud of smoke she couldn't even see through.

She finally got it stopped and hesitantly got out and opened the still smoking hood and looked at it. This stupid car had been the one thing that she'd successfully stymied her parents in in nearly her whole life. They hated it with a passion and she was relatively sure that was the reason that she'd insisted on not selling the car, even during the eighteen months of her mission to Portugal.

The car had been a total pain from the first day she had brought it home, but she cheerfully put up with its incredible lemonness because she knew she was in charge for just this one, petty little issue. It wasn't a money thing, or a college thing, or even a loyalty to the Honda corporation thing. It was that sweet, satisfying little thing called control. Her parents had never been able to get rid of this ugly silver problem, and she had almost learned to love it at the same time she cheerfully wanted to swear at it on a regular basis.

Fo had finally caught on to why she wouldn't part with the car after about six months of struggling with it. Ever since then he'd been totally on board whenever she needed help with it which was ridiculously often. Usually, he simply insisted on driving everywhere and would talk her into taking his or letting him run her if there was ever a safety issue involved.

Here in Montana she'd only ever had to drive it a handful of times, but it had never failed to break down even one of those few times. However, this was the first time it had ever pulled a full scale explosion. It had actually been quite frightening. The whole car had shaken.

She was still standing there looking at the smoke wafting off into the breeze when Luke appeared over the hill beside the road on a big bay horse. He tied the horse to the rail fence and slipped through to come and look into the engine with the same easy going attitude he approached everything else with.

When the car quit smoking and they could see better what was going on, he took out a pocket knife and then reached into the engine and pulled up a thick black hose that had a tattered end and sliced off the ragged part. Then he took a quarter out of his pocket and used it to loosen a hose clamp that he slipped over the end of the black hose, pushed it back onto something in the engine and then tightened it back up. With that done, he finally broke his silence. "Have you got any water in here anywhere?"

She dug into the back and got out the gallon jug she carried in case of emergencies and he used it to pour into the radiator. When he'd emptied it in, he said, "When I get in tonight I'll get you some more coolant, but you should be able to make it home fine with this much."

"You mean it's not finally dead forever?"

He smiled. "No, unfortunately. You only blew a radiator hose. It'll live to strand you many more times I'm afraid." With that, he calmly walked back over, ducked through the fence, got back on his horse and rode away.

Lindie had been right. He could fix anything. He'd just fixed an explosion with a pocketknife and a quarter.

He was as good as his word and that night after dinner when she wended her indirect way back to her cabin, Luke was there pouring engine coolant into her car for her. He looked up as she approached from around a nearby shed and asked, "Where have you been?"

"Up at the house, why?"

He nodded toward the shed she had just skirted. "Why are you taking the long way home lately?"

She felt slightly foolish, but leveled with him anyway. "Uh, well. I don't have to stop and visit with Tyree if I take the long way home."

He tightened the cap on her radiator and shut the hood. "I wondered if you were trying to avoid Chase. Does Tyree bother you?"

"Mmm. He doesn't bother me really. He just creeps me. Know what I mean?"

Shaking his head with that almost smile, he said, "No."

"He hasn't done anything to bother me, but he kind of makes my skin crawl. Sorry, that sounds rude, I know. I can't help it."

"Charlie, you don't need to apologize. Doesn't it occur to you that what you refer to as making your skin crawl could be a prompting to stay away from him?"

She met his eyes. "Yes, actually. I'm sure of it, in fact. That's why the funky route home. It just sounds a bit off the deep end when I voice it that way."

He picked up the empty coolant jugs. "Better off the deep end than sorry. Watch yourself and if I can find a half way plausible reason, I'll send him packing. He's not a great hand anyway." He set out toward the main house and then said over his shoulder, "Good luck with these fancy wheels."

She could hear him chuckling to himself as he went.

****

The half way plausible reason to get rid of Tyree became apparent sooner than later. The very next day when Charlie and the kids were headed to feed the piglet she caught the strangest smell coming from one of the sheds as she went past it. She could swear she was smelling marijuana smoke.

Just then Tuckett walked out of the shed and when he saw her he immediately looked guilty and hurried in the other direction. Charlie was horrified. She told the kids to wait for her right where they were and she opened the door of the shed and went inside. The smell was far stronger inside the closed shed and there was still the haze of smoke hanging in the air.

She wasn't surprised when Tyree stepped out of a stall and greeted her almost lazily. It was no great feat to figure out Tyree had been in here smoking pot with Tuckett. The air in the shed was nearly suffocating and she was instantly furious. She was so mad she decided to calm down and talk to Luke about this before deciding how to handle this situation.

Under the circumstances she wasn't afraid of Tyree and certainly didn't feel the slightest need to be civil to him

70

when he made some suggestion about the two of them getting together later. Still mad to the core, she slammed out of the door and gathering up the children she headed on toward the pig barn. She was going to cook up a ranch hand and serve him for dinner!

When the little pig was well fed, she took the kids back to the house to Madge and went in search of Luke. Richard was in the great room pulling wires out of the back of the entertainment center. She could hear him grumbling as she started to go past, and she asked, "Is something wrong, Richard?"

"Oh, this whole television system is on the fritz and Madge asked me to look at it, but really I need Luke to do it. He can fix anything. Have you seen him? This whole ranch is going to fall apart when he finally leaves here. I wish that he wanted to stay. I can't imagine why he would want to go off and be an accountant of all things."

Charlie hesitated and then said, "Actually, Richard, Luke dreads when he's going to have to leave here. He doesn't want to be an accountant. The only reason he's studying accounting is because it'll pay the bills when Chase takes over here."

Richard stopped what he was doing and stared at her. Finally, he asked, "When Chase takes over here? What are you talking about? Why would Chase take over here?"

"Luke knows that eventually you'll hand the reins here over to Chase because he's the oldest son, just like all the other generations of Langstons have. He feels like when that happens, he'll have to leave. The accounting degree is simply his plan for an occupation for when he has to find a way to make a living after he leaves here."

Richard was still staring at her aghast. "Luke told you that? Luke honestly believes that?" She nodded and he said a mild expletive and went on, "My own son Luke? Who I talk to every single day of my life? Who I thought I had the ultimate father son relationship with, thinks I'm turning this place over to Chase?"

He began to swear again and sat down heavily in a chair and Charlie wondered if she'd made a big mistake telling him as he continued to mumble, "How can he possibly think I'd turn this place over to Chase? It's all I can do not to kick Chase out because he does so little around here. Chase would destroy this place in a month." She shrugged and waited to see if he was going to yell at her or cry.

He didn't do either, but he turned to her and asked tiredly, "Is there anything else this earth shaking you've figured out since you've been here that I'm missing and need to know?"

Charlie hesitated. He seemed to honestly want to know, but some of the things would be likely to rock his world. He saw her hesitation and said, "Go ahead and tell me, Charlie. They're my children. My greatest treasures. I love them and I need to know."

"Okay..." She sat down in the chair next to him. "Do you want me to be brutally honest? Or politically correct?"

He sighed, but then said, "This is Montana, Charlie. We don't do politically correct. Let me have it."

Nodding, she began, "Well, I guess you should probably know that Lindie's baby is Chase's and Luke isn't truly in love with her, but he's going to marry her because he feels it's the only honorable thing to do. Lindie actually wants to give the baby up for adoption and go to college, but she can't get that through to Luke."

Richard closed his eyes and bowed his head quietly, but then a few seconds later looked back up. "And."

"Um... Tuckett is smoking pot with Tyree, but I'm going to kill both of them before you have a chance to, so that's a moot one."

72

At this Richard sat forward abruptly. "Smoking pot! Tuckett? You're kidding!"

She shook her head sadly. "I wish I was. I'd been wondering if Tuckett was smoking. Regular smoking, but I just caught the two of them not half an hour ago. I was looking for Luke to tell him when I came in here."

Richard put a hand up to rub the back of his neck. "What else?"

"Actually, since you already know about your wife's shenanigans, that's about it. Fo finally has a girl he really likes. That's earth shaking, but it's a good thing. Madge has an on-line fling going, but I think she's being smart about it so that's all okay. Other than the fact that Jamie thinks he wants to be a ballerina, I think everything else is under control."

He sighed and then cracked a halfhearted smile. "Oh, that's all I need on top of everything else. A son who's a ballerina."

Luke came in from the garage right then. He laughed and asked, "Chase wants to be a ballerina?"

Richard shook his head. "Not Chase, Jamie. Have you got a second Luke? There are some things Charlie and I were just discussing that I think you need to be in on."

Luke looked from one to the other and Charlie said almost guiltily, "I hope you're not going to want to kill me later, Luke."

She got up to go and added, "When you're through here with your dad, would you come find me? I'm going to need some help murdering Tyree and then trouncing Tuckett." As she walked out the door, praying for all she was worth, she could feel Luke's eyes burning into her back.

They were still talking earnestly when she came back in two hours later to start dinner and when the kids came in laughing and squealing, Luke and Richard headed into the office and shut the door behind them. Charlie started in praying silently for them again and began getting ready to grill steaks for dinner.

Dinner was long over and the kids down for bed, but she still hadn't seen Tuckett. Luke and Richard were still cloistered behind the office doors and Charlie had begun to worry in earnest. She wished Fo didn't have a date tonight so she could talk to him, and finally decided to go find Lindie. At the very least, she should admit to her what she had told Richard earlier.

She found Lindie at her parents' home across the way and they both laughed when Lindie asked her if she wanted to go shopping and walk home. Sitting on the porch step, Charlie told Lindie about her conversation that afternoon with Richard. Lindie took it calmly and patted Charlie's hand. "Don't worry, Charlie. Remember when you told me everything would work out the way it's supposed to eventually? Sometimes a little wake up call is necessary. Maybe not pleasant, but necessary."

"I know. I felt I needed to be honest with Richard when he asked, but I'm afraid Luke's going to want to kill me."

Lindie smiled. "I've known him my whole life and to my knowledge he's never killed anyone yet. A couple times he's wanted to come close with Chase, but he's pretty hard to rile." She put a hand to Charlie's shoulder. "I think you're safe."

After a while, Charlie took the long way back to her cabin and sat in one of her porch rockers in the dark and looked out across the valley. One more time she began to pray silently to herself that all would be well with these people she had grown to love like her own.

Almost an hour later when Luke quietly materialized out of the darkness, for a second he almost scared her. He stepped up on the porch and settled himself into the rocker next to hers without saying anything and she wondered for just a minute if he was angry with her, but the silence was comfortable.

When he finally did break the silence, all he asked was, "How do you know what pot smoke smells like?"

She shook her head and began to laugh softly. "I've been worrying and praying for hours for you and that's all you're going to ask me?" She laughed again. "No, I've never smoked pot or anything else, Luke. I simply went to high school. Unfortunately there were those who did." She lazily rocked her chair and after a minute asked, "Are you really mad at me?"

"No. I'm grateful to you." The quiet stretched out, broken only by the creak of her rocker.

Finally, she asked, "Did Tuckett ever come back?"

"No. Neither has Tyree. Tyree had actually asked me for tomorrow off earlier and he's gone. I think Tuckett is here somewhere. He's just worried he's gonna get crowned."

"He's right to worry. I'm going to tan his hide once you and Richard are through with him."

Luke smiled. "I'm sure that's the reason he hasn't come back. Dad and I don't scare him. You terrify him."

They rocked in silence for another while and then Luke said, "I talked to Lindie." When Charlie didn't say anything after a few minutes he continued. "Why didn't you tell me she wanted to put the baby up for adoption? Somebody should have told me."

"It wasn't truly my place."

"But you told my dad."

"I was worried someday you'd both be bitter at each other for getting married. I know you were trying to help her, but someday she would have met someone who would have made her wish she'd waited until she fell in love to commit. And you'd never have been truly happy would you? And it would have made it hard to ever be friends with Chase someday, wouldn't it?"

"It will still be hard to be friends with Chase someday. It's all I can do to tolerate him. We don't have much in common. But you're right. Marrying Lindie would have been a mistake."

"So did you call it off?"

"Yes. She's going to put it up for adoption and go to college. Dad's going to pay her tuition and expenses out of what would have been coming to Chase."

"I feel like I should apologize to you."

"Actually, I came to thank you."

She was still so unsure. "I've been praying for you. I was worried I'd made a mess of things."

"Things have been a mess, Charlie, but you didn't do it. Things have been a thousand percent better since you came."

She thought about that for a few minutes and then said, "I'm glad. I really love your family."

"We really love you too."

She had no idea how to respond to that and they rocked on in silence that lasted, but it was an incredibly sweet and comfortable long silence. Theirs had been an easy friendship that had just gotten a lot easier. The guilt Charlie had been feeling about falling in love with him was gone and it was a good feeling. A great feeling.

Sometime later Fo appeared out of the darkness too and pulled up another rocker to join in the easy quiet. Charlie wanted to ask about his date, but it felt wrong to interrupt the peace of the night and she decided to wait until the next day.

She wasn't even sure what time it was when the two of them peeled themselves out of their chairs, but it had been long enough that the peace had settled into her bones. Even when they were gone she was loathe to end this sweet night, although now that she was alone, the peace seemed to have dissipated. Now she was just incredibly tired and was tempted to nap for a second in her rocker.

Finally, she got up to go feed her little pig. The million stars over Montana may have been casting a spell, but little piggies still needed her to go to market. She was later than usual and gathered up her bottle and headed out into the ranch yards that seemed darker to her with everyone gone to bed. It was almost a little nervousing.

As she let herself into the barn and turned on the light, she was startled when Tyree came through the door behind her, shut it and said silkily, "I thought I'd see you here tonight." His eyes were much more alert than they had been this afternoon and there was no mistaking the appreciative gleam in them as he glanced her up and down. She suddenly wished she'd brought either Luke or Fo with her this time.

"I usually come and feed him." Knowing that she'd never come here late alone again, she tried to act nonchalant about him being there, and stepped away from him to call the little pigs out of the hole in the fence. When the runt made it through, she picked it up and went to put the bottle in its mouth, but Tyree grabbed her. He put a hand over her mouth and though she tried to wrestle free, she couldn't break his hold as he began to tell her close to her ear the things he planned to do to her just now.

The little pig began to squeal for all it was worth where it was being crushed between them and Charlie started to fight even harder. She knew she was in trouble, and though she was trying to keep her head, deep down she was horribly afraid. She was strong and in great shape, but Tyree was much bigger and stronger, and there wasn't much she could do to get away no matter how hard she was trying. He was hurting her face. And her arm where he was wrenching it felt as if it was going rip right off at the shoulder.

With the little pig still squealing, Charlie jerked her head back and got just enough room to bite Tyree viciously. In the process, she accidentally stepped on more of the little pigs that were milling around her feet. They set up a wholesale ruckus and then the mother got into it as well.

When she bit him, Tyree jerked his hand away swearing angrily and she screamed. She was able to get the bottle hand free and she raised it, swinging as hard as she could. She caught him on the side of the head and was almost ashamed that she hit him hard enough that the bottle shattered on impact. It showered both him and her and the whole squealing pig family with milk. He went down in a heap and the piglets at their feet got even louder when some of them were half buried under him.

Luke and Fo and Tuckett all three came flying in the barn door at almost the same second as Charlie bent to try to rescue the squished baby pigs from Tyree's unconscious body. She fished three or four of them out and by the time all the babies were back in the hole and safely cowering beside their seriously upset mother, Tyree's head had begun to bleed profusely from a gash where she'd decked him with the bottle.

While it was all happening, she'd been able to focus on fighting him, but as soon as the barn fell into silence, she began to shake. Fo and Tuckett leaned down to try to stop the blood pouring out of Tyree's head, and Charlie turned away as she started to cry uncontrollably. She tripped over the broken glass bottle and stepped out the door of the barn. Once out of the circle of light, she leaned her head against the barn wood and sobbed.

A gentle hand touched her and pulled her back, and she turned and buried her face against Luke's chest as he quietly wrapped both arms around her. For a minute he simply held her and then softly asked, "Are you all right?" She nodded, but couldn't stem the tide of tears that ran down her cheeks or control the shaking that was making her teeth chatter.

Presently Fo came out and tried to get her to speak to him. Even with him talking to her it was several minutes before she was able to get herself even partially under control. Fo went to touch her on the shoulder to get her to look up at him and she winced and started to cry harder all over again. Whatever Tyree had done to her shoulder was excruciatingly painful and she cried all the harder when they tried to ask her just what had happened.

Finally, Luke sat on the edge of the feeder and pulled her right onto his lap and tipped her chin up and said gently, "Charlie, you're okay now. I've got you. Fo's right here. Calm down and get control of yourself. You're okay." He put a big hand softly on her hair and pulled her head against his shoulder again. "You're okay. We've got you. You're okay."

Somehow his direct bluntness, and his telling her she was okay over and over made it through, and she was able to nod and pull herself together somewhat. She wiped her tears and looked up and then closed her eyes and concentrated on taking several deep breaths to steady herself. When she opened them, Richard and several more of the hands were there and Luke and Fo were both looking at her intently. Gently Luke asked her the same question he had started out with, "Are you all right?" She nodded. "Are you hurt?" She nodded again.

With her good arm, she tried to push away and Luke helped her to stand up. They bumped her other arm and she winced again. "Something is wrong with my shoulder. He was pulling on it so hard." She felt her lip quiver again and Luke reached a hand for her other shoulder.

"You're okay, Charlie." She looked up into his eyes and took another deep breath and turned away from them as the tears welled in her eyes again. Luke reached for her good arm and he and Fo led her away from the crowd that had gathered.

Richard and Tuckett came up to them and Richard said, "A deputy Sheriff will be here in a few minutes." He looked at Charlie. "Are you up to answering questions?"

She nodded through the tears she couldn't seem to stem and Luke said quietly, "He hurt her shoulder. After she talks to the Sheriff, we need to take her in to the emergency room."

Richard looked at her with the saddest eyes, "I'm so sorry about this Charlie. I never dreamed you weren't safe right here in the ranch yard. I'm so sorry."

Looking up at him, she shook her head and tried to tell him without her voice cracking, "This wasn't your fault Richard. And I'm okay." She glanced over at Luke and he met her eyes and reached up to gently wipe the tears from her cheek. She turned back to Richard. "While the police are here can we have them search Tyree's stuff and bust his butt for possession as well and get rid of him for a good long time?"

"You can be sure we will." Almost as one, the four of them turned and looked at Tuckett and he looked down.

Charlie sighed as she struggled not to cry. He glanced up at her again and she said tiredly, "I'm disappointed in you, Tuckett. You're smarter than to smoke. Especially drugs. If my shoulder wasn't so hurt I'd trounce you right this minute. As it is, I have about half a mind to haul your butt off to jail too."

Richard added, "I may do it for you Charlie. It would about be what he deserves. Tuckett Lawrence Langston, if you ever pull something like that again there will be repercussions you'll regret for the rest of forever."

Tuckett looked up at Richard and then at the rest of them. "It'll never happen again, I promise, Dad. I didn't even really want to do it anyway. I should never have hung out around Tyree." He turned to Charlie. "I'm sorry about tonight Charlie. I had no idea he would hurt someone like this. I'm sorry we didn't get here sooner."

She reached up and patted his face with her good hand and said as her tears began to fall again, "It's okay, Tuck. Just don't ever do something that could hurt you so, so much ever again. You're too good a kid to get caught up in a mess like drugs."

The sheriff showed up then and Fo and Luke stood by her as she answered his questions. Fo was horrified and Luke was furious when she glanced at them and then haltingly told the deputy the things Tyree had been threatening to do to her. She could feel the anger roll off of Luke. She was glad Tyree was already locked into the back of the squad car so Luke couldn't get at him and wondered if he was mad at her as well.

By the time she had answered the sheriff's questions it was after one o'clock in the morning, and her shoulder was hurting her so badly she could hardly take a deep breath. Luke and Fo saw the officer off and then gently helped her load in to run in to the emergency room to have it checked.

It was her left arm and as they went to pull out, she said tiredly, "You guys both have to work in the morning. I can run myself in. I can drive fine with my right arm." Both of them looked at her as if she was on drugs herself and she said, "Then at least one of you stay here. I don't need both of you."

They talked about it for a minute, and because Fo was the one that had to be in to the very hospital they were headed to the next morning at seven, he got voted to go to bed while Luke took her in. They pulled out and down the gravel road in the deep darkness of early morning and she tried not to wince when he hit a chuckhole. He turned the radio on low and she tried to focus on the music to forget the pain and prayed this trip would go quickly.

The hospital was on the near edge of town and Charlie had never been so thankful for a gentle, steady, strong arm to help her out of the truck in her life. Once inside, the attending physician asked her how she was feeling. When she started to cry again as she hesitantly admitted that she was miserable, Luke put an arm around her shoulders. The doctor hooked her up to an IV and gave her a dose of morphine for the pain even before he sent her to have an MRI taken of her shoulder. The pain relief was so welcome and she was so tired and upset that as soon as the pain subsided, she closed her eyes and went to sleep on the exam bed while Luke stood beside her.

The next thing she could remember, Luke was trying to wake her up to load her back into his truck in the parking lot. On the way home, he started to explain to her what the doctor had said, but then he was waking her up in front of the main ranch house to bring her inside. He brought her one of Angela's silky night gowns that she could get on over the sling they'd put her arm in and then helped her into a vacant guest room. He sent her to bed with the promise that someone would check on her if she needed anything in the night.

****

It was dark. Someone was there. She knew that Tyree was there, but she couldn't get the light to go on, or move to run. No sound would come out as he suddenly grabbed her. She tried to scream. There was no sound but that of her terrifying struggle. She hit him with the bottle, over and over, but he only laughed and wrenched on her shoulder and she couldn't scream. She couldn't scream.

Luke's quiet voice cut through the fear and his touch helped her to wake up and realize that it was just a nightmare. Pulling her to sit up, Luke sat right on the bed to hug her, telling her over and over that she was okay and that he would be there to protect her. She closed her eyes and clung to him as she tried to calm herself. It was only a dream. Luke was here and Tyree wasn't. She was safe. Luke was here.

With a shuddering breath, she could feel herself calm and settle back into the cottony oblivion of the medicine. Luke was here. He would protect her from Tyree.

In the middle of the night, she woke again and at first didn't know where she was. Between the pain and the strange place and the half awake flashbacks of the night before, just for a few moments she was horribly frightened and cried out. Luke answered her. The sounds of both her voice and his were intensely comforting after so many times trying to scream without being able to.

Struggling to wake, she sat up and put a hand to her chest. She tried to will her heart to stop pounding and her breathing to slow as she realized again that Luke was right there with her in the chair beside her bed.

He touched her and spoke to her quietly, then stood up next to her bed and pulled her over to lean against his chest until her heart quit racing so. He was telling her she was okay again and after a second, she laid back and calmed down, knowing she was fine with him there beside her. Part of it must have been whatever they had given her at the hospital the night before because she wasn't usually the type to be afraid like this.

The pain was brutal again and when she finally was aware of where she was, she went to get up to go to the kitchen to take something. He stopped her with his voice low there in the dark and asked where she was headed.

She let out a big breath. "I have to go take some ibuprofen. I'm dying, Luke." She stood up and then staggered slightly and leaned against the wall for a second while she got her balance.

Reaching for her good elbow, he gently pulled her back. "You get back in the bed and I'll bring you one of the pain pills they sent with you last night."

Absolutely grateful for his gentle care, she carefully eased back onto the mattress. "Thank you, Luke. You're a saint, do you know that?"

A few minutes later when he came back, he handed her a glass of milk and a pill and a couple of pieces of cheese and some crackers on a small plate. "You're going to need to eat with it or it might make you sick." She took it and within only a few minutes she could begin to feel that wonderful weightlessness that helped to ease the pain.

She knew he was still awake with her and when it had dulled to an ache, she tried to turn on her side with a sigh of relief. "Thank you, Luke. For everything. Good night."

Chapter 6

When he knew Charlie was finally sleeping soundly with the pain under control, Luke got up and went to the great room and stretched out on the couch. It was four-fifty in the morning, and though he had cat napped the last couple of hours beside her bed in the recliner, it had been an incredibly long day. And what an amazing day! If only Charlie hadn't been so harmed.

This morning he'd been engaged and had thought someday he'd end up a CPA off in a city somewhere. After his talk with his dad this evening, he now knew the whole ranch would be left in his own hands one day. He wouldn't be the only owner, but he would be the only one in charge of its stewardship and the feeling that gave him in his heart couldn't even be explained. This land was in his blood and he loved it to his very soul. The thought of someday leaving it had made him heartsick.

And as much as he cared about Lindie, knowing that someday he'd be free to marry someone he chose was like releasing him from a lifetime of bondage. Only knowing what Tuckett had been caught up in, and the fact that Charlie had been assaulted could taint the sweet taste of happiness and freedom he'd been given last night. It made him feel guilty to be so grateful when she was hurt and had been so scared earlier. And he still wanted to string Tyree up. He had to fight down the urge to destroy Tyree every time the attack entered his head.

He thought back to that afternoon weeks ago when he'd picked up the phone to hear Charlie's sweet voice saying something about her mother being a tough bird when she'd called to talk to his dad about coming. He'd had no idea then that that funny phone call would change all of their lives in such a huge way. From the very second she'd shown up here everything seemed to shift in a positive direction. She had to be the most dynamic and yet real girl he'd ever met and he enjoyed her thoroughly.

He considered how he had felt when he'd realized she and Fo weren't a couple. Then that knowledge had been incredibly frustrating because of his commitment to Lindie. Tonight, so much had happened so soon after they had decided to call off getting married that he hadn't even had a chance to explore his feelings, but nothing had ever felt so right as the hug he had given Charlie tonight when she was so scared and hurt.

Thinking again of what had happened with Tyree made him feel sad and angry all over again, but it had been a sweet balm to that sadness to be able to help her at the hospital and then here at the house tonight. Even hurt and drugged, she was good and kind and grateful and he was pretty sure he'd been permanently swept off his feet by a happy, quirky girl with long legs and blonde curls. Now he just had to figure out how his whole family could continue to function when she went off to law school this fall. He wasn't sure any of them could live without her anymore.

****

Charlie knew the little girls were here with her, but it was hard to cut through the chemicals in her brain that made her so woozy to tell them good morning. She could hear both Madge and Richard quietly encouraging them to let her rest and then she heard Jamie's cute little voice, but she was so tired. After a while she heard Luke's low, sexy voice and even this out of it she could hear the fatigue in it. He had taken such good care of her last night when she was hurt. The attraction she'd been trying to forget all these weeks had blossomed last night into something warm and sweet that made her want to smile even with her pain medicine and the frightening memories. He was a truly good, truly gorgeous man.

****

She had no idea what time of day it was when she finally woke up. It felt like morning, but the sunshine slanting through the blinds wasn't right somehow. And there were no birds. There were usually tons of birds singing in the morning. She groaned and pulled herself upright and began looking around for her clothes. She could remember Luke handing her Angela's night gown, but that was about it and she really didn't want to parade around the house in it.

The throbbing from her shoulder that had finally woken her ratcheted right up to full blown pain when she sat up, and she decided she'd waltz into the kitchen as is anyway to find some pain medicine. Just as she was about to step out into the hall, she glanced into the adjoining bathroom and saw her clothes. She was relieved until she actually got in there and went to put them on. In the ruckus last night, she'd forgotten she'd been showered in pig milk replacer, not to mention having handled multiple piglets. Her clothes were covered with sticky white spots and smelled like a barn yard.

Seeing a robe on the back of the bathroom door, she opted for it and dropped her clothes back into a wad on the tile. She put one arm into the robe and draping the other side over the sling, ran a hand through her wild curls and headed for the kitchen. The house seemed to be abandoned and the way she looked, she was glad for that as she poured a glass of orange juice and added bread to the toaster.

She was just reaching for the ibuprofen when she heard a sound and looked up to see Chase coming up the stairs from the basement. He still gave her his signature come on look and she rolled her eyes as she went to shake out the pills. He advanced into the kitchen and said, "Hey, Charlie. Heard you had some trouble, huh? Last night. You okay? You look absolutely edible when you wake up."

Charlie laughed half heartedly and shook her head as she glanced down at herself. *What an idiot.* "Chase, you are a complete dork sometimes. Do you think I could borrow some sweats and a t-shirt?"

"Sure. I'll bet you'll look hot in my clothes. It'll kind of turn me on the next time I wear them."

With the pills half way to her mouth, she stopped and stared at him in disgust. "You know what Chase, never mind. I'd truly rather just walk home in this robe than risk kind of turning you on. Keep your clothes." She took the juice and pills and turned back for the bedroom she'd been sleeping in. *What a double idiot.*

Luke appeared at the office door as she went to go past. He had a ridiculous grin on his face and she knew he'd heard their exchange. She rolled her eyes and shook her head. "Please tell me you're not going to say I look edible."

"What and risk being called a complete dork? Actually, you look thrashed. Would you like something stronger than Ibuprofen?"

"Do I have to smoke it?"

He laughed right out loud. "Go back into the kitchen and get your toast and I'll see if I can get Ahnold to go back to pumping himself up in the weight room. Then I'll find you some of Dad's sweats. Even with Tyree gone, you headed across the yard in a nightgown is probably asking for trouble. You do look kind of edible."

She gave him the look. "Stow it, Luke."

He laughed at her again while he was bringing her the little pharmacy bottle of pain pills, and then said to Chase, "I don't get the impression she's in the mood for romance, Chase. You'll have to try later when she's loopy again. Go back downstairs and leave her alone." Chase looked from one to the other of them and then headed back down the stairwell.

She took the pills and said, "Thanks. I think thanks. Now he'll probably be watching to see if I really get looped. Why did you tell him that?"

Luke leaned against the counter and watched her. "I'll be looking out for you. He knows it. But he left, didn't he? And you have to admit, they do make you pretty snockered."

"Snockered?" She rolled her eyes again and laughed. "You're both nuts. They do not make me snockered."

"Whatever you say, my edible friend. Only don't be around him when they take effect because I'm here to tell you, you're a bit out of your head on them."

"A bit out of my head only sounds marginally better than snockered. Did I do something questionable last night? Why are you hassling me?" She took a bite of her toast.

"You mean you don't remember making a pass at the doctor?"

"Funny Luke. You've been living with Fo too long. I've never made a pass in my life."

"Oh, really? I'm going to remind you you said that if a certain Dr. Greg Nichols calls you today." He didn't look like he was joking and she studied him, wondering what she'd done when she was snockered.

"Um, I didn't even have the pain pills when I was around any doctors did I?"

He shook his head, "No, but they'd given you morphine. It made you just a touch amorous." He grinned again. "You didn't really get all that snockered until we were back here and I gave you some in the night."

She continued to watch him, beginning to get worried. Amorous sounded terrible. Finally, she said, "You can't hold things I did when I was snockered against me. I can't be held responsible when I'm a bit out of my head."

When all he did was laugh and leave to head toward his dad's room, she began to get a lot more worried.

He came back in with the borrowed clothes and then leaned on the counter again and said, "Did you understand any of what Dr. Nichols told us last night? About your shoulder?"

She became slightly paranoid when she couldn't for the life of her even remember this Dr. Nichols; let alone what he'd said or what she'd done. "It's all a bit hazy. Could you remind me?"

He grinned, but didn't tease her anymore. "You're shoulder was dislocated. They call it separated. It's highly painful, but should heal fine. The splint for a week or so and then therapy and you should be good as new. But as soon as it doesn't hurt so badly you need to be moving it. Apparently if you don't start using it after about a week, it will begin to lose mobility permanently. He said it should start to feel better within a few days but those first days are going to be bad. Sorry."

"But no surgery or torn tendons or any of that ugly stuff?"

"No. Which is good. He said shoulders can be tricky, but you were in great condition." He grinned again. "Or maybe what he said was that you had a great figure. Maybe I'm getting it all mixed up."

She swept up her crumbs and picked up her dishes. "Just so you know. I'm planning to be mad at you when I feel better about teasing me when I'm snockered. That's not very fair."

"Who said I was teasing?" He looked at her with a deadpan face for a second and then smiled and headed back into the office and said over his shoulder, "Madge took the kids to a museum for the afternoon, in case you are wondering. For the time being we're not going to expect you unless we see you, so you can take your time until you feel up to small people. I'll be here in the office all day if you need anything." She heard him chuckle as she went back to the bedroom to change.

Glad Tyree was gone and she could walk straight home, she headed back to her little house. Lindie was in her parents' garden as she went by and she hugged Charlie and told her how sorry she was for what had happened. When Charlie got back to her cabin, she dressed in her own comfortable jams and lay back down. Her shoulder was ridiculously sore and she was grateful for the medicine, even if it did make her snockered. As she fell asleep, she thought again about Luke teasing her. She hoped she hadn't truly done something questionable last night.

****

She was fighting the bad dreams, trying to wake up again, and needing more pain medicine when Fo knocked on her door and let himself into her house with a steaming plate of dinner. Dragging herself up, she put on a robe and walked out of her bedroom to greet him. She knew she must look a sight when he laughed and said, "Man, Chuck, you looked wasted! You look like you've been partying for days." He gave her another grin and added, "It's too bad Dr. Nichols can't see you now. He said hi, by the way."

Wondering again what had happened at the hospital; she shook out a pill and tossed it back with a glass of milk as she eyed the plate he was carrying. He handed it to her and held her chair for her at her table before going back to the drawer and bringing her silverware. As she began to eat, she admitted to him, "It's no surprise I look wasted. I keep having these nasty flashback nightmares about Tyree. It must be the medicine. If I didn't need it so badly, I'd go without just to be able to sleep decently."

He pulled out a chair across from her and sat down. "Give it some time and hopefully it'll get better. I was talking to my mom and she told me to tell you hi and to take really good care of you." He paused for a minute and then continued soberly, "She said something like this could be a big deal emotionally, Charlie. How are you? Honestly?"

She tried to shrug her one good shoulder and act nonchalant about it, but the tears welled up in her eyes unbidden and she had to be more honest with him. "It shook me up so much more than I thought it would." She started to wipe at her tears with her hand and he got up and handed her a napkin. "Sorry." She wiped her eyes and was embarrassed as the tears continued to fall as she tried to eat. Finally, she whispered, "I was so scared, Fo. He was so strong. I couldn't get away from him. That's the most vulnerable feeling you can ever imagine. It was awful."

He stood up and came over to stand beside her and rub her good shoulder as they heard a knock at her screen door. Luke poked his head in and was just about to say something when he saw her tears and quietly came inside and approached the table. He didn't say anything, just looked from one to the other of them. After a minute Charlie tried to smile through her tears and Fo said, "I'm glad you're here, Luke." Fo glanced down at Charlie and squeezed her shoulder again. "If I go out tonight, would you watch over her for me? It might be best if she had some company." He looked down at Charlie and asked, "Should I break my date? Do you need me to stay here with you tonight?"

Shaking her head, she tried to shut off her tears and smile. "Heavens no! Once you've finally asked someone out, I'm not going to be the one to break it! I'm fine. Maybe a little emotional. Go have fun. When do we get to meet this girl?"

He was watching her like a hawk and then finally seemed to decide she would indeed, be okay. "Soon. I definitely need your opinion. I'm just waiting long enough that she doesn't assume you and I are an item the way everyone else does." He put a hand on her head and ruffled her wild, tousled curls. "Take care of yourself. Call me if you need to." He looked up and met Luke's eyes. "Take care of her for me, Luke. She's my main life organizer. I can't be having her out of commission."

Luke smiled down at her. "I'll babysit her for you. Go on your date. But I want to meet your girl too."

"Forget it, dude. She wouldn't even look at me again. You stay here and babysit and keep your distance." With that, he walked out the door and let it cheerfully slam behind him. Luke pulled out the same chair Fo had been sitting in and sat down.

For a second or two he only watched her and she self-consciously wiped at her eyes again with the napkin. "Sorry. I'm not sure where these tears are coming from. How has your day gone? Did you get a nap after your short night?"

He shook his head. "Not yet, but I'm working on it. How's the shoulder? Are you staying ahead of the pain?"

"Yes and no, I take the pills and then fall asleep and then don't wake up until it's bad again, but I'm okay. Have you already eaten? Do you want to share mine?"

"I ate." He paused again and then said quietly, "Madge thinks we need to get you some counseling after last night. What do you think? She said this might be a big thing to deal with psychologically. Do you want me to find you someone?"

At his question, the tears filled her eyes again and she covered them with her napkin and took several deep breaths. "Sorry." After a minute or two, she shook her head and ran a hand through her hair. "I think I'm okay. If I can just get a handle on the pesky nightmares. Or maybe they're daymares, when I'm napping. Which is it?" He didn't answer her lame attempt to joke. He was still watching her and she had to softly admit the same thing to him she had said to Fo, "He was so strong I didn't think I could get away and...I was scared." After another uncomfortable minute he got up and came to stand beside her just as Fo had done.

He put a hand on her shoulder and gently asked, "Would it help to talk about it? Or would it help to completely try to get your mind off of it?"

"Get my mind off of it. Definitely. Let's change the subject. Tell me what went on around here today."

For the next few minutes he told her about the little ones reaction to the museum and how they had taken care of the piggies without her and even how Tuckett had been the model of a perfect teenager all day and she finally honestly smiled. Having the pain pill start to take effect helped her heart almost as much as his conversation did.

When he went back to his chair and sat down again, she asked, "Do you think we could watch a movie? I'm too looped to do much, but I'm sick of sleeping. Are you still working or are you done for the night?"

"I'm done. I'll feed the little pig late, but other than that I'm through. Sure, we could watch something. What are you in the mood for?"

"You pick. Just nothing rated R. Something that will keep me from thinking."

"I don't watch Rs. Are you thinking action, comedy or chick flick?"

She yawned and got up to rinse her plate. "Surprise me. Can we watch in the bunkhouse?"

"Absolutely. Bring your pillow and we'll find you a blankie."

****

When Fo showed up at eleven thirty, he had to smile at the two of them there on the cowhide couch. Their movie was still rolling, but both of them were dead to the world. Luke was leaning against the end of the couch and she was snuggled over against his chest with her feet curled up beside her and her pillow had fallen to the floor in front of them. Fo sat down in the recliner and watched the last part of My Big Fat Greek Wedding, wondering if his best friend hadn't finally found her prince charming. Luke was strong enough to deal with her all powerful family and keep her from getting squished by them quite nicely. Still, knowing her, she would be hesitant to acknowledge she'd found him.

As the credits began to roll, he woke the two of them up and as he looked at her tired eyes, he said, "I've been thinking about you tonight, Chuck. Would you like a blessing? Would that help you?"

She sighed and nodded her head gratefully. "I would love that. Would you guys mind?"

Luke gave her a gentle, tired smile. "Anything for you, Charlie."

****

All the next day she lay around trying to fight either the pain or the snockeredness. By the following day she was absolutely stir crazy and showed up in the Langston's kitchen bright and early, determined to do her best to pull her weight. Luke watched her quietly as he told her good morning and she wondered for a minute if he was going to send her back to bed. He must have understood that she needed to be up and going because he only took the platter she was carrying one handed and set it on the table without commenting.

Richard did try to talk her into taking at least another day, but he too must have understood she needed to get busy so that she didn't have so much time on her hands to think. He finally said, "Well, welcome back. We've missed you terribly. Haven't we kids?" The little ones all answered enthusiastically and Jamie gave her a hug around her leg that nearly tripped her as Richard went on to his children, "Charlie still isn't feeling so great. And she isn't supposed to be using her arm yet. Can you guys take good care of her for us today?"

Evie said, "Well take good care of her, Daddy. And we'll even feed Wilbur all by ourselves."

At this Luke interjected, "No, you won't Evie. Don't you go up there without an adult. You know the rules. That mother pig could hurt you. I'll help you. Or Tuckett will."

The kids were disappointed, but didn't question him as Richard asked, "Who's Wilbur?"

Madge answered, "Wilbur is their piglet, Richard."

Relieved, Richard said, "Oh, good. For a minute there I thought we'd gotten yet another dog."

Placidly, Madge assured him, "No, thank goodness. Six is plenty. It's only a stinky little porker that I understand likes to dance."

For a second Richard looked around the table perplexed. "Likes to dance? Do I dare ask what you mean, Madge?"

At his question Charlie and Luke exchanged a look as Elsa said innocently, "Oh, he does like to dance, Daddy! He loves it when I twirl him when I'm giving him his bottle!"

Without skipping a beat, Richard replied, "Yes, I imagine he does." He turned to Luke and asked, "Do pigs get motion sick, do you suppose?"

Luke met Charlie's eyes with a smile. "I believe Charlie was concerned about that as well. Did you ever call the vet, Charlie? What did he say?"

Smiling, she assured him, "You thought I was nuts when I wondered and there was no way I was asking someone else. At any rate, the piggies seem fine in spite of twirling. It's the ballet outfits I worry about. They haven't looked the same since the pigs were born."

Jamie pitched in from his high chair, "Can I get a twirly skirt, Daddy? Evie and Elsa won't share wif me. They're mean."

Richard took him out of his high chair and wiped his face with his napkin as he said soberly, "This is just one of the great injustices of life you're going to have to face I'm afraid, Son. Girls never share their twirly skirts with their brothers."

Jamie wasn't mollified by Richard's air of hopelessness. "Aw, Daddy. Can't you make 'em share? I can twirl good as bof of 'em."

"I'll bet you can. How is your little pig doing anyway? Is he getting along okay?"

At this Jamie beamed. "He's jus great! He's never gonna die now. We maked him heowfy!"

Richard looked at Madge and asked, "Heowfy?"

The housekeeper answered placidly, "Healthy, Richard. The piggie is now healthy."

Nodding, Richard turned back to Jamie. "Of course. I'm so glad he's healthy."

Everyone smiled at Jamie's cuteness until Elsa told him matter-of-factly, "Yes, he is too gonna die. What do you think pigs are for? He's going to grow up and be turned into meat. That's why we raise pigs for. Just like our cows."

Jamie was horrified and burst into tears. Richard hugged him as he grimaced at Elsa. "Elsa, that's enough. Don't." He turned back to Jamie. "Jamie, she's right, but you know we raise animals to help feed people. That's why we have them. People need food. It's okay, don't cry."

Tears ran down his little cheeks as he sobbed. "I don't want to kill Wilbur! He's my fren. I don't want to kill Wilbur!"

Richard got up and put the devastated little boy over his shoulder and said gently but firmly, "That's enough, Jamie. Stop. You're too big a boy to behave like this. Remember how big you are getting?"

Jamie lifted his head and perked up. "I am big now, amn't I, Daddy?" Then he remembered what Elsa had said and his face fell into tears again. "But I don't want to kill Wilbur!"

Rolling his eyes behind Jamie's head, Richard said, "Maybe Wilbur won't be made into meat. Maybe he'll be one of the daddy pigs. Settle down." Heading for the front door, Richard said, "Excuse us. We're going to see if there are any trucks in the sand pile." As soon as he said that, Evie and Elsa got up from their chairs and Charlie was thrilled to see them pick up their plates and take them to the sink before they too headed for the front door.

With all three of the little ones gone, the table became remarkably peaceful and Tuckett smiled and said, "I'm being really quiet now, amn't I Luke?"

They all laughed as Charlie began to get up and one handedly clear the table. "I think I'd like to keep him little forever. He's so adorable."

Chase headed for the stairwell and Luke nudged Tuckett as he went past. "Yeah, Tuckett was that adorable when he was that size too and now look at him. His hair grew into a poof ball."

Charlie put her one good arm around Tuckett's waist. "He's still adorable. In a Shetland pony kind of way. What are you doing today, Tuck? Are you free to help me grocery shop? Or are you working with your dad?"

"I'm working with Dad in the morning, but I could help you this afternoon if you need."

"Good. Plan on that then please. Until I get my other arm back, I need all the help I can get. In fact, if it's all right with you, let's go have lunch with Fo at the hospital while we're in town. Can you be ready a little before noon?"

"Sure, whatever." Tuckett took his own plate to the sink and then went out the door and Luke picked up what was left of the breakfast and followed Madge and Charlie to the kitchen.

Standing beside Charlie at the sink he asked, "Do I detect an ulterior motive in taking Tuckett grocery shopping?"

"Am I that transparent? I thought I'd run him through the cancer wing and let him see up close and personal what will happen to him if he smokes. If the patients don't mind, that is. Maybe we can scare the need to ever light up again right out of him."

"That's a very good idea. Are you sure you're up to it?"

"No, but I get the easy part. You get to help him research what pot does to the male reproductive organs." She smiled up at him as she began to load the dishwasher.

He looked shocked at that. "I do?"

"You do. We need to scare the drugs out of him, too."

"Do I know what pot does to the male reproductive organs?"

She smiled again. "If you don't now, you will."

He turned toward the door. "How do you know so much about pot?" He paused and then added. "Or male reproductive organs?"

"I simply listened in health, Luke. I promise, I've never dabbled in either. There are some great websites about medical stuff." She grinned at him. "Good luck!"

He went on out the door shaking his head and Madge laughed with Charlie when he was gone. "Tuckett was the one you wanted to scare, but right now I think Luke's the one worried."

"Ah, it'll help him practice for being a good father."

Madge sighed. "He get's plenty of that around here I'm afraid. Sometimes I wonder if he'll ever be able to get married and settle down with a wife without having to still be the other parent to these little ones."

Charlie considered that for a minute. "You may be right, Madge, but life brings all kinds of issues to everyone. Hopefully, when Luke finally does marry, his wife will understand and help him through what's on his plate."

The older woman looked at Charlie for a long moment before she went on, "I 'magine things will work out all right eventually. Luke's a good man. The best. I expect that he'll end up with a great woman to work beside him, come what may." With that, Madge went back to

wiping down the counter as Charlie thoughtfully went
search of the little ones to get them ready for their swim.
lesson.

Chapter 7

Charlie had known that the trip to the hospital would bring some surprises, but she didn't realize she would be the one surprised. As she and Tuckett walked into the hospital cafeteria, where she had arranged to meet Fo for lunch, she was nonplussed when a brown haired doctor in scrubs, looking to be in his early thirties stood up from Fo's table as well and greeted her warmly, "Charlie! It's so good to see you again. How is that shoulder coming along?"

Charlie glanced at Fo in confusion before noticing the name on the doctor's staff ID tag that hung around his neck. Dr. Greg Nichols. She tried to smile and act nonchalant as she began to worry again. Luke had joked about her making a pass at a Dr. Nichols. She could feel her face flush as she tried to tell herself making passes wasn't her style, even when she was a little drugged. She had to qualify that thought though. How did she know how she acted when she was under a chemical influence? She smiled bravely and stuck out her hand to meet his. Oh, well. What was done was done and all she could do now was her best to rectify things, if in fact there was something to rectify.

This Dr. Nichols was apparently well acquainted with Fo. He joined them for lunch, making no secret of the fact he wanted to further his friendship with Charlie. She knew Fo could sense her hesitation and was grateful for her and Fo's ability to almost read each others thoughts, when he communicated that this guy was relatively okay. She'd have to pick Fo's brain later and see if he had any idea just what she'd done that night at the hospital.

She made it through the lunch and then her foray into the scary world of lung cancer was a resounding success. They'd stopped at the nurse's station and when Charlie explained what she had in mind; one of the nurses nodded her head and said, "I'll bet Mr. Nelson would be more than happy to meet with Tuckett here. Come with me."

She had set off with Charlie and a very tentative Tuckett behind her. This Mr. Nelson had indeed, been more than willing to try to discourage Tuckett from ever inhaling anything. He was in the advanced stages of lung cancer and was basically being kept comfortable until he passed away in a mere handful of days from what his doctors expected.

He looked as if he was dying and breathed through a device implanted in his neck because his throat and mouth had been so damaged as well. It was all Tuckett and Charlie could do to understand him as he struggled to speak. If Charlie had wanted a graphic example of why Tuckett should obey the Word of Wisdom, she couldn't have asked for anyone more convincing. For more than half an hour this kind and regretful man struggled to talk with them before he finally closed his eyes in exhaustion and they headed back to the Taco Rocket. It was a much wiser and more sober Tuckett that held the door for Charlie as she climbed into the driver's seat.

Charlie was tired and had had no pain medication in too long and the drive to the grocery store was quiet after what they'd just seen. When she pulled into the lot they sat for a minute and then, finally, she simply looked over at

Tuckett and he met her gaze evenly without saying a word. Nothing needed to be said after that.

She swiveled to open her driver's side door with her right hand and Tuckett asked, "Are you sure you're up to this, Charlie? You don't look so good."

She gave him a weak smile. "No, I'm not sure, but we need groceries. We'll hurry and get only what we need for a day or two and go home and I'll take something. I can't take anything when I'm driving. That would be as dangerous as driving drunk." Finally, she got the door open and they hurriedly shopped. But she still wished that Tuckett had his license by the time they got loaded in and headed for home. The shoulder was positively miserable.

For the first time, she was totally disgusted when the Taco Rocket stalled on the gravel road long before they got near the ranch house. She put her head right down on the steering wheel and wanted to cuss the little car that had been her symbol of rebellion against her parents' power for so long. She hated to admit it, but it was long past time she got more dependable transportation.

After gathering her purse, she was gingerly starting to get out when Luke pulled up behind them in his truck. She had never been so grateful to see anyone in her life, and it wasn't just that he looked absolutely masculine in his boots and jeans and chaps. Without saying anything, he helped them load their groceries into the back seat of his truck and then he held the door for Charlie to climb into the front with a sigh.

As they pulled away, he looked over at her and asked, "You okay?"

She shook her head. "I'm sore. Sorry. I thought I could do it, but it was too much. Thanks for rescuing us. Our ice cream would have been soup."

He glanced in the rearview mirror at her car fading into the dust and gave her a lazy smile. "Would you be terribly offended if I bought you a car for the summer to run ranch errands like this? It might be nice to be able to make it all the way home from time to time."

"Usually I would be, but today you could buy me a Porsche and get away with it. Every ounce of rebellion I own has leaked out."

He chuckled. "You must be sore. I don't know that I've ever seen you without that feisty little attitude. I think I'll take advantage of it to give you a car, but a Porsche might be pushing it in these mountains. You might be better off with a four wheel drive and some clearance. Mud or snow would leave you just as stranded in a Porsche as your dead Honda."

With a tired laugh, she said, "I was kidding about a Porsche, Luke. I was kidding about any car. Let me get home and take something for this shoulder and tomorrow I'll be happy with the Taco Rocket again."

He and Tuckett both busted up. "The Taco Rocket? I'd have thought anything Rocket was a bit of a misnomer, but I must be mistaken. I'm sure it's faster than it looks."

From the back seat, Tuckett interjected, "It's not. Hurry and buy her the new car. I never know if I'm going to make it home when I go with her. She should call it the Molasses Road Kill."

Charlie closed her eyes and said tiredly, "I'll let you get away with that today, Tuckett, but tomorrow I'm going to be defensive again, so plan on it. Fo and I had an incident the very first day I bought it with flying Mexican food. I was figuring out how touchy the brakes were. Thus the nickname. That car has gotten me through college and a mission."

"Hey, I didn't know you could take a car on your mission! Where did you go? I hope I get the same mission. Maybe I'll take a Corvette!"

She smiled and opened her eyes. "You can't take a car on your mission. I just meant that the Taco Rocket and its accompanying rebel streak help me make it through some of the struggles. At first Portugal felt like another planet. It's silly, but that car makes me feel like I can deal with stuff better for some reason."

Luke looked over at her. "Maybe you'd better keep the car. Or get another one that makes you feel just as capable. What is it about the Taco Rocket that makes you feel stronger?"

She gave him a sheepish smile, closed her eyes again, leaned her head back and admitted, "That my parents hated it. They wanted me in a respectable, new, little Mercedes sedan. It was the first battle I ever won. I think it's still the only battle I've ever won."

Luke said, "Dang, now you're making me feel guilty for wanting to replace your junker car. We're all going back to Connecticut for some retirement reception for Fo's dad. Are we going to get to meet your parents?"

Without opening her eyes she said, "I don't even know for sure that I'm going to go. I know that sounds so uncaring, but I'm not sure I'm up to dealing with them right now. Plus, you're forgetting Elroy. I have to deal with him as well. As wimpy as I am about standing up to them, I'm likely to be engaged against my will before I get back here."

Luke chuckled. "I'm having a hard time picturing you so easily manipulated. Are you sure you're not embellishing here? You could just elbow him like you do Chase and he'd get the message, don't you think?"

Charlie tried to turn and ease the pound in her shoulder. "Like Chase has gotten the message. Plus, Elroy's an attorney. I'd probably end up being sued and engaged." She opened her eyes as they rumbled across the bridge and sighed gratefully when Luke pulled straight to her house first thing, then got out to help her out.

On her porch he was surprised when she had to dig a key out of her purse to get in. "Wow. I think this is the first time in my life that someone around here has locked a door."

"Sorry. I guess it's the big city girl in me. Give me a second to take something and I'll come up and put the groceries away and start getting dinner."

For once, the administrator came out in him toward her. "No, you won't. Take something and put some ice on your shoulder and go lie down. We can handle the groceries and dinner. I'll even send you a plate. Just get a handle on the pain and relax. Honestly, you shouldn't be back at all yet."

She looked up at him and then turned to go into her kitchen and take the pill bottle out of the cupboard. "Don't be so bossy. I'm too sore to argue."

"So don't argue. And I am your boss theoretically. So mind me. Go to bed. I'll send Fo up to check on you."

She laughed at the dichotomy between his stern words and his gentle voice. "You can't make me believe you're anything but a softy, so give it up. But I'll be good anyway. Gratefully. Thanks for bringing me home. Maybe tomorrow I'll be more up to things."

As he shut the door behind him she stared at it for a moment. He was incredibly sexy when he was bossy. She took the pill, got the recommended ice and went into her bedroom to change and lie down. While she waited for the painkiller to kick in she thought about their conversation. It probably was time to get a new car, but she didn't have to tell her parents about it just yet. And she couldn't not go to Fo's dad's big to-do back east. It would be rude and cowardly anyway.

When she finally felt the blessed relief, she gratefully let herself drift off to sleep, enjoying that dreamy, almost happy distance from reality. Luke was really adorable. She should be more careful about how she was feeling about him.

****

Luke must have taken her seriously about how her willingness to drive a different car would fade the next day, because when Fo came to check on her when he got home from work, she was stunned when he asked whose new SUV was out in front of her house. She dragged herself to the door and wondered if she'd taken too many pills and was hallucinating. There was a shiny, pewter GMC Yukon with new stickers in the window parked beside the rusting Taco Rocket in the gravel parking.

She went out and walked all the way around it with Fo at her heels, and finally, she whispered, "He didn't really."

"Who didn't really what?" Fo was mystified at what was going on.

She sighed and went back into the house and collapsed onto the couch. "Your cousin, the lunatic. That's who. For thirty seconds I admitted that I ought to get a more dependable car and he has that thing brought in. I should never have discussed cars when I was so sore. Now look what he did! How am I ever going to resist that?" She looked up at him and almost felt weepy again. "How wealthy are these guys? He had to have simply called and ordered it. There's no way he even had time to have gone and gotten it."

Fo laughed. "That's yours? Wow, you must have been sore!" He laughed again, shaking his head. "You may have finally met your match, Charlie. Which is a good thing. Now I won't have to worry about you every single time you go anywhere. Quit acting so pitifully woeful.

That's a gorgeous vehicle! Let's go out and look at it. C'mon."

She shook her head. "No. In the first place, I'm too tired and in the second, I should make him return it. Who calls and orders something like that? What? Did he think he was calling Dominos? Oh, it almost makes me mad, except he's so dang sweet about everything." She hid her face with a pillow and this time she did start to bawl.

Fo looked at her warily, then sat down next to her on the couch and asked hesitantly, "Charlie?"

He sounded so worried that she looked up at him and smiled through her tears. "What?

"You're kind of freakin' out on me here. What's going on? Why did Luke buy you a truck and why are you crying over it?"

She wiped at her eyes frustratedly. "Oh, I don't know on either count. The Taco Rocket quit again and Luke hauled Tuckett and me home, and I hadn't had enough pain medicine because I was driving, and I admitted that I should get something more dependable, and he asked if I'd be offended if he bought something safer for me to drive for the summer." She finally wound down and took a deep breath.

"And what did you tell him?"

She groaned. "That he could buy me a Porsche if he wanted to today, but tomorrow I'd be perfectly happy with the Taco Rocket again. What I meant was just that I was having a weaker moment, and tomorrow I'd be fine. I never dreamed he'd buy me a new SUV. I mean it's not mine. He said it was for me to drive this summer on ranch errands, but still. Now what do I do?" She fairly wailed the last.

Gently, Fo asked, "Since you're already bawling, can I be mean and say that, truthfully, if Tuckett was my son, I wouldn't want him riding in your car, no matter how much

I trusted your driving skills. Heck, I hate it when you drive it at all, but I don't want to hurt your feelings. I just try to always make sure I know where you're headed in case I have to come rescue you. That being said, they probably only want their children to be driven as safely as possible. Take the Yukon graciously for the kids' sake. At the end of the summer you can always drive away from here in the Taco Rocket with your pride intact." He ended with a grin and she had to smile back.

"You were right. That was mean. And do you truly think I'll be able to face that rusty Honda after driving in relative luxury for more than a month? The Taco Rocket's days are probably numbered."

Fo grinned. "Honestly, I hope you never end up driving away from here. I think you should marry Luke and live happily ever after right here in Montana, but I would never dare actually tell you that. So..."

She looked at him wide eyed. "Fo! You're crazy! You have love on the brain. Luke thinks I'm as much of one of the guys as you do, and I'm headed back to Utah to school. Can you even imagine the tough old bird if I announced I was staying in Montana?"

"How do you know Luke thinks of you as one of the guys? He must think something good about you. He just bought you a truck! And what do you think about him? Isn't that the real issue here? Law school doesn't even matter to you."

She looked up at him and leaned her head back against the couch again with a sigh. "I'm not even going to answer that on the grounds it might incriminate me. I should never have come here. Why didn't you tell me your cousin was gorgeous and sweet and smart and... and everything. I liked him even before he was unengaged. I felt terrible."

He laughed and put his arm around her and pulled her to lean against him. "What. It's not so bad. I think the world of him. What's wrong with Luke?"

"Nothing. Except he's a Montana rancher. Apparently a rich Montana rancher and I'm a Connecticut law student. And you know staying here isn't an option. My parents would send in the FBI if I even considered it. Not to mention the fact that Luke doesn't know I exist, except that he needs to rescue me regularly."

"Oh, quit whining. You're positively sniveling. Listen to you. What's wrong with a rich Montana rancher? You just said he was gorgeous and sweet and smart. And I think quite a bit of him frankly. I think he's perfect for you. He could deal with you and keep on ticking. If you know what I mean."

She eyed him suspiciously. "No. I don't know what you mean. Explain yourself Forest Eldridge. What's wrong with me?"

"Nothing. That's the problem. Can you imagine a regular Joe mediocre attorney trying to keep up with you? He'd be intimidated in seconds. You need someone that can keep up with both how competent you are, and can match your strength. That makes it a lot harder. There's not one man in ten million that could do it. Luke could."

"Strength." She gave another big sigh. "I'm so strong that I can't even *not* go to law school. That's pretty strong isn't it?" She put her feet down off the coffee table. "I guess I'd better get up and make my plane reservations to go back east. As much as I'd like to stay here, I know I need to go. Do you know when everyone else is flying out? I'll try to get on the same plane."

"Richard bought your ticket days ago with the rest of ours. I told him you'd worry about it and finally decide you had to go and he bought it so you're all set."

"I guess you do know me. How many days are we staying there?"

"Two or three. I'm not sure. We'll have to ask them. I told Richard to get you a hotel room too so you could use the excuse that they need help with the kids. That way you won't be so toasted by the all powerful by the time we leave again."

"Thank you, but isn't that overkill or petty or something? I ought to be able to spend time with my own parents. You'd think I was three."

He looked at her steadily. "Charlie, it isn't that you can't handle spending time with your parents. You can handle it fine. You just don't enjoy it. And honestly, they would rather be doing their own thing too, don't you think? It's simply more pleasant this way. It's not ideal, but I truly believe they are to blame. You try; they just never stop to consider your wants or needs. You have good parents, Chuck. Only they're frankly more interested in their careers and appearances than in happy, healthy relationships with their kids."

She shook her head. "No, it has to be my fault as well, Fo. They get along fine with everyone else. Well, almost everyone else."

"No, Charlie, they don't. The only ones they get along that great with are the ones that also focus on career and appearances. The eternities aren't necessarily a priority there. I mean they're good people, don't get me wrong. But the prophets don't say get a powerful career and put your kids in daycare."

She gave him tired smile. "When you put it that way it reminds me that it's okay to disobey your parents to follow the Brethren."

He patted her hand. "You're an incredibly smart and strong woman, Charlie. And you have your head on straight. Trust your own judgment on the important stuff.

You and I both know your priorities are much more in line with what the Savior wanted than your parents' are. What you need to do, Charlie, is stop feeling guilty for growing up and growing away. Quit apologizing for making good choices. Yes, I think it's good not to fight with them about it, but that only makes it even more okay to separate yourself some. Stay at the hotel and don't feel guilty about it. We'll go to lunch with your parents and have dinner. And we'll dress up and play the appearances game a couple of times for them, but we're not going to be bullied or feel guilty for you making your own decisions."

His pep talk made her laugh. "You're so good for me. I needed to hear that. Could you tell me that same thing on the flight over?"

"Sure. But it's gonna cost you. Have you already eaten?"

She shook her head. "No, and I'm starving. I haven't had anything since lunch. Speaking of lunch, how did Dr. Nichols know me? Did he say?"

Fo grinned at her. "Luke said he didn't think you remembered, but I thought he was kidding. You really don't remember?"

Hesitantly, she admitted, "No, and it worries me. Luke teased me about making a pass at him when I was on morphine, but I don't even remember him. I've always reacted strongly to drugs. Usually, I only have to have like half a dose, but that night I was tired and upset as well, and they must have given me a whopper dose. I hope I didn't do something questionable."

He thought this whole thing was funny. "That's something else we'll have to ask Luke about. In the mean time, Dr. Nichols definitely wants to get better acquainted with you." He laughed and she grimaced. It made him laugh again and say, "He's not so bad. He's not a member, but maybe you could convert him."

They both looked up at a knock on her door. Luke pushed open the screen door and poked his head inside. "Anybody home?"

Charlie answered, trying to ignore Fo's grin, "We're home. Come on in."

Luke walked in carrying a plate covered with tin foil. "Sorry, Fo. I didn't realize you were here or I'd have brought two plates. Have you eaten?"

"Not yet. I'll go find something in a minute. We were just talking about you. We have some questions for you. Well, Charlie does. Did you really buy her some wheels?"

Luke looked from one to the other of them, then handed her the plate and went to find her some silverware. "She said she needed something more dependable." He handed her the silverware and went back to bring her a paper towel and a glass of milk.

She took his offerings graciously, but then said, "Luke, hadn't we better talk about this? I feel terrible. I was only being whiny because my shoulder hurt. You didn't need to do that."

He hesitated to answer her and Fo said, "I was just telling her that if Tuckett was my kid, I wouldn't want him riding in the Taco Rocket, so I've been working on her. And she's reasonable, even when she's rebellious."

Luke grinned. "Is that true? You're reasonable even when you're rebellious?"

She looked up from peeking under the foil. "I suppose."

"You don't sound very enthused about being reasonable."

"I just know where this is headed and I feel completely guilty about that shiny, new SUV out there. And I'm certainly not going to disagree with you when you brought me such marvelous dinner. Thank you."

Luke waved a hand and sank into the chair beside them. "You're welcome. Don't feel guilty about the Yukon. We'll use it around here somewhere. How's the shoulder? You look better than you did earlier."

She nodded. "It's much better, thank you. I'm sorry that I over did. How was Tuckett after we got back? It was a pretty graphic hospital visit today."

"Tuckett was fine. At least until we got on-line after dinner to look at the marijuana residues. Between the two of us, I hope he truly won't dabble in anything ever again." Fo was looking from one to the other of them, but Luke went on. This time with a teasing grin. "He did mention that you had an enthusiastic lunch with Dr. Nichols. How did that go?"

Charlie rolled her eyes. "Honestly, Luke. What did I do that night in the hospital? I need you to tell me. I didn't even recognize him and he greeted me like a long lost friend."

Fo smiled at her distress and asked Luke, "Why is she looking so guilty here, Luke? Did she do something really questionable the other night?"

Looking from one to the other of them again, Luke shook his head. "No. She just was a little too willing to lean on the good doctor. Literally. I had to kind of get possessive that night, because he was far too willing to be leaned on."

Charlie put a hand to her forehead in embarrassment. "Really?"

Luke smiled. "Really."

"Oh, I'm so sorry. They must have given me too much. I'm not usually that way, I promise."

Fo laughed at her. "So the real Charlie finally comes through. They say your true character comes out at times like that."

She threw a couch pillow at him. "Oh stop. You know I'm not like that."

"Apparently you are deep down. Why else would you snuggle up to someone you don't even remember?" She reached for another pillow and he stood up. "I think I'll go in search of that dinner now."

He walked toward the door, but before he ducked out he said to Charlie, "Bye, Toots." To Luke he said, "Watch her. She's on pain meds and it makes her cuddly."

The screen door slammed as the couch pillow hit the jamb and Luke laughed at her too. "You're actually a pretty good shot. You didn't even spill your dinner." He went and retrieved the pillow. "What else did you want to know? Fo said you had questions. Plural."

"We were wondering what the travel plans were for Connecticut. I was getting ready to make my flight arrangements, but Fo said your dad already got my ticket. Do you know what the dates are?"

"I think we leave early Thursday and return Saturday night red eye. Will that work for you?"

"Anything is fine. I'm actually not very thrilled to be going and it makes me feel so guilty. Fo was just giving me a lecture about it."

"Why don't you want to go back there? Is it Connecticut or the tough old bird?"

She sighed. "Birds plural. I truly do love my parents, but I'd as soon not have the confrontation. We simply have different goals. I'm glad I'll be staying in the hotel with your family. That way I can escape more gracefully, although I'm going to get busted that I'm working at the ranch. I told them it was a corporation."

"It is."

"I know. I wouldn't lie to them, but it's still going to be suspect to them. What I'm doing right now doesn't carry the proper amount of clout for an Evans."

Luke was quiet for a minute and then asked, "Would it help to know that you've improved the quality of life for our family dramatically?"

"Yes and no. I'd like to hear it, but I'm not the one bothered by the lack of status. I love it here. I don't want to be one of the all-powerfuls. That's what Fo and I call the whole bunch of them. My mother would die to hear this, but someday I just want to be a mom. I'm not embarrassed to say that, but I don't want to fight with anyone about it."

"Would it work to have it out with them once and for all? Or is that only a pointless argument?"

"It would be pointless, I'm afraid. They would never actually accept that I know what's best for me against their wishes. It's better simply to avoid the issue. Only I can't avoid the issues without avoiding my family. It makes me feel terribly guilty. That whole eternal family thing haunts me. I'll probably burn for being so rebellious."

"Was Fo lecturing you to stop avoiding your family or to stop beating yourself up about it?"

She smiled that he was so astute. "To stop beating myself up. That's easier said than done, but I'm working on it."

"Life in general is easier said than done, Charlie. Working on it is all we can do. Just never quit working on it."

****

The next day went better. Charlie showed up to help with breakfast again, but this time she and Madge arranged to have someone else do any driving so Charlie could take pain medicine when she needed it. It had been four days now since that night and she was hoping the pain level would back off soon.

She spent the morning after breakfast working in the garden with the three little ones. They were at long last harvesting as well as still weeding and watering and the kids had finally caught the vision of what their little garden was all about.

Jamie had a hard time not trampling the plants and he had dirt around his mouth from eating green beans right off the vine, but he seemed to be fine with that so Charlie didn't get too uptight about it.

Somehow the little piggies had learned to push out the wood blocking the hole of their pen and go on safari. Charlie looked up to see one of them rooting around in the garden beside where Jamie was picking his beans. They were both so cute she decided to go get the camera before she went about containing the little pigs.

She put the piglet back, but honestly, the little pigs were so cute that she didn't mind them being around. And the garden was easier to contain than the piglets, so she put up a quick fence of electric posts and wire a few inches off the ground and then, when they were working in the garden she'd simply turn it off for the duration. It worked well for a few days until the piglets got even more out of control. Finally, when one of them followed Jamie into the house for lunch one day they had to be incarcerated.

Charlie hadn't even realized it was inside until she heard Richard roar from the office. She and Madge rushed in to see what the problem was and got there just in time to see Luke make a dive behind a desk and surface with a little black and white squealing piglet and an adorable two year old boy. Luke gave Charlie a wry smile as he headed outside with his catches. She could hear him lecturing Jamie as he went about how real life wasn't like the movies.

Luke fixed the hole in the fence and there were no more piglet incidences and they quit giving them the supplemental bottles at the same time. It wouldn't be but another couple of weeks until they were weaned anyway and their Wilbur would be sent off to wherever he was to go.

Chapter 8

Charlie got her splint removed and started her physical therapy and after that first week, her shoulder did get markedly better. It was still sore, but at least she could begin to start using it again and was completely off the pain medicine except for some Ibuprofen.

She had been right. The Yukon was heavenly to drive compared to the Taco Rocket and she didn't miss being stranded on the highway one bit. It probably would be awful to go back to her lemon at the end of the summer, but she drove the SUV gladly anyway. When she and Lindie went into town, Lindie asked her if she wanted to park it and walk back in the last little ways just to tease Luke and they laughed again

The day finally rolled around to travel back to Connecticut and they all boarded the airplane together to make the big trip. It was the longest plane ride the little ones had been on even though they flew fairly often, so the adults were hard put to keep them entertained for the whole six plus hour flight. Richard eventually had Jamie in his lap and the others took turns playing card games and clapping games with the little girls. The fact that Charlie didn't necessarily want to arrive in Connecticut made it all rather miserable for her.

When they finally stood up to deplane, Fo gave her a sympathetic smile and she mentally lectured herself to have a better attitude. She was making some headway until as they rode the escalator she glimpsed Elroy waiting at the top of the concourse. Her better attitude was hard pressed to survive and Fo looked even more sympathetic when she excused herself to go talk to him. She met Luke's eyes as she turned aside and his raised eyebrows went a long way toward helping her to laugh at this whole situation. This truly was insane.

Even though she had never been a party to the whole marriage scheme, Elroy opened his arms to greet her and she only felt slightly guilty when she sidestepped him neatly and began to dig in her purse for a tissue as they greeted each other. She had never once given this guy any encouragement and she wasn't about to start now. She still had no idea why her mother had decided he was the man for her. Other than the fact that he was quite good looking and successful and had a high status job, there wasn't one outstanding thing about him that Charlie could see.

He had come thinking that he would be taking Charlie home to her parents' house and she was more grateful than ever to be able to say, "I'm sorry, Elroy. I'm going to be helping with the children at the hotel. I guess my mother didn't understand that. I so appreciate your coming here to get me, but I'm afraid it wasn't necessary. I'll just ride with the others." Right then Fo called her and she took the call and then turned back to Elroy with a smile. "I'm sorry; they're all waiting for me. Be a dear and tell Mother and Daddy I'll see them as soon as I can. Would you? Thanks, Elroy. Gotta go."

She smoothly walked out of the building and stepped into the waiting rental car and waved to Elroy as she settled into the seat beside Luke. Fo was driving and they headed off into traffic as she breathed a heavy sigh of relief. "Thanks Fo, for heading him off at the pass so smoothly. Mother's going to be ticked, but thanks."

"Anytime. Elroy is looking very successful these days. He finally looks comfortable in that suit." Fo turned to Luke and explained, "He used to look like a little boy at church who was having a hard time sitting still."

Tuckett cracked up in the front seat and Charlie had to remind Fo, "Mind your manners, Forest Eldridge. What would Jesus say?"

"Jesus would be honest with the guy and tell him that you aren't going to be marrying him in the next century or so and let him get on with his life. Quit leading the poor doofus on."

"He's a very successful attorney, Fo. I don't think doofus is truly the word is it? And who's leading him on. I moved to the other side of the country if you recall. And he's in as much of a tight spot as I am. After all, he'd have to tell the tough old bird no as much as I would. You should feel for the guy."

"I said tough. Not old. You make it sound worse than it was. Can we eat before we unpack? I'm starving!"

Tuckett seconded that sentiment, "I'm with you, dude. Let's call Dad and have him meet us in the restaurant."

Luke interrupted them, "We probably need to help Dad with the kids, Tuck. I'll bet Angela is about crazy by now. She's not used to being around them and can't take it very well. Dad would probably appreciate us taking Chase off his hands as well. Let's get the bags headed to the rooms and we'll take the kids and go eat."

Tuckett turned back to Luke with a grin. "I'll take the kids. You get Chase."

Luke grinned back at him. "Be nice, Tuck. Or I'll make you babysit him while he exercises."

They were in three suites. Richard and Angela and their children were in one, Luke and Chase and Tuckett in another and Charlie and Madge in a third.

After dinner, she and Fo and Luke went to see her parents. She hugged them as she came in and felt guilty when her mom held on for an extra moment. Her parents were polite, even though Charlie knew they had to have been miffed she hadn't come with Elroy, but they didn't pay much attention to Luke after he was introduced. He seemed okay with that, but Charlie was disgusted with their poor judgment as far as eligible men were concerned. Luke was a hundred times the man Elroy was, but lacked the proper clout in their opinion. Their priorities were screwy and she was grateful when she and Fo and Luke were headed on to Fo's parents'. They visited for a while and then dropped Fo. She and Luke returned to the hotel.

On the drive back, the ride was quiet and Charlie was dying to know what Luke had thought of her parents. He didn't say anything and even at the hotel he only small talked in the elevator. She decided the whole tough bird issue must simply be in her head and resolved to not be so worried about the next day or two until they were headed back home to Montana.

Elroy showed up bright and early the next morning to take her to breakfast and Charlie didn't have the heart to turn him away when he'd obviously taken work off two days in a row to see her. But she did commit to herself to make it clear to him this was the last time she was going to feel obligated to accept a date she hadn't okayed in advance.

As they walked down the hotel hallway on the way downstairs, she met Luke coming back up in his swimming suit with the little girls and Jamie. He smiled at her in passing and she couldn't help but compare his quiet, confident, dark muscular good looks with the polished, business suited man who accompanied her down the hall. It was hard to even imagine fitting into the slick legal world Elroy lived in anymore. She'd never been much of one for the shallow cocktail party scene and now, after Montana, this life of expensive business suits and even more expensive watches felt positively foreign to her.

Several times as they ate Elroy made reference to when she finally came home and they "settled down". This whole deal became weirder than ever to her. Was Elroy content to just wait for the four years of law school in Utah? The idea of hanging out waiting to marry someone for four years was mind boggling to her, especially when Elroy had never actually discussed the topic of marriage with her. She thought about having to wake up next to this guy for the rest of her life and just the idea depressed the heck out of her, even knowing that it wasn't a possibility.

She listened to him small talking through breakfast and finally, after having put up with him for an acceptable length of time, she thanked him and excused herself to go back upstairs to help with the kids. After telling him good bye, she was disgusted with herself all the way up the stairs for not telling him out right that she wasn't marrying him. Ever.

Luke answered the door when she knocked at Richard's suite and he gave her a heart stopping smile as he let her in and asked, "How is Elroy this fine morning?"

She couldn't help but smile back. "Marvy, Luke. You can wipe that grin off. Please tell me your dad is in desperate need of assistance this morning. I used him as an excuse and I need to be honest."

"In that case, he's in dire need. Actually, he does need help, but it's with Chase." He grinned again. "Will that be a problem?"

He asked it far too innocently and she nudged him with her elbow. "What does he need help with Chase for?"

"Uh, apparently there is some kind of high school softball tournament in town. Dad was just trying to convince Chase the players were off limits. Chase can't figure out why."

Charlie rolled her eyes. "That's not very funny, Luke. Especially after Lindie's baby. With a high school girl he'd go to prison. This is serious."

Luke nodded. "Believe me, Charlie. I know that. That's why Dad needs help. He's about ready to put Chase right back on a plane."

"Chase's twenty seven years old. God Himself won't *make* him behave. He has to decide to behave on his own doesn't he?"

"This may come as a surprise to you, but self discipline isn't Chase's strong point. From time to time, we have to make him. Dad might actually have to put him on a plane."

Charlie sighed. "Being in Montana won't guarantee good behavior, will it?"

"No, but at least that way he won't embarrass the whole family or get shot by an irate father."

"I doubt that would be as much a risk here as it would be in Montana. But then again, Chase could temp a saint. Seriously, what can I be doing this morning?"

He came up to her and looked at her frankly and asked, "How is the shoulder? Are you up to going to the ocean with the kids and me? Maybe riding the ferry and going to the aquarium? How much are you up to?"

Raising her arm, she moved it gingerly all around and then admitted, "The arm is still sore, but honestly I'm much more up to going to the coast with you and the children than not. I need you to need my help."

He rubbed the shoulder she was stretching. "And I do. I need you desperately, both with the kids and with knowing where to go and what to do here. How soon can you leave?"

"Anytime. Just let me grab my purse. Thank you, Luke."

****

Charlie had been to the Maritime Aquarium a number of times, but it had never been like this before. Being there with Luke and the children made it seem a whole new experience for her. She tried to see the displays and the different tanks through the eyes of a Montana child and it was as amazing to her as it was to the three little ones. Being with Luke was more comfortable than she ever dreamed she'd feel after only knowing someone for a couple of months. His calm, happy demeanor and the way he treated both her and the children definitely didn't quell the way she'd been feeling about him.

When she caught herself watching him and admiring the way his shirt stretched across his shoulders when he leaned down to hear something Evie said, she had to mentally put the brakes on. She needed to get a handle on these feelings or she was going to be a mess when she went back to school. She took Jamie's hand as he went across to look at a tank set up as a tide pool and wondered if it wasn't already too late. Law school was stretching out there more and more lonely by the minute.

She shook herself out of her reverie when she heard Luke's low, sexy chuckle near her ear and realized Jamie had both of his sandals off and was trying to climb up into the tide pool tank while she still held his hand. Luke looked at her as he gently took the two year old off of the stone wall he beginning to climb. "Those thoughts are somewhere far from this aquarium. What are you thinking about while Jamie goes wading?"

She turned and looked at Luke's long legs in his faded jeans and didn't dare tell him what she was really thinking. "Just thinking about school. Sorry. I didn't realize he was going in."

When she mentioned school, Luke met her eyes for one long look, but she couldn't face those green eyes and had to look away. It was going to be hard enough to climb into the Taco Rocket and drive away without him knowing how she was feeling as well. The rest of the afternoon she spent waffling between enjoying being with him and trying not to feel so good about being with him, but it was hopeless.

Riding the ferry in the breeze off the water, with him standing beside her at the rail while the kids sat on the bench below them, made it all the harder not to imagine her and Luke, with kids of their own doing this same thing some day.

A gull cried as it wheeled in the spray and as she turned to look at it, the wind caught a curl and blew it across her lips. She reached to brush it out of the way, but Luke's calloused brown hand beat her to it, and she looked up into his eyes as he gently smoothed the curl from her face. Glancing down from her eyes to her mouth, he softly ran a thumb across her bottom lip and her stomach did some little gymnastic thing as he did it. He looked back up into her eyes and gave her that easy smile before he turned away to answer a question for Elsa. The electricity of the moment was gone again as quickly as it had come, but the butterflies it had loosed in her heart were still fluttering like mad and she had to work to be able to breathe. She had no idea what that casual touch meant to him, but she had never felt like this before. It scared her.

Her lip tingled all the rest of the boat ride and even during the drive back to the hotel and as they walked in the glass front doors, Evie asked her, "Are you sick, Charlie? You've been very quiet."

She glanced at Luke, carrying a sleeping Jamie beside her and knew he'd been watching her as well and she tried to brush it off. "I'm fine, Evie. I'm just thinking, but thank you for asking. The party tonight is going to be fun, isn't it?" The little girls went off chattering about how excited they were and Charlie was able to try to get some semblance of a normal state of mind back before they made it up to the hotel rooms. But she never was able to get Luke off of her brain, even when she was back in her own room and dressing.

****

The reception that night was fun in some ways. The little girls thought they had died and gone to the prom and that Jamie was their own personal prom king. They were all three dressed for it in their lacy little dresses and a suit and tie and they were unbelievably cute. After the dinner they wanted to dance and Charlie stayed near them on the dance floor. It was supposedly to keep tabs on them, but Luke stayed nearby as well and Charlie was definitely enjoying her duties when he danced there with her. She tried to laugh and maintain her cheerful distance, but when the band played slow songs it was heaven to be in his arms. All of her earlier ideas about keeping her distance went out the window and it was all she could do not to melt. The best she was capable of was trying not to let it be obvious.

Chase came by occasionally and tried to get her to dance with him as well, but she politely declined him every time. Even though she tried to pretend that she was only being sociable to Luke, she definitely drew the line when it came to purposefully letting Chase get his hands anywhere near her.

Several times Fo came by, but there were always either girls he'd known forever with him or new girls that someone had introduced him to, and Charlie hardly even got to talk to him all night.

When her parents showed up, they had Elroy in tow and when they located Charlie on the dance floor, they brought him with them there as well. Her parents began to dance and she dutifully danced with Elroy, telling herself it was just for this one song. That song was followed by another slow one however and she found herself being maneuvered away from the others to a more secluded corner where Elroy apparently finally felt the need to discuss their future.

At first, Charlie didn't understand what was going on, but when he stroked her hand with his and leaned in to kiss her temple she began to wise up fast. She was just pulling away to put more distance between the two of them when Elroy said, "Charlie, there's something I've been meaning to talk to you about." She looked up at him wondering what exactly was coming when he went on, "You must know your parents have spoken to me several times about taking care of you."

At this, she stopped dancing altogether and pulled away from him. "Yes, I've been meaning to talk to you about that as well."

"Oh, good. Then you know what I'm about to ask you."

She looked up at him and knew she needed to stop him before he asked something he'd be embarrassed about when she told him unequivocally no. "No. I don't know what you're going to ask me, but you need to know, Elroy. I'm not really interested in having any kind of relationship just now. Especially not one that my parents have any say in. I'm heading to law school here in a few weeks and that will take years. I know my mother has a tendency to want to micromanage my life and she thinks she's in charge, but I'm simply not interested. I'm sorry."

He only smiled serenely and, completely unconcerned about what she had just said, replied, "You're mother told me you would probably say something like that. Don't worry. I'm incredibly patient and have no problem waiting for you to deal with whatever you need to to arrange to come back here for law school and your internships. And trust me; I do understand your hesitation. Take all the time you want until you feel comfortable with me. Your mom has told me about how you sometimes need extra encouragement in making decisions."

Charlie's mouth dropped open and she looked at him in disbelief. He hadn't taken her anymore seriously than her parents usually did. For a long time she had assumed he was a bit simple, but he wasn't. He was merely as power crazed and out of touch with reality as her parents and the rest of her family.

Just as she was about to tear into him and let him have a piece of her mind right there at the reception, Luke danced over to her with Elsa and Jamie in his arms. He whispered something to the children and then set them down to dance together as he said to Charlie. "I've been looking for you. Isn't this the song you said to save for you? Come dance with me and save me from these two will you?"

Without even waiting for her answer, he stepped neatly in front of Elroy and took her in his arms and then subtly danced her away from the speechless attorney. Elsa and Jamie followed them and soon they were back over on the other side of the small dance floor near where Fo was dancing with a very animated Evie.

Charlie literally sighed with relief and Luke smiled hesitantly down at her and asked, "Are you as thoroughly disgusted as you looked over there, or am I reading you wrong?"

She leaned into him instinctively and asked, "Does it show that clearly? I'm sorry."

His breath fanned her heated brow as he spoke. "I'm not sure if I rescued you or him. What did he say to you?"

"I don't know that I can even tell you without wanting to swear. I tried very politely to tell him I wasn't interested in any kind of a relationship, and he replied that my mother had told him I would say that. He said my feelings weren't a problem. That he could wait until I arranged to come back here to go to school and that my mother had warned him I'd need help making my decision about him. That he could wait. He didn't even begin to consider that I could actually decide for myself that we weren't going to have a relationship."

Luke chuckled at her outrage. "After knowing you these last weeks, I have a hard time picturing them assuming things like that. You haven't seemed very indecisive to me."

She thought about that. "Elroy doesn't even know me. And I don't truly think I am indecisive. It's just that they're so unbending and so self assured, they don't stop to consider the fact I might have a brain or that I'm not a child anymore. I don't think it's ever crossed my mother's mind I might have an idea of my own that could be viable."

He gathered her into his arms more tightly almost as if to hug her and said, "Maybe what you need to do is simply get married. They'd never wonder about arranging your life again."

Charlie laughed and it felt good to let the frustration go. "That's a great idea, Luke. But I've spent most of my life learning to be pro-active and not basing my decisions on what someone else does or wants. Wouldn't marrying almost in revenge be just a trifle foolish?"

He smiled down at her. "That would depend on who you married."

His green eyes looking down at her with the little smile lines starting around them and talking about marriage, even in an off hand way, made her a bit breathless. For a second there she wasn't thinking all that clearly. Then Luke chuckled again and Charlie looked up to see what he was laughing at. "The tough old birds aren't very happy about me rescuing you. I'm not sure, but I believe the look I just got could be considered a glower."

Still more than a little outraged at Elroy, Charlie moved even closer to him and said, "Yeah, well, here's to being rebellious. Let's turn our backs to their glowering, shall we? Being rebelliously pro-active would dictate that I not let them and their scheming ruin my night."

Luke laughed again and turned away from her parents. "Now, I've read a few books in my day, but rebelliously pro-active sounds suspect to me. You're not taking those pain pills again are you?"

She smiled and relaxed against him. "You're missing the spirit of the thing." She paused for a second and then said, "You know you shouldn't talk about marriage so casually. My parents may not understand the seriousness of it all, but you should."

Just then he turned to avoid another couple and then looked down and met her eyes. "I wasn't speaking casually, Charlie. They certainly couldn't keep trying to marry you off if you already were."

She gave him a lopsided smile. "You're forgetting that he's a divorce lawyer."

Luke shook his head and laughed. "I guess there is that. Maybe we'll have to figure something else out." He looked all around the hotel ballroom and wondered aloud,

"How long do you suppose we have to stay here to be considered polite?"

"Aren't you having fun?"

"I'm fine, but doesn't that deep conversation between your parents and Elroy look like a war party powwow to you. They're cooking something serious up. Maybe we should discretely leave. Do you feel strongly about staying?"

Charlie shook her head and looked over to where her mother and father were in a decidedly serious looking conversation with Elroy that included numerous glances in her and Luke's direction. None of them were looking too happy and she had to wonder if Luke wasn't right.

He danced her over to the side of the floor and whispered, "Why don't you act as if you're headed to the restroom and I'll tell Fo's parents thank you and good night and collect the three little one's. We'll take them back to Dad and Angela's suite and either get them ready for bed or take them down to the coffee shop and get desert or head for the pool. Where would your parents be the least likely to look?"

"It'll never work, Luke. They'd call out hotel security looking for me if I didn't answer my phone."

"So just tell them you took something for your shoulder, which would be true and don't worry about it."

"Actually, they don't know about my shoulder, but maybe lying low for the night would be fun. There's a theater next door. I wonder if anything is playing that the little kids could see. I'd be hard to find in the dark."

He looked surprised and asked, "You didn't tell your parents?"

"No. I didn't think I should."

"I would have thought it would have been nice to have someone to talk to about what happened."

She shook her head. "Me tell my parents I'd been assaulted in a pig barn feeding the runt in the middle of the night? No. They would have been horrified and simply insisted I come home immediately and raised a fuss. I talked to Fo. And a little bit to you. My parents wouldn't have even wanted to know that one."

The look he gave her almost made her feel guilty for not telling them, but he didn't say anything else about it, just whispered to her as they neared a side door, "I'll meet you at the rooms in a few minutes. See ya."

She slipped out the door and it made her smile to think Luke was helping her elude her parents and their chosen betrothed. Maybe she should have been making it harder for them to find her all along. She was half way to her room before her phone rang.

****

Luke had joked with her about hiding from her parents and their intended in-law, but the tender kiss he'd seen Elroy give her on her temple when she'd been dancing with him hadn't really been a laughing matter. That one little gesture had ticked Luke off and surprised him at the same time. He was usually pretty slow to rile, but somehow that kiss had been a wake up call. He'd known he cared a great deal for Charlie, but hadn't realized how much until then. It had made him positively territorial and he'd been hard pressed to hide the slow burn he felt rise inside him. At least the kiss had made her move straight away from the guy. Luke's smile came back when he thought about the look of total disgust he had seen on her face as he'd come up to them.

He collected the kids, bade Fo's parents good night and made his way from the ballroom. He hated to encourage the rift between her and her family, but there was no way he could stand by and watch that pretty boy in the expensive suit and Italian shoes claim her. He didn't understand her unwillingness to confront her parents and put a stop to all of this, but at least he could help ease her tension about them tonight.

Surprisingly, the kids were tired and were perfectly happy to head on up to the room to get ready for bed. Charlie peeked out of her own door as they approached and came across to his dad's suite and helped him get them changed and into pajamas and get ready for bed. Their teeth were brushed and prayers were said when his dad and Angela showed up with both Fo and Chase in their wake. Tuckett was staying at Fo's parents' house with a cousin and he'd stayed downstairs, and Madge had actually struck up an acquaintance with one of the men from Fo's dad's company. She had stayed downstairs as well.

It was only nine o'clock and Luke was stumped as to why his dad and Angela had come up so early, but from the less than happy vibes he was getting he wondered if Angela hadn't been up to her usual antics and his dad had called her on it. At any rate, his father took his parenting seriously and would have been up sometime relatively soon to be with his small children anyway. That was probably bothering Angela as well. She hated that sort of responsibility.

With the kids settled in, the four young adults headed next door to the theater to find out what was playing and Charlie seemed to take an almost childish pleasure in turning her phone to silent and then putting it where she couldn't feel it vibrate. She should have been doing this kind of thing for a long time. She seemed to feel like it was a bit petty, but it was still preferable to being dominated ruthlessly.

She smiled gratefully when Fo and Luke neatly sat on either side of her as they took seats in the darkened theater to keep Chase from hassling her. It was great to be able to watch over so smoothly. Fo had always looked out for her, but now Luke helped and it was like being her own personal Guardian Angels. As they sat and shared popcorn and milk duds back and forth, the only thing he wished for was that cowhide couch back home that let her lean comfortably against his shoulder.

****

When they got out of the movie, there were several messages waiting for her from both of her parents and Elroy. The last one was from her mom demanding Charlie call tonight no matter how late it was and she didn't sound very happy. Charlie sighed knowing that tomorrow she was in for one of the discussions she had come to dread. She wondered if the confrontation Luke had asked about was finally going to happen, but she turned off her phone for the night anyway. She owed that to the Langstons. This wasn't their problem; the least she could do was spare them the dramatics tonight.

She was still feeling that way the next morning at breakfast when she took the inevitable call from her mother. Charlie let her vent for a moment or two and then calmly said, "Mother, I appreciate your feelings, but I'm in the middle of a family meal just now. So we'll have to finish this later. Please forgive me, but I have to go."

Norma Evans wasn't amused. Her voice could be heard by everyone at the table as she replied, "Charlene Marie Evans, I will not be treated like this! You and I have some things to discuss and we will do it right now!"

Again Charlie calmly said, "No, mother. We won't. I have to go. Love you." With that, she pressed the end button and then completely powered the phone down. Turning to the others, she apologized and tried to feign that all was well. "Sorry about that. So what are you doing today, Evie and Elsa?"

Luke was looking at her with that deep, quiet way he had as the little girls began to enthusiastically tell her their plans for going to the ocean. Inwardly she sighed. It would have been great to go with them today, but she knew she had about twenty minutes before her very irate mother would appear to demand her discussion. She had to protect this good family from the inevitable theatrics that resulted when her power monger mother felt thwarted and Charlie hurried to finish her breakfast and then excused herself. On the way out of the room, she asked Richard if he could manage without her for the time being and then went to wait at the curb for her mother. At least if she was inside a vehicle to vent her wrath, everyone else wouldn't have to be subjected to her as well.

Charlie was surprised when Luke pulled up beside her in one of the rental cars. He rolled down the window and looked at her for a minute with concern and then asked quietly, "How can I help you, Charlie? Do you have to face her? Will it do any good? Or can we keep dodging her until we get on the plane tonight? Will she be mad enough to follow you back to Montana?"

Charlie tried to smile, but it wasn't working very well as she replied, "I don't know how you can help me, Luke. It won't do any good to face her, but I don't know what else to do. I'll go to law school to avoid dealing with them, but there's no way I'm marrying someone to please them. I can't do it and I won't."

"Then get in."

She hesitated and he went on, "If facing her won't help anything then don't. If she catches up to us before we leave tonight, I'll take her on with you. Get in."

For another second or two, she wondered if this was wise and then she opened the door and slid into the seat beside him and he smoothly pulled away just seconds before she glimpsed her mother coming the other direction in her Lexus. She thought to herself, *blessed be the peace makers.*

They rode in silence for a few minutes and then Luke volunteered, "Fo said she was tough. He wasn't kidding."

Charlie felt she needed to defend her. "She's not as bad as she sounds. She doesn't very often decide something that I go absolutely against. And when I'm clear across the country it's much less confrontational." He gave her a sad smile and she went on lamely, "Her hardness has helped her become very successful professionally."

He pulled onto the freeway. "I'm sure it has." After another short pause he said, "You've done a great job at turning out more gentle and undemanding. That can't have been easy."

After thinking about that she admitted, "Thank you. I didn't want to turn out like her. You're right. It hasn't been easy. I would have died without Fo. He has always understood and helped me. And my mother adores him, so that comes in very handy. I think she thought we would get married after our missions and she's been very disappointed. I suppose that's the reason for Elroy."

"Why Elroy? What is it about him that they like?"

"I honestly don't know unless it's that he has that respectable occupation they crave, but he's still manipulatable. That's the only thing I can figure. The whole idea of marrying a divorce attorney is bizarre to me. Even if I was madly in love with him I wouldn't go there. As it is though, he just gets on my nerves. I'm sure he's a nice guy and that I only have a bad attitude because they're pushing him."

"He doesn't have to go along with their scheming. Even if he wasn't a divorce lawyer, you couldn't marry someone that has no backbone."

"Maybe he has a backbone. Maybe he truly is attracted to me. Who knows? He doesn't even know me, but I guess there's a chance."

Luke sounded skeptical when he said, "There's a lot to like about you, Charlie, but are you sure he doesn't think you'll come with a chunk of Momma and Papa's cash and cash equivalents?"

She shook her head and smiled at his bluntness. "That was harsh, Luke. I'm not that undesirable. Am I?"

"Of course not, Charlie, but don't sucker into this even a bit. This is not how eternal marriages are forged."

"I know that."

"Good. Don't forget it when the tough old bird gets militant and the chips are down."

He was so earnest he made her laugh. "You sound just like Fo when he gets wound up. I can finally see some resemblance."

"Well, are we right?"

"Yes, you're right. I don't question whether you're right. I just have the hardest time with that whole families are forever concept. It's hard for me to figure out how to follow the prophet about families, and then follow the prophet about everything else when my family has a slightly different take on so many things like women's roles, and succeeding in the home and worldliness, and seeking first the kingdom. When I say it out loud like this it's easier, but when I'm actively trying to avoid my family I feel so guilty. It feels as if I'm going backwards or something."

His voice softened. "I can see what you're saying, Charlie, but you aren't responsible for the choices they've made. Remember that pro-active stuff? You need to do what you think is right, regardless of what they do or don't do. And you need to remember you aren't a little girl anymore. You're a grown woman who is wise and strong and good and soon you'll be the matriarch of your own family and leading them is much more important than obeying your mother when she's a few degrees off course. I don't mean to be disrespectful of your mother, but from the little I've seen, you are by far the wiser woman and better disciple. Trust yourself here. You're so confident when you're helping others. Trust that same whatever it is that has helped my family so much for yourself."

He paused for a few minutes and then said gently, "It's your gift. It's precious and valuable. Don't hesitate to bless your own life with it, Charlie."

The incredible strain this whole mess brought her and his gentle tone, coupled with the respect he was voicing was more than she knew how to process and she was embarrassed when she started to cry, but there wasn't a thing she could do about it. She pulled a tissue out of the little box on the floor of the console of the rental car and tried to turn her face to the window so he wouldn't see her emotion.

They drove in silence for a moment and then he pulled the car onto a turnout and stopped and killed the engine. He put a gentle hand on her arm. "Don't turn away from me and cry, Charlie. It's okay. None of this is your fault. I knew you were having a hard time of it, that's why I came for you in the first place. Come here."

She turned to him and he pulled her into a hug and stroked her back as she cried. He put a gentle hand onto her head and said, "You know what helps me, Charlie, when things feel overwhelming and I wonder why God gave me the set of issues that He did? Sometimes if I count my blessings and then remember that even though my deal doesn't seem very fair, it's better than what some others have, then I'm actually grateful for my portion. You know, your mom may be tough, but at least you have her. My mother passed away, which is heart breaking, but Tuckett's took off without a forwarding address. Can you imagine?

At least your mother cares enough about you to get militant. Tuckett struggles with feeling completely unlovable."

Charlie sniffled and cried even harder. "That's horrible. She doesn't keep in touch with him at all?"

"Not that I'm aware of. She walked out when he was six and the only correspondence I've heard of was the divorce papers. All she wanted was alimony."

She looked up at him. "How sad. I'll bet he was a corker when he was six." She wiped her eyes. "You're right. I am grateful for my tough old bird. But would it be ungracious to say I want to do a lot of things differently with my own children?"

He smiled at her and wiped at a stray tear with a finger. "Not at all. That's the goal of every worthy generation isn't it? To do better than the last. Maybe by the time the Savior returns we'll be down to fine tuning and the children will all be raised flawlessly. In the mean time, we all have our own set of struggles." He put a hand back on her hair and let her lean on him again. "Are you going to be okay now?"

She nodded against him. "Yes, I'm fine now. Where are we going?"

"To the coast. We'll meet Dad and the others. Is that okay with you?"

"It's great. Thanks for talking me into getting into the car. What are we going to do at the coast?"

"All the things that we can't do in Montana. Walk on the beach and play in the sand and beach comb and look at the tide pools." He stopped to smile. "We're going to let Jamie wade in them this time."

She laughed and leaned up and wiped her nose. "Sorry about yesterday. My mind has been a bit preoccupied this trip. How far ahead of the others are we?"

He reached and started the car back up and pulled back onto the highway. "Probably a half hour or more. Is there any certain beach we should go to? Or is there something else you'd like to do in the mean time?"

She thought about that and then said, "Yes. Yes, there is. If you truly want to do what you can't do back in Montana then we need to go find some things for lunch." She looked around. "Take the next exit here in Derby. I think there's a market that will have what we need. And let's call your dad and tell him to head for a place called Silver Sands State Park. It's just south of Milford. That will be the most kid friendly place nearby that I know of."

They stopped and she bought a blanket and a pot and corn on the cob and a number of spices and lemons and butter. On the way to the check out she added paper eating ware and a roll of paper towels.

When they got closer to the ocean she had him stop again at one of the little shops on a pier and she bought live lobsters and muscles and shrimp packed in ice, and then when they got to the beach, she parked their gear and walked along gathering up drift wood until the minivan carrying the others showed up only a few minutes behind them.

The little kids thought gathering the firewood was a great game and soon they had all the wood she would need and they spread out to do the things they couldn't do back home.

Chase laid out a towel and stretched out on it and watched the girls on the beach around them as Luke and Charlie and Tuckett and the little ones played in the surf for a while and then went exploring tide pools and finding ocean treasures. Jamie had so many treasures in the pockets of his shorts that they soon began to sag and he was sporting a plumber's crack when Luke suggested he park a load of the neato finds near Charlie's gear.

After climbing around rocks and drift logs and the sea wall with the children, Charlie finally climbed up onto a point of rocks and sat down where she could watch the children and the ocean and the various boats and birds that moved out there. Even as busy as this stretch of Atlantic ocean was, there was always something about the ocean that was eternally intriguing. The power of that huge expanse of water and the unending consistency of the waves that frothed up onto the slick were almost hypnotic. No matter how often she came to the ocean, it never got monotonous to her.

She sat watching the kids and the surf and the muscles in Luke's thighs as he bent to inspect something the girls were looking at. The way he had rescued her today had put her world back on keel more effectively than even Fo had done it over the years. Not only had he gotten her out of the situation, but then he had comforted her and even talked her into not feeling like such a failure as a daughter. True, she still had to resolve things with her parents, but she no longer felt as if she had done some unpardonable travesty by standing up for herself and refusing to be bullied.

The problem with Luke's unshakeable strength was that the more Charlie was around him, the more she cared for him and respected him, which wasn't a bad thing except for the fact she was supposed to be walking away from him in a few weeks to return to Utah and law school. She already felt so strongly about him that leaving Montana was going to kill her.

She watched him laugh with Jamie as they ran from the waves and then lean down to pick him up when the wave washed him off his feet. He was so gentle and sweet with the kids that she couldn't help but wish she didn't have to leave at the end of the summer at all. It would have been incredibly nice to just stay working for the Langstons indefinitely. Nice enough that she'd probably do it if she thought there was any chance that something could develop between her and Luke. But there were so many things to preclude that.

In the first place, he was a rancher through and through and would certainly want a wife who had been born and raised to that kind of life, and would understand what he needed in a help mate. Not only that, but he had just barely been given back his freedom. The relief that had brought him had been obvious. As willing as he'd been to help Lindie out of a bad situation, there was no doubt about how much happier he was to be free of that commitment. You could see it in his face almost as soon as the engagement had been called off.

Those two things were enough to make Charlie know her chances with Luke were relatively nil, even without the fact that he was intimidatingly wealthy and heart stoppingly gorgeous. It was no wonder that women usually reacted to him exactly the way Summer Harmon did every time she showed up.

Charlie tried not to think about how he had made her feel this morning when he'd hugged her, or yesterday when he'd touched her lip on the ferry. She had to admit she had it bad for a tall, dark and handsome Montana rancher and as good as he made her feel, she also felt slightly panicky about falling so foolishly.

She was just thinking she had better get a handle on her feelings when Luke himself climbed up onto her rock and sat down next to her close enough his shoulder brushed hers. For a minute or two he only sat and looked out over the expanse of the sound before them and the striking skyline of Long Island across the way. She glanced down to double check that Richard and Angela were with the little kids before she turned to study Luke's profile against the blue of the summer sky.

Maybe it was a good thing she was leaving soon. Time spent with him never failed to make her more conscious of him and how he made her feel. She turned back to look out at the ocean and wondered again about what he had said that morning concerning being grateful for our own particular circumstances. Her parents had made her a bit miserable this last day or two, but at least she hadn't come here for the entire summer and been up against this for months. And she would always be grateful for the wonderful experiences she was having this summer. Even if she ended up with a shattered heart out of the deal, this had been the time of her life. She had to be honest about that. Dealing with her mother for a short time only made Montana all the sweeter.

Earlier Luke had spoken about losing his own mother in an almost matter-of-fact way, but it had to have been devastating to him at the time. She glanced up at him again and wondered at the man he had become in spite of such a traumatic loss. It was no wonder Chase had developed some negative attributes and it was just as much of a wonder that Luke had become such a rock.

She leaned against his shoulder and hesitantly broke the silence, "Tell me about your mom."

He was quiet for so long she worried she had offended him and she looked up at him again wondering how to undue the damage. He glanced down and into her eyes and she could see the pain that still haunted him. She hurried to take back her request. "I'm sorry. That's none of my business. Please forgive me."

He simply reached over and took her hand and held on to it firmly as he turned to look back at the sea. "It's okay, Charlie. I miss her, but the memories are good. I almost hate to admit this to you, but she was the best mother I could have ever asked for. I loved her dearly and always knew she felt the same way about me."

His thumb unconsciously stroked the back of her hand. "It's not like she never had to discipline us or anything. She definitely wasn't a pushover. But she was gentle and kind and Chase and I and Dad were her life. She was as solid and dependable and honest as Angela isn't, and I was blessed to have her until I was eight."

Charlie leaned her head against his shoulder again and said, "I'm sorry you lost her, Luke. It must make it all the harder to have known the best and then had to lose her. What did she die of?"

"She had pancreatic cancer. She died within three months of when they found it."

"I'm sorry." That was all she knew to say, but she knew he didn't doubt she meant it.

There was deep sadness in his voice when he said, "Me too. I miss her."

Again they sat in silence, broken only by the cries of the gulls and the sounds of the boats out in the sound. The kids had settled into the sand and were beginning to build a sand castle with Richard while Angela lounged beside them on a blanket. Tuckett was helping them construct a moat around their structure.

It was almost eleven and Charlie knew she probably ought to get down there and start building her fire to make their shore lunch, but she was loathe to leave Luke and the companionship she was feeling here beside him right now. She never failed to be surprised that she was as comfortable with Luke after only a couple of months as she was with Fo after nearly twenty years. Her and Luke's easy friendship was almost uncanny.

****

Luke sat there on the rocks beside her wishing they had all day to bask there in the mild New England sunshine holding hands. He knew she had been troubled about this trip and after hearing her mother's raised voice on her phone this morning he could understand, but he was enjoying this mini vacation immensely. It was great to have the time to spend beside her without a million other responsibilities demanding his attention. Even saving her had been enjoyable, both last night dancing and this morning. It was awful to see her cry, but it had been heavenly to hug her. And just now holding her hand was ridiculously pleasant.

At length, he let go of it, stood up, brushed the sand off of his shorts and reached again for her hand to pull her up beside him. "Come on, we'd better get started on your seafood. If we don't get Jamie fed soon, he'll go down for a nap hungry. You can tell me what to do to help you."

He kept hold of her hand as they climbed down from the rocks and he almost wished they had to climb over more stuff to get back to her gear so he wouldn't have to let it go.

He helped her get her fire going and then shucked the corn while she seasoned the water and sliced lemons into it. Once the pot of water was boiling, the lunch only took a few minutes to finish and then they all sat around on drift logs and enjoyed authentic Connecticut seafood, as fresh as you could get it without pulling it out of the water yourself. It was heavenly and the little kids had tiny rivulets of butter running down their chins before they were satisfied and ready to crash on their towels for a nap.

Richard volunteered to clean it all up and Luke and Charlie and Tuckett had a game of Frisbee at the edge of the surf while he did. Madge was thoroughly enjoying the down time with a thick novel, a lounge chair and a beach umbrella for shade and Luke wasn't surprised when a few minutes later she too had gone to sleep.

Tuckett threw the Frisbee and bounced it off the slick and Charlie and Luke both went after it, but just when he thought he had it, she put on a burst of speed and snagged it cleanly out of the air right in front of his hand. She laughed as she bumped into him and the curls that always framed her face fell out of their clip. She tossed him the Frisbee as she twisted the mass of blonde waves back up and secured them once again and then kicked water at him as she lunged for the disc again.

He laughed at her in return when they collided. She went down with a squeal into a sneaker wave that soaked the knit shirt she wore over her long shorts, and he reached down to help her back up as the wave receded. "That had to be refreshing, even as warm as it is today."

As she stood up, he swallowed hard. She'd looked good dry, but holy cow! His world rocked on its axis. Now the wet clothes hugged every curve, and she looked more desirable than if she'd been wearing a scanty bikini. *Man... He had to get a handle on this attraction issue.* They hadn't been running that much, really, but... Her femininity made him literally struggle to breathe. It must be the exercise. Except that the urge to kiss her was almost overwhelming again.

A stray tendril of her hair escaped and blew across her cheek and he thought about how much he had wanted to kiss her yesterday on the ferry. It had taken all of his self control to turn away. He started to reach up and brush the tendril back, but then before he actually touched her, he stopped himself. They were playing with fire here this afternoon. As he dropped his hand back to his side, she looked up at him and he could see the smile stall on her face.

For a second her emotions were exposed and he could see the questioning deep in those incredible eyes that matched the sky over the ocean. It made him want to kiss her again, just to let her know how he felt about her, but he couldn't. She was feeling so bullied already. The last thing she needed on her plate was someone else trying to manipulate how she felt.

He thought again about her leaving to go to school and it made him heartsick. He'd never in his life enjoyed being around a person the way he did with her and it made him want to beg her not to go when fall semester started. He'd have done it too, even if only for his family's sake if he didn't know she was pulled so by her own family's expectations for her.

He gently touched her cheek and then turned away with a sigh. He couldn't do this. Just a simple game on the beach was making him crazy. He fell harder for her every day and it was setting him up for disaster. Huge disaster. And she wasn't immune either. She was going to be hurt as well. When they got back to Montana he knew he had to try to stay away from her so he didn't fall any harder for her. He knew it, but he hated it. The day she climbed into her stupid Taco Rocket and drove away was going to kill him.

Chapter 9

Charlie reached up and adjusted the tiny fan above her seat on the plane and then turned out the light that shone down on her. It was a little before nine p.m. Connecticut time and although she had managed to make it clear onto the plane without that dreaded discussion with her mother, she was still tired and discouraged.

She took a deep breath and closed her eyes as the plane began to taxi toward the runway, wondering if she'd honestly be able to sleep during this long flight across the country. All afternoon and evening she'd been trying to figure out just what had happened there on the beach between her and Luke when she fell to make him look at her the way he had and then sigh and turn away. It was as if the fun and the friendship had offended him. He had pulled away from her so hard afterward that she was positively lost.

As they were loading into the cars, she had asked him out right if she had done something to offend him and although the look he had given her was almost soul searching, a moment later he had simply shaken his head, assured her she had done nothing and sighed again as he climbed in behind the wheel.

Then Chase and Tuckett had climbed in with them so she wasn't even able to ask him about it as they drove back into Waterbury to catch their plane. He'd been polite and helpful and kind, like he always was, but she could just about swear he'd decided something about her that subtly held their easy friendship at bay. It wasn't even anything she could put her finger on. It was simply a silent, invisible door he had shut on his smile toward her.

Now, seated beside him on the plane, she wondered if he'd even speak to her on the long flight home. As the plane lifted off, she swallowed the lump in her throat, determined not to cry in front of him again, even though that's what she felt like doing. Feeling the tears well up behind her closed eyelids, she willed herself to think of something else to counteract her discouragement. This had to be a culmination of the other things going on in her life right now with a few hormones thrown in for good measure, but regardless of what was causing it, she really didn't want to cry right now.

Without opening her eyes, she reached up and brushed away the one tear that overflowed and escaped, then turned her head toward Fo's side so her emotions wouldn't be so apparent to Luke.

****

Fo Eldridge sat in the big air bus with his two best friends on the planet and wondered what in heaven's name was going on in his world. Luke was a silent bear, and Charlie was sitting beside him quietly crying and hoping no one was noticing. What the heck had happened since he'd last seen them laughing and joking with each other? He wanted to lean over and shake them both and demand an explanation, but that didn't appear to be much of an option on this packed flight. He sighed like both of them had. This was going to be a long, long night.

****

Charlie had been right. There hadn't been a lot of sleeping going on for her on the flight home to Montana. She honestly tried, but thinking kept getting in the way. Her thoughts ranged from wondering what had happened with Luke, to wondering what was going to happen with her mother and father, to wondering why she was still planning to go back to Utah to law school, to wondering if maybe she shouldn't just go somewhere different than all three places and start completely over with her life.

Luke obviously wanted nothing to do with her all of a sudden; she didn't want to go home to Connecticut ever again after this last fiasco of a visit and law school held no intrigue for her whatsoever. She wished they didn't have church first thing in the morning. It would have been nice to talk to Fo for a while about the whole mess. Thinking about Fo made her even more tired. It was beginning to look like maybe he truly had found his princess charming and while Charlie was thrilled for him, she was also wondering if there was life after Fo eventually did get married.

When they finally made it back to the ranch it was three forty in the morning and as she prayed and laid down on the bed that felt heavenly spacious and comfortable after the flight, she dearly hoped the little ones would be as tired as she was and would sleep the morning away instead of popping out of bed as usual.

****

It was not to be. She felt as if she'd only been asleep for seconds when the phone she'd put under her pillow began its ringtone. She answered groggily to hear Evie's cute little voice asking, "Charlie, will you come help us make some breakfast? We're starving and Madge has a headache and Daddy and Lukey and Tuckett had to go out and take care of some cows early."

Still wondering if she could focus her gritty eyes to make breakfast, Charlie answered, "Sure, sweetie. I'll be right there, what did you have in mind?"

"Oh, we already started making it. We're having waffles. We just don't know how to get them to stop running out of the sides of the waffle cooker thing. That's why we called you. Do you know how to get it to stop doin' that?"

Charlie sat straight up in bed. "Who's we?"

"Oh, me and Elsa and Jamie. We were going to surprise you!"

"You have. Where's your mom?"

"Hmmm. I'm not sure where Mommy is. I'll bet she's gone on a plane somewhere. Do you want me to go look for her?"

Pulling some warm up pants on, Charlie replied, "No. Don't worry about finding your mommy. Just go get Elsa and Jamie and take them out to the sand box and wait for me there, okay? I don't want one of you to get burned in the kitchen."

"Oh, Jamie already got burned on the waffle thingy. We put some of that blue stuff out of the cold thingy in the freezer on it and he's gonna be fine. He says the blue stuff is fun and tastes like Jell-O."

Charlie hit the door of her cabin running. "Evie! Don't let him eat the blue stuff! Take them outside. I'll be right there. Don't touch anything else."

When she finally did reach them in the sand box, Jamie had decided the blue stuff in the cold thingy also made great sand mud and that the sand mud felt funny when it squished through his toes. Charlie picked him up and inspected the burn on his pointer finger and was immensely relieved to find it was wonderfully minor. He was quite offended when she confiscated his cold sand mud and shoveled it into the garbage dumpster and then washed his hands and feet off with the hose. When she was relatively sure they were out of the woods as far as ingesting anymore cold blue stuff, she left them playing in the sand and squared her shoulders to brave the waffle kitchen.

It was even worse than she had feared.

They had literally emptied the set of cupboards that housed the baking supplies, as well as two dozen eggs, a jug of orange juice and two bottles of jelly. They had mixed and spilled and walked around in a concoction that would have rivaled any mad scientist's lab, hands down.

Unsure of where to even begin the clean up, Charlie glanced down the hall toward Madge's room and decided she needed to check on her first and call poison control. She slid as she went to step across the mess on the kitchen floor and would have fallen except for coming up sharply against the countertop on the far side of the room. Rubbing her hip where she'd banged it, she was slipping out of her sandals to head to Madge when Luke asked from the kitchen doorway, "Are you okay?"

Charlie spun around to face him, self consciously running a hand through her undoubtedly wild curls as she did so. "I'm fine, thanks. It's the kitchen that isn't. Are they still safely in the sand box?"

Luke gave her a tired smile. "Not exactly. Jamie just threw up in the sand box and it made Evie and Elsa join him. I sent the three of them to the hose."

Charlie picked up the phone book and tossed it to him as she headed for the hallway. "Call poison control." She handed him the blue gooey wrapper from the cold pack Jamie had tasted. "See if whatever is in this is toxic. Jamie says it tastes like Jell-O. I need to see about Madge. They said she isn't feeling well." She rushed from the room and after groaning about the way Luke had just seen her, she knocked and went into the older woman's bedroom.

She quietly approached the bed and when Madge wearily raised her head, Charlie asked, "Madge, the kids said you weren't feeling great. Are you okay?"

Madge bravely smiled, but then shook her head and admitted, "I'm afraid I overdid yesterday Charlie. I've given myself a migraine. And after what I've been hearing from the kitchen I'm also afraid there might be a disaster in there. How bad is it?"

Charlie chuckled. "Uh, well, that would depend on if you're using the Richter scale or not. The kitchen's fine. What can I do to help you? Do you have anything you take for migraines?"

Madge sounded almost feeble as she answered, "I do, dear, but it's still packed in my suitcase in the garage. Would you mind bringing my bag in?"

Luke spoke from the door, "I'll grab it, Charlie. You stay here with her."

Charlie turned back to Madge. "What do you need with the medicine, Madge? Do you need to eat with it?"

"No. No food or drink, thank you. I'd never keep it down. I simply put the little tablet under my tongue. Then dark and quiet for a few hours. Will you be all right with the children without me this morning?"

Luke appeared with the suitcase and set it on the nightstand and he and Charlie dug through it looking for the medicine. They were standing side by side with their heads together and when the medicine was found, Luke helped Madge sit up as Charlie carefully handed her one of the pills.

She looked terrible and was hesitant to even open her eyes. Charlie was proud and grateful when Luke quietly asked, "Madge, would you like a blessing? That's always helped in the past."

She nodded gratefully. "I would appreciate that very much, Luke. Is Richard around? Or is he gone somewhere?"

"He's gone, but I could go find Anthony. He's in the north pasture if you want."

"No." She shook her head. "Just you will be wonderful. Thank you, Luken."

Charlie quickly sat down in the chair beside the window and Luke gently put his hands on the elderly house keeper's head and gave her a short, but powerful blessing of comfort and peace. When he was finished, he leaned down and kissed the older woman on the forehead. "You rest, Madge. Get feeling better." He rose and left the room and Charlie patted Madge's hand and followed him.

Luke was waiting for her in the hall. "Poison control said the blue stuff shouldn't be toxic, but it might make him sick to his stomach. I guess we already knew that. How much did he eat? Do you know?"

"I'm sorry, I have no idea. I was still home asleep when they called to say they'd been making waffles and Jamie had been burned and thought the blue stuff tasted like Jell-O. I hurried, but... The damage had been pretty much done."

They stopped to take in the hurricane that had hit the kitchen. "Pretty much. Waffles huh? What do you suppose the popcorn and spaghetti were for?"

Charlie nodded to the peanut butter smeared across the counter and the top of the still smoking waffle iron. There were popcorn kernels and spaghetti sticks and various types of pasta and dried beans stuck into the peanut butter in a spiral pattern. "Decoration. Waffles are an art, you know."

Just then Richard walked in the far door and stopped stock still and stared. "Holy Toledo!" He looked at the mess for several seconds and then turned around and headed into the living room where he opened a cupboard near the entertainment center.

Charlie whispered to Luke, "What's he doing?"

Luke grinned. "He has this saying that's kept us all alive from time to time. Don't get mad. Get the camera. He's digging for the camera."

"Oh." Charlie stopped and looked down at the t-shirt she had slept in, her warm up pants and bare feet. "I think if there's a camera involved, I'd better slip out the back and go get dressed. I wonder where the kids are."

Luke looked her up and down and grinned again. "You got a problem with being immortalized on film looking positively edible? You know that's what Chase would say about you."

She shook her head and laughed. "You got a problem with being called a complete dork? That was what I called him, I believe."

Luke groaned. "I remember that now. No. I do not want to be a complete dork, thanks."

Just then, Elsa came running in, hit a broken egg on the floor, slipped and landed full length in the thick of the mess. Evie and Jamie were right behind her. They all three went flying and Charlie was both appalled and couldn't help laughing at the same time. She'd never seen anything like this.

The front door slamming brought Luke's head up, and he made a lunge for the other kitchen door just in time to keep the three dogs that were following the kids from taking a mud bath in the mess as well. He chased the dogs out and Charlie latched the door lock and they hurried back to the kitchen. Richard was standing in the living room door quietly filming the kids as they tried to help each other up, only to slip and fall right back down. The three of them were so caught up in trying to get up and help each other they didn't even realize they were being either watched or filmed.

By the time they were finally all three on their feet and out of the worst of the goo, Charlie and Luke were in stitches and there was no way Richard could keep the video camera steady as he laughed while he was filming. The kids all turned to look at the adults as if they had lost their minds and then they looked at Charlie and Evie asked, "Can I have a tubber? I feel yucky."

At this, Richard roared with laughter and Luke and Charlie laughed so hard they had to lean on each other. Finally, Charlie was able to contain herself enough to tiptoe across to the bag drawer and take out the roll of plastic wrap. She carefully took the roll out and then taking the end of the plastic, she stuck it down into the edge of the worst of the mess on the kitchen floor and then with a flourish, she tossed the roll toward the front door and let it unravel all the way across the great room floor. She followed it and carefully strung it out the front door that she propped open. Then she grabbed the dogs before they could go inside and said to the children. "All right, you three. One at a time. Walk across the plastic and come out here. You're going to have to start in the hose and at least get the big chunks off before you can go into the bath tub.

Miraculously, they all three made it across the plastic except for one minor crash and burn as Jamie stepped onto the plastic walkway. Richard followed them out and began to help them hose off again. Luke disappeared as Charlie headed back into the kitchen to try to figure out where to even start. Moments later, Charlie busted up laughing again when Luke showed up with a snow shovel and a huge rubber garbage can.

After searching around, they found some big lawn and leaf bags to line the can with and they started in.

They had the floor mostly scraped when Richard came back through with three soggy children wearing only their underwear. By the time Richard had them bathed and dressed; Luke and Charlie had finally found the countertop and had mopped the floor clean. Richard went across and pulled out two boxes of cold cereal and took it and the kids to the dining table and came back to get bowls and milk and spoons. Jamie started to cry. "I fought we were having waffos."

Richard picked him up and began to help him into his high chair. "Oh, no you don't. We've had all the waffle making we can take for one day. Which cold cereal do you want?"

Charlie laughed when Luke said, "That looks really good. I'm starving. Have you eaten yet?"

She shook her head. "I haven't even woken up yet. Shall we join them?"

He glanced around the kitchen. "I think it's safe to leave it for a few minutes. At least as long as the dogs can't get inside." He nodded at the door. "After you."

Halfway through breakfast, Richard looked up and said, "Good heavens! It's Sunday!" He glanced at his watch and then shook his head. "Oh, I am so glad I didn't have a speaking assignment today. The jet lag and then that kitchen have made me forget everything. We completely missed church!"

Luke finished his bite and said drily, "Ok, so the ox wasn't in the mire, but the spaghetti was definitely in the peanut butter. And I'd hate for Jamie to throw up and set off a chain reaction in the chapel."

Sighing, Richard said, "Yes, that's all we need, isn't it? We'll just have to have some personal worship here at home."

By the time Chase and Angela appeared between noon and one, the house was returned to its usual level of organization and except for the priceless film footage, you would never even know to exactly what depth of destruction the three little ones were capable. Luke and Richard were long gone again and Tuckett had gone back to bed.

Charlie fixed a late lunch and then checked on Madge again. When there was nothing more she needed, Charlie dragged her tired body that was jet lagged and every other lagged, back to the great room where she asked Angela, "Is there anything else you need me to do this afternoon, Angela? Are you going to keep the kids with you here?"

Looking up from where she was reading a magazine near where the children were watching a Veggie Tales movie, Angela waved her manicure at the three partners in destruction. "We're fine thanks. We're just going to hang out until dinner. They'll watch a movie. They'll be fine. They can't get into too much trouble. I'll watch them."

"Perfect. I'll have my phone if you need me." Charlie rolled her eyes as she wended her way back to her house. *They can't get into too much trouble. Where was she when they needed help making waffles?*

As she walked past the bunkhouses she thought back to how normal things had been between her and Luke this morning in the kitchen. It was as if in the crush of things he hadn't had time to mentally shut the silent, invisible door on their easy friendship. She knew when he had time, he might shut it again, but for this morning his casual acceptance of her went a long way toward mending the hurt of yesterday. Leaning together to find Madge's medicine had been as comfortable as ever, except for the fact that his nearness affected her heart rate now much more than it had in the beginning.

Just as she was unlocking her door, her phone rang and she knew instantly it was showdown time with her mother. Much as she hated to face this, she gamely pushed the send button and said cheerfully, "Hello, mother."

The moment of silence on the other end of the line did nothing to allay her dread, but surprisingly her mother simply said, "I'm glad to see that you'll take my call, Charlene. Did you make it safely back out there, then?"

"Other than some jet lag, we all made it here in one piece, thank you."

It was obvious that her mother was attempting to use some diplomacy as she continued, "Give it a day or two and you'll feel fine." Then she added sternly, "I want you to know, young lady, that I don't intend to take the kind of disrespect from you that I received when you were here."

In as smooth a voice as she could muster as tired as she was, Charlie replied, "I'm sorry you took it as disrespect, Mother. But you must admit I can't marry someone I feel nothing for. And I am twenty-three years old. I'm old enough to decide my own agenda."

"This has nothing to do with deciding your own agenda. You and I both know you sometimes have issues with making decisions. The least you could do is spend some time with him and see if you'll like him. He's a wonderfully sharp, young litigator."

"That's actually the problem, mother. I have no intention of ever spending time with a man whose life's work is breaking up marriages. That's repugnant."

"Oh, don't be obtuse, Charlene. The marriages are over long before Elroy gets involved. He only facilitates the split."

"Whatever you say, Mother." She decided to change the subject. "How is Shelly feeling with her pregnancy? It must be draining to keep up her workload at the office the way she does."

"Actually, she lost the baby a few weeks ago. I think it was a relief to her. She didn't feel the timing was right, what with Roger being made a partner just now. They're going to try again in a year or two."

Wondering if anyone was going to mention it to the sister in Montana, she asked, "Mom, isn't she like thirty?"

"Thirty-one, but I think they only want one or at most two. She'll be fine. Are you going to find the time to come out again for a visit before you start school? And have you been thinking about transferring to a law school closer to home. Elroy told me he had spoken to you about it in hopes of being able to get married sooner."

Charlie rolled her eyes, but simply said, "I'm not sure what my plans are yet. I'll phone you when I know for sure. I'm pretty busy here, so we'll have to see."

"I've been meaning to talk to you about that, Charlene. Those people seemed to think they could expect you to help with their children as if you were some kind of domestic help. You shouldn't let them manipulate you like that. It's demeaning. And I didn't approve of the way Fo's cousin acted as if he owned you, either."

Shaking her head at the idea that the Langstons could hold a candle to her family in the manipulation department, Charlie assured her, "I think you got the wrong impression, mother. He definitely doesn't treat me as if he owns me." *I wish he did.* "It's been great talking to you, Mother, but I'm beat. Is there anything else you needed?"

"I only called to remind you that your behavior last weekend was not becoming of an Evans. I expect you to do better in the future."

"Yes, Mother."

"And you need to be more attentive to Christopher Elroy or you're going to drive him away, even as patient as I know he is. He truly is perfect for you, dear. Trust me. I'm your mother and I know what you need."

Not willing to admit defeat or push either, Charlie replied calmly, "This is all so premature, Mother. I have four more years of school. Let's argue in a few years about this, shall we?"

"Well, if you'd be realistic and switch to a school closer to Elroy's practice, you wouldn't have to wait so long. Being married is really quite nice you know."

"I'm sure it is. Tell Daddy hello. Love you."

"I love you, too. Charlene. Think about some of these things, would you?"

"Sure, Mom. Take care."

"Goodbye, Charlene."

"Bye, Mom."

With a sigh, Charlie mumbled, "Does she have any idea how hard it is to even get accepted to a law school? Transfer. So I can marry a sharp young divorce litigator. My word. She's a lunatic."

She prayed and then climbed into bed even though it was only mid afternoon. She knew she shouldn't do this as far as getting her body back into Montana standard time, but she was dead. She couldn't wait until tonight to let her body rest.

****

She slept soundly until sometime deep in the middle of the night and then she started having strange broken dreams about Tyree that didn't quite let her wake up, but wouldn't let her rest either. Finally, she had such a vivid nightmare flashback about the night that Tyree had hurt her that she woke up with her heart racing and the damp sheets in a wad at the foot of her bed. She sat up with a hand to her chest and tried to think her way to calmness, but she couldn't seem to break the hold the fear had on her psyche. It took several minutes for her to realize there was a breeze wafting through the cabin.

That was strange. She had been dead tired when she'd lain down, but she didn't remember opening any windows. She got up and wandered into the other room in the dark and was even more fearful when she realized the cabin door was standing wide open. As she went to close it, she tripped over something on the floor in front of it and she screamed as it moved.

Whatever it was gave a low whine and she realized it was one of the dogs that had come in and was sleeping curled up just inside her door. She reached down to pet him and found that he was actually a comfort to her in her fear and she decided to leave him inside with her. She closed the door with a slam and threw the dead bolt and willed her heart to slow as she leaned down to pat the dog again. "Sorry I stepped on you, Pilgrim. You scared the tar out of me though."

She went back to bed and laid there trying to calm down and get back to sleep, but it wasn't working. Tonight the cabin that had been filled with such a sense of peace from that very first moment seemed to be fraught with a sense of urgent foreboding. She tried to tell herself it was only a bad dream, but the fear persisted. She prayed fervently for a sense of peace and when the feeling got even worse as she said amen, she followed what felt like a prompting and got up. She grabbed the pillow and quilt off of her bed, called the dog to come with her and headed out the door at a jog toward Fo's bunkhouse. At the door she paused feeling foolish and then felt that urgency again. She quietly opened the door and she and the dog slipped inside and she locked the door behind her.

It took a moment for her eyes to adjust to the dark, and then she crept to the cowhide couch and sank onto it gratefully. Instantly, she felt the reassurance that she was safe. She still felt slightly foolish, but she put a hand on the dog's head and the fear dissipated in moments. She was able to close her still weary eyes and finally go back to sleep.

Chapter 10

At first light, Luke was up and although he was still tired from the jet lag, he headed for the shower, knowing it would help him to beat the fatigue and wake up. He was clear into the bathroom when he did a double take and backed up to look over at the couch. He ran a hand across his tired eyes, but he wasn't seeing things. That really was Charlie's blonde tousled curls he was seeing lying there in a wadded quilt with a dog beside her. He stood there and looked at her for a minute, wondering what was up with this. If he hadn't known she was even more tired than he was he would have woken her up and asked what was going on.

He continued on to the shower and as the steamy water pelted him awake, he thought about the girl lying in there. She had gotten to him in a way that was both wonderful and terrible. Being with her made everything in his life brighter and more vibrant, but knowing she would be leaving in a few weeks was like pulling the plug on the energy in his life. His head told him he needed to keep his distance, but when he'd tried after wanting to kiss her on the beach yesterday it had been awful.

Not only had he felt lonely and discouraged, but he knew his sudden change of attitude toward her had left her wondering what she'd done wrong. She'd cried as they boarded the plane, and he knew she hadn't slept on the whole flight home. He'd been able to cat nap, but every time he'd looked over at her she'd been staring out the window into the darkness, wide awake. Still, it was foolish to fall any deeper. Wasn't it? And it wasn't only him. He knew she wasn't indifferent to him. He'd seen the blue fire in her eyes on the ferry.

That was what scared him the most actually. She would be hurt as well when she left. And her life had enough struggle to it. The last thing she needed was something else pulling on her. Especially another something who had the baggage he had. It wasn't as if he was ever going to be able to marry someday and be a carefree newlywed. He had the ranch to run and a whole passel of little brothers and sisters he helped to raise. Heck he even had an older brother he helped to raise. Sometimes Chase was the biggest baggage of all. He certainly had been in Lindie's case.

Still, it would have been so nice to let himself fall in love with Charlie. For just a second he let himself day dream that she'd be willing to forego the whole law school issue and stay with him here in Montana forever. He could see that so easily. He could see her growing old beside him, keeping him entertained and organized. He could see that in a second.

With a long sigh, he turned off the water and toweled off. He shouldn't let his mind wander like that. It was only torturing himself. She had to go and he knew that he couldn't even ask her not to. If it was bad enough that she felt she needed to actually go through with this law school thing then he needed to leave her alone. She wasn't a spineless person. She must truly need to do this.

On the way back out of the shower he paused to look down at her again. She was really, really beautiful. Even in her sleep she truly did seem edible. He heard Fo come up behind him and take the same double take he had. He followed Luke back to his bunk where she wouldn't be able to hear them and whispered, "What's she doing here?"

Luke shrugged. "You've got me. I got up and went to shower and found her there, just like you. I didn't even hear her come in. What time did you get in last night?"

"Midnight. Twelve thirty. Somewhere in there. She wasn't there when I came to bed. Did she bring the dog in?"

"The dog and her quilt and pillow. Does she show up like this often at your apartment?"

Fo looked up at him in disgust. "Of course not. Something is wrong. She wouldn't just show up here in the middle of the night for no reason."

Luke had already suspected that, but he'd been hoping he was mistaken. After giving Fo a long look, he asked the question that had been bothering him since he'd first found her there. In the lowest voice Fo could hear, he asked, "Is Tyree still in jail?"

Fo looked up at him in surprise and he could see the thought get through to him. He shook his head and whispered back, "I assumed so, but I don't know. I hadn't even considered they'd have to let him out on bail and that he'd come back."

Luke glanced over at her and then asked, "On your way into work would you call and find out? You can do it more unobtrusively than I can. Then let me know what you find. In the mean time, I'm going to go up and look around her house. If she wakes up, keep her here. If he's still in jail, I don't want to scare her unnecessarily. She doesn't need to know I'm looking around."

As Luke went to turn and go out the door, Fo asked quietly, "What's up with you two anyway? Why were you not speaking on the trip home?"

Luke considered this and wondered what to tell him, knowing that Fo was her best friend as well as his. Finally, he shook his head and said sadly, "I just like her way too much is all. I don't want to make her miserable. Her mom did enough of that."

Fo's brow creased and he asked, perplexed, "I don't get it. You don't want to make her miserable, so you stop speaking to her? You saw how that worked. She cried half the way home. I thought you two had had a big fight or something out at the coast. No?"

Shaking his head, Luke admitted, "She was amazing at the coast. Too amazing. I couldn't even breathe when her shirt got wet." He sounded as guilty as he'd felt and he looked away. "Twice this trip I wanted to kiss her." He shook his head again and reached for his chaps and began to buckle them on. "She's leaving for her stupid law school, remember?"

Fo nodded, still not looking as if he understood very well and Luke continued. 'Remind me about that the next time you see me looking a little dazed would you. It's hard to think with no oxygen and I don't want to hurt her. Or me. She's way too nice a girl to toy with."

"What do you mean toy with? You're not like that."

"What else would you call it when we both know she's leaving in a few weeks?"

"It's not as if she wants to go to law school, Luke. She hates the whole idea."

Luke shook his head. "She plans to go, Fo. That's the bottom line. You and I both know she's made the decision."

"Well, maybe she'd change her mind, if she had a good enough alternative. Why don't you offer her one?"

"What? So she can hang around here while I work sixteen hour days? In her spare time she can raise my little brother and sisters? And dodge my older one? Oh, that's a great life. I'm sure she'd choose that alternative."

He picked up his rope and gloves and turned to leave and Fo forgot to whisper when he said, "You're a jerk, Luke. She's twenty three years old. She has the right to make her own choices."

Luke looked over to where her silky hair still lay against her quilt. "She has. She's chosen law school. And you know what? She'll be a great lawyer. Just like she's great at everything else." He stared at the locked deadbolt on the bunkhouse door with a frown and then said over his shoulder to Fo. "I'm going up to her house."

As he walked up to her cabin, he felt as if he'd turned up the vacuum on his energy leak to high. Talking to Fo about how hopeless falling in love with her was, made it all hurt even worse. Or maybe it was seeing her there asleep. He'd wanted to stop and sit down and touch her. At any rate, the attraction was stronger than ever and that computed into discouragement that stung.

Everything at her house seemed normal. She hadn't locked the door when she'd fled and he let himself in and poked around, but nothing seemed out of place. Her house smelled like her and he breathed in deeply, wishing that even smells didn't evoke attraction.

He went back outside and walked around the little house but the grass had been mowed recently and there was nothing to indicate what had scared her. Outside her bedroom window he noticed the blinds didn't completely cover the opening. There was only a small strip at the edge exposed, but he resolved to discretely change out the blinds anyway. He wouldn't put it past Tyree to come sneaking back and spy on her.

Climbing into his truck, he went to pull out just as she emerged from the bunkhouse door with her pillow and quilt in her hands and the dog standing beside her in the doorway. He looked up and their eyes met. He desperately wanted to get back out and go talk to her and find out what was going on and if she was okay. But there was this little nagging voice in his head that said that was only another excuse to be with her, which was foolish and likely to hurt them both in the long run.

He hesitated for a moment and then nodded and put the truck in reverse and backed out; hating himself for the way her face fell when she understood he wasn't even going to say good morning. As he drove away, he tried to tell himself that was kinder than the alternative, but somehow his heart didn't truly believe it.

****

Charlie started to wake up, and she could hear them talking quietly over by Luke's bunk, but she couldn't really hear what they were saying, still half asleep as she was. But she did hear Fo call Luke a jerk and say something about letting her make her own decisions. She had no idea what they were talking about, but she knew Fo sounded disgusted and Luke sounded tired.

Just as she was going to roll over and get up, she heard Luke's comment about how she had chosen law school and would make a great lawyer as he strode out the door. He sounded utterly disgusted with her choice, even if he was giving her a compliment, and her heart fell while she tried to figure out what they had been saying.

It must have been that Luke thought she shouldn't go back to law school because the prophet recommended LDS woman put home and family first. Law school involved a lot of years of effort if what she really wanted was to walk away from a career and raise a family.

She laid there sad and wondering what she truly did want. Oh, she knew what she wanted, but if she couldn't have Luken Langston, what then? Was she seriously willing to go back and take on a commitment like becoming an attorney simply to keep from being hassled by her parents? And if not, then what? She was now educated and a returned missionary, but she was glaringly single. That had never bothered her, but now, after falling in love with Luke, she almost felt as if she needed to consciously work to fall for someone else to protect herself and move on.

She rolled over and sighed and sat up. She needed to get home to her little cabin where she could read her scriptures and pray for the insight she so desperately needed.

When she put her feet on the floor, she realized she'd gotten a sliver running here in the dark last night and she put her foot back up to look at it, but the light was too dim to see it clearly. She stood up and stepped on her tip toes to protect the sore spot as she folded her blanket and then picked up her pillow. She gave the bunkhouse one last look around, wondering where Fo had gone. She'd heard Luke leave, but she hadn't heard Fo go out at all.

As she took a step and the floor creaked, he poked his head out of the bathroom with shaving cream covering half of his face. "Hey, you. To what do we owe the pleasure of your company last night? What time did you show up here?"

She set down her bedding and walked over to him. "I don't even know what time it was. I'm sorry I bothered you guys, but for some reason my house was terrifying last night."

She was glad he looked honestly concerned and didn't tease her. "What do you mean? What was terrifying?"

"I don't know. I'd been having these weird dreams and then I had nightmares about Tyree again. Then when I woke up for some reason in the middle of the night, the door to my house was standing wide open and that dog was lying just inside the door. I shut the door and locked it, but I was still so scared there. I couldn't seem to get a handle on it and finally, when even praying seemed to make the urgency worse I bailed and came up here. I probably shouldn't have. It looks terrible, but I was 'a mess."

He shook his head. "It's okay, Charlie. If you felt you should come then you should have. Don't blow off the Spirit if that's what it was. What do you think happened with your door? Do you think you just didn't shut it tight?"

It would be so easy to say that and they wouldn't think she was a nut, but she knew she hadn't simply not shut it tightly. "No, Fo. I didn't lock it because it was only mid afternoon when I laid down, but I'm sure I shut it tightly. It would have come open when I was puttering around there before lying down if I hadn't." She paused and then looked at him again and said, "What's weird is, why would someone open it in the middle of the night? It had to have been late, late. There were no lights on anywhere on the ranch except the security lights. Even the dairy barn was dark and quiet. Why would someone do that?"

"I don't know, Charlie. Maybe someone was trying to tease you. You know, like getting toilet papered or door bell ditched. You don't have a door bell." She looked at him and he said, "Okay, that was stupid, but I honestly don't know why someone would do that."

Hesitantly, she voiced a question she hated to even consider. "Is Tyree still locked up? Or has he been let out on bail?"

She knew when he didn't immediately toss the idea that it was a possibility. "I'm not sure. Let me finish shaving and I'll call the sheriff's office and find out." He glanced at his watch. "Actually, I'm going to be late. I'll call on the way to the hospital and call you back and let you know what I found out. Will that work?"

"Sure, that'll work. Just please find out he's still in jail. Okay?" She said it jokingly, but in a way she was serious. She so didn't want to let something like this ruin the sweet peace she had found here in this land of the big sky. She picked her bedding back up and headed for the door. "Have a great day at work. And tell what's her name hi. See ya."

She stepped out the door just in time to see Luke fold his superb physique into his pick up truck. She hesitated on the step, assuming he'd say hello to her, but all he did was pause for a second and then back out and pull away. She almost felt as if she'd been slapped.

So much for their easy friendship. She'd begun to believe he cared for her other than simply as one of the guys, but apparently not. Apparently really not. That silent invisible door had been slammed shut. He didn't even want to know why she'd showed up in the middle of the night.

She couldn't help the tears that filled her eyes and she felt like a fool as she walked back to her house unable to stop them. What was going on here? For months things had been so new and fun and she'd had the time of her life here with Fo and Luke. What had all of the sudden happened to them? She was incredibly lost and the fact that she had fallen into full blown love while he had suddenly become allergic to her killed her heart, not to mention her ego.

That he was usually so kind and caring made this complete disregard and cold shoulder come straight out of the blue. She had no idea how to come to terms with it.

She made it to her porch and although she was once again afraid to go inside, she pushed the door open and walked in anyway. What did it even matter?

Showering and scripture study helped. It was a few minutes that she could be still and try to listen to God and she asked Him why and then said, "Never mind why, please just help me be strong enough to make it through whatever You have in mind for me." She didn't understand, but she'd never been one to wallow in defeat, and she wasn't going to start now.

As she dressed to go up to the house and pitch in, she mentally pep talked herself that she was, indeed, strong enough to do this and that, in time, she'd figure out what she needed to be doing with her life. Looking in the mirror, she knew she still looked tired, and her eyes were puffy from all the crying the last day or two, but she couldn't help it. She put on the shirt she felt the prettiest in, hoping it would help her make it through at least breakfast without melting like the wicked witch of the west.

She put her quilt back on her bed and made it and went to put on a pair of earrings and noticed one of her favorite iridescent blue turtle earrings was missing. She searched all around and even turned the entire jewelry box upside down and dumped it out, but it wasn't there. The hair on the back of her neck stood up when she finally had to face the fact it was gone.

She had been wearing those earrings yesterday and she absolutely knew she'd taken them both off and put them on top of the box when she came home and went to bed. She knew she'd seen them sitting there as she brushed her teeth the last thing before she lay down. She hadn't misplaced one. Someone had taken it. It was a simply stated fact, but one that left her shaken and afraid. Someone had been in here last night with her. Who would do that and why? Those questions only deepened the fear.

Going to the door, she turned before walking out to look back and glance around the quaint little cabin. She had found such peace here. She closed her eyes and prayed. Please God, don't let me lose that precious, tenuous peace.

As she walked up to the ranch house, she phoned Fo and when he picked up, she didn't small talk. Just asked, "Hey, Fo, what did you find out about Tyree? You didn't call me back."

He paused and her stomach tightened. Somehow she had known it, but he confirmed it. "Actually, he's out on bail. He got out only a day after they took him in, but they don't think he'd ever risk doing something like coming back there."

She thought about that and then asked, "Do you really believe that?"

The best friend who never kept things from her hesitated and then quietly answered, "Of course not. Do you?"

"No. He was in my house last night. One of the earrings I put on top of my jewelry box yesterday was gone this morning. I know exactly where I put it, and the other one is still there, but one's gone."

"You're sure?"

"I'm sure."

"You need to tell Luke."

She couldn't help sounding bitter when she admitted, "I can't tell Luke. We're not speaking. I'll go in and get a restraining order if the police will give me one. And I'll get a gun and I'll be fine. I'll be more careful about locking the door though."

"Why are you not speaking?"

It took her a second to answer. "I honestly don't know. Something happened in Connecticut to make him dislike me. I've thought and thought about it, but I don't know what I did. Maybe it was my parents. Or Elroy. Maybe he's just sick of me and can't wait for me to leave. I don't know. But don't tell him about the earring. I'll handle it."

This time he was the one who hesitated. "Okay, Charlie, but he runs this place. He truly ought to know what's going on. Don't you think?"

"I don't think this has anything to do with the ranch. I've gotta go. Thanks for digging for me. Have a good day."

When she walked into the kitchen, first Madge asked her if she was okay and then when he and Luke came in, Richard asked her as well, "Charlie, are you okay? Are you sick?"

She brushed off his concern. "I'm fine. Some jet lag is all. How are you feeling? Back on Montana time yet?"

Richard took the platter of bacon and eggs she was carrying. "Give me one more day and I'll be good as new."

They all visited through breakfast and she felt as if she'd done okay as she cleared the table afterward. Hopefully, no one had even noticed that her heart was smashed and her peace of mind had been brutally ripped away this morning.

She rolled her neck as she waited for the water at the kitchen sink to run hot before she rinsed the plates. She could do this. The only one who seemed to have a problem with her was Luke. Everyone else still acted like she was welcome. All she had to do was find a way to push the thoughts of Luke out of her head and finish out the summer. She could do this. She was fine.

The children helped as they were around her that day, and when Richard asked after her again that afternoon it helped as well. She simply had to remember to count her blessings and not be too hopeful about the future right this minute. All she needed was some time. Once she'd adjusted her mindset, she'd be just dandy.

That night, she went straight to her cabin after dinner and was surprised to find the same dog Pilgrim lying on her front porch. After locking the door securely, she checked to make sure all the windows were locked and then slipped out of her clothes and showered. It had really helped this morning. Maybe the soothing hot water would help her state of mind again tonight.

As she got out, she pulled out a new book she'd been meaning to read. With all the fuss of the trip and what not, she'd never even opened it, but surely a good read would help her shake her nerves and sadness tonight.

She took the book into her bedroom and pulled not only the blind, but the drapes as well and settled in to read. It was a good book, but she was still so tired and put it aside before it was even nine o'clock. She turned out the lights and prayed and turned onto her stomach and pulled her pillow into her arms, grateful that last night's fear hadn't reappeared.

The next afternoon, she truly did go into town and arrange to have a restraining order placed on Tyree. She had to file a police report about someone being in her house two nights before, but thankfully, the officer who helped her didn't push too hard before agreeing to process the order.

On the way home, she stopped at a sporting goods store and bought a small handgun. The paperwork for this actually took longer than the police paperwork and she thought about what she was doing as she waited. She'd never in her life considered buying a firearm, even though she'd actually been taken to a shooting range once on a date. Six months ago, she'd have never dreamed of owning a gun, but after the fear she felt over Tyree, she hoped it would make her feel more secure.

The salesman who helped her make her selection asked her if she was familiar with how it worked and when she admitted she would need some practice, he didn't hesitate to offer to help her learn. Even though the last thing she wanted right now was another guy's attention, she accepted. He seemed nice enough and she truly did need the help learning to use her new purchase. She arranged to go to a shooting range with him that Friday evening and then took the heavy little black pistol and drove back to the ranch. As barbaric as it seemed, knowing she had a weapon there in her house with her did help. She was able to lock her doors that night and feel as secure as she had before that ugly night with Tyree had ever happened. Even though she had no intention of ever shooting anything, it was very reassuring.

****

She hadn't mentioned she was going to be going anywhere on Friday and when her friendly shooting instructor showed up to pick her up, Fo looked surprised and for some reason, Luke almost looked mad as they drove past the bunkhouse on the way out. The gun range was interesting, and other than her date thinking he had to put his arms around her to show her how to hold it properly, the evening felt like a success. She knew how to load and unload the gun and how to shoot it properly and felt she could handle it if she ever needed to. She also knew the friendly gun salesman did absolutely nothing for her romantically and she smiled noncommittally when he said he'd call as he dropped her back at the ranch.

Fo showing up at her house as soon as he got back from his date, didn't surprise her a bit. She'd known he'd be up to investigate when she drove past him on the way out. He dropped into his porch rocker and offered her a half package of Oreo's. "You got any milk? Luke and I are out at the bunkhouse."

"Of course I have milk. What are you thinking?" She got up to go inside to get the milk and cups. "Is he coming this way too? How many cups do I need?"

"He's long gone to bed. It's just me."

When she came out and handed him the milk, he asked, "So, who was the guy?"

After explaining about the gun, she went in and got it to bring it out and show him. He only looked at it for a minute before he locked it back in its case and then looked back at her and shook his head. "I never thought I'd see the day Charlie Evans was packing heat."

"Oh, give me a break. I'm not exactly packing it. It's like a really expensive dose of Ambien. I'm hoping I'll be able to rest easier with it and so far it's worked."

"Whatever works. Just be careful. So apparently you weren't overly excited by the company tonight?"

She sighed. "Not to speak of. Has Luke ever said why all the sudden he's allergic to me?"

"Yes." She looked over at him. "But, I can't tell you what he said."

"What? You're kidding. You'd never hold out on me. C'mon Fo. It's me, Charlie."

"I know it's you, Charlie, but this truly would be betraying a confidence this time. You'll have to ask him yourself."

"Do you think he'll tell me?"

"No."

She was silent for a minute while they rocked and then she said, "I don't think so either." After another time, she admitted to him, "I almost wish I hadn't come here, now."

"I thought you were loving it. Until Tyree at least."

"I was. Even after Tyree. But knowing Luke wishes I was gone is awful. I tried so hard to be immune to him,

Fo, but it was hopeless. He's just too darn adorable. Now it makes me heartsick."

Fo hesitated and then said, "I don't think *wishes you were gone* is exactly how I'd describe what's going on here."

She sighed. "It's been a week, Fo. He only has anything to do with me when he accidentally forgets to ignore me."

"Don't you think it's just that he's been busy after taking a few days off?"

Charlie glanced over at him and rolled her eyes. "Nice try, Fo. Can you at least tell me what I did that was so bad?"

He hesitated again and then said, "I'm sorry, Charlie, but you seriously are going to have to have this conversation with him."

"I thought I ranked over anyone on the planet with you. What's up with this? And I already asked him. He wouldn't tell me."

"It's not that you don't rank, Chuck. If this was someone else. Just another guy, I'd tell you in a heart beat. But this seems too... Too... I don't know. For real or something, to take a chance on messing up for the two of you. If someone is going to mess it up, it's not going to be me. There's too much at risk."

Sadly, Charlie said, "Actually, apparently there's nothing at risk. I'm going to focus on helping out as much as possible for the next three weeks until I leave without getting in his way. He went from absolutely friendly to absolutely cold in like three seconds the other day on the beach. I don't have a clue what I did." She paused and then said, "Never mind. How was your date? I've never seen you like this over a girl."

He watched her for a moment, and then grinned. "It's almost a bit scary isn't it? I don't know, Charlie. I'm thinking forever with Amy is not nearly long enough."

"And what is Amy thinking?"

"That's what scares me. She thinks I'm wonderful. I keep worrying she's going to find out what I'm really like and run."

She leaned across and nudged him. "You're one of those that gets better the closer you look. You know that. Do you actually think this is her?"

He rocked back in his chair. "I don't know. We've only known each other for a little over three months, but it feels so right. Does that make any sense?"

"You're asking me? The romantically moronic one? I just told you the only guy I've ever seriously felt lovesick over is allergic to me. I'm definitely not the right one to ask."

"Honestly, I don't even need to ask. Everything seems too good to question much. We've even talked about getting married. Right now we're both just saying we need to give it some time and make sure. I'm going to go finish my last semester back in Utah and we'll see what happens. The hospital has offered me a permanent position if I want to come back."

She reached across and took his hand and gave it a squeeze. "I'm so happy for you, Fo. I mean, I'll miss you to death, but I've been praying you'd find her. I hope it all works out perfect for you."

He squeezed her hand back. "I hope that same thing for you, Charlie. I do think you and Luke would be so good together, but I guess none of that is up to me. All I can say is, I think he's the greatest man on the planet and that he's worth fighting for. He's definitely worth giving up stupid law school for."

"I'd give up law school in a second for him, Fo. But I don't think that would fix his sudden aversion. It has to be something more than that. It's not like he's breathing down my neck, begging me to stay."

He let go of her hand and went back to rocking. "No, he's not really a begging kind of a guy, is he? He's more of a self sacrificing kind of a guy so that he doesn't get in the way of people's dreams."

"I don't understand what you're saying, Fo."

All he did was sigh. "I'm saying this has to be a conversation you have with him." He got up to go and she raised her hand to catch his as he continued, "I can tell you he was way not happy to see your personal shooting instructor tonight. That's a good sign, isn't it?"

"I haven't a clue, at this point, Fo. All I know tonight is I'm tired now."

"Go to bed, Charlie. Lock your door. I'll pray for you. For both of you."

"I'll pray for both of you too, Fo. Night."

****

The next morning, Charlie was in the office, trying to figure out why the computer wasn't interfacing with the printer when she felt a hand on her shoulder as she leaned over looking at the back of the tower. She automatically swung an elbow to dissuade Chase from getting any cozier than just the hand on her shoulder. As she turned to see Luke doubled over sucking air she was horrified. "Oh, Luke. I'm so sorry! I thought you were Chase. Please forgive me. Are you okay?" She turned and put a hand on his arm and looked up into his face. "I'm so sorry!"

With a groan, Luke attempted to say, "Remind me never to surprise you again. Geez. For once I actually feel sorry for Chase."

Charlie shook her head. "Don't. He deserves every elbow he gets. One of these days I'm going to take Tae Kwan Do. Are you all right?"

Luke tried to smile. "Yeah, just a little short of oxygen. But then you've always had that effect on me. I'll talk to Chase and tell him to leave you alone. What are you doing?"

"Oh, this computer is foinging out again. It's not speaking to the printer. Do you think you could look at it?"

"Foinging? Do I know what that means?"

She looked at him, wondering how to take his comment about oxygen. "Yeah, you always have that foinging effect on us girls. I'm sure you know."

He laughed. "Whatever." He reached over and turned both the computer and printer off and then they both sat there silently for a minute while he waited to turn them back on. As they powered back up, he leaned over like she had been to check all the cords. He pushed them all to make sure they were tight and she couldn't help but watch the muscles of his shoulders stretch the fabric of his shirt as he moved.

Trying to take her mind off of how attractive he was, she decided to try again to have that conversation Fo had talked about last night. "Luke, are you ever going to tell me what I did at the beach to offend you so much?"

He looked up and met her eyes for a long moment and then went back to inspecting the tangle of wires coming from the computer. "I told you then you didn't offend me, Charlie."

She folded her arms over her chest and leaned back against the desk. "So then what's going on? Because you like me when you forget that you've decided not to like me." He glanced up again and she challenged him, "Deny it."

Before he answered, he did something with the mouse and the printer kicked in as he looked up and said quietly, "What's not to like, Charlie? I think it's stopped foinging. Call me if you need me again."

As he went out the door she called after him, "Cow pie." She could hear him chuckle as he walked down the hall and she muttered to herself, "Double cow pie. How am I supposed to have a conversation when he won't converse? It's not just the computer that's going to foing."

"What are you grumbling about in here?" Richard came in and sat down at his desk.

"Oh, nothing. I just want to whack your son."

"Well, do what you have to do. We try, but Chase is a hard head. What did he do this time?"

Charlie felt slightly sheepish remembering how hard she'd elbowed Luke. "It was Luke actually, for once."

Richard did a double take. "Luke? Oh, no. He's the one child I have that typically stays out of trouble. What'd he do?"

Still muttering, Charlie said under her breath, "Nothing, dang it." To Richard she admitted, "He just won't be honest with me about what I did in Connecticut that has offended him so much. He's hardly spoken to me in more than a week. It's awful. Sorry I'm whining."

"Ah, whine all you want. Did he get that thing working?"

"Of course. You know him. He can fix anything except my peace of mind." She shut the paper drawer on the printer with a bit to much force, took a deep breath and tried to change the subject. "I'm taking the little ones in to the pediatrician to get some vaccinations this afternoon. Can you sign these releases? And do you need anything from town?"

Richard smiled big at her as he signed where she indicated. "Just your peace of mind, Charlie."

"I'll work on that. Maybe a big hot fudge sundae would help. I always wanted one after I had to get shots when I was little, but my mother never had time. I think I'll stop and get the kids one if they're good."

"I have heard hot fudge does wonders for peace of mind."

"Enough fudge sauce can fix anything. You no longer mind if someone doesn't care about you. I believe I'll try it."

The smile faded from Richard's face and he asked, "Are you sure that he doesn't care, Charlie? Or is it that he cares too much?"

She wrinkled her brow, trying to understand what he was saying. "Why would he quit speaking to me if he cared too much?"

"Because you're leaving."

She thought about that and then shook her head. "No. Luke is too confident to let that bother him without at least saying something. It has to be something else. I know when it happened. I just don't know what I did. It was at the beach that afternoon. Maybe he'd simply had enough of my family."

"Or maybe your family is why he doesn't feel he can pressure you to stay. Maybe he thinks you already have enough people trying to manipulate you."

Turning to the office door, she said, "I can't matter too much then, can I?"

****

The conversations with both Fo and Richard had been thought provoking, but somehow the idea that Luke was giving her the cold shoulder because in actuality he wanted her to stay didn't seem plausible. If he actually wanted her to stay, wouldn't he at least hint that? Fo's comment about how Luke hadn't been very happy about her date was intriguing as well and when she saw Dr. Nichols on the way into the pediatrician's office and he asked her out, she said yes. It would be interesting to see

Luke's reaction. At the very least she could enjoy a night out with a pleasant man.

Charlie had been honest with the little ones about where they were going and why. Her mother had never mentioned vaccinations until the syringe appeared and Charlie had always felt as if that was dishonest somehow. Charlie told them about the shots, but she also downplayed it and told them if they were brave they were going to go get sundaes with all the extras and not surprisingly, the vaccinating went fine.

Jamie cried for a moment, but then was so thrilled with his Winnie The Pooh Band-Aids and the sticker he got he forgot all about just having been poked. The only problem with the girls' reaction was the minor argument over who got the Belle sticker and who had to settle for Snow White.

They got huge sundaes and Charlie knew she'd hopelessly spoiled their dinner, but she'd also treated them the way she wished she'd been treated as a child. It was a good feeling to know she was making a difference for these kids, even if it was only in a small way.

****

If she was hoping for a reaction from Luke when Dr. Nichols showed up to pick her up, she was thoroughly disappointed. When she emerged from the main house to greet him, he and Luke were standing on the porch talking like they were old friends. As they left, Luke simply whistled for the dogs and then got into his truck and headed for somewhere on the ranch, absolutely unconcerned that she was going out. So much for seeing if he cared.

Dr. Nichols took her to a concert at an outdoor amphitheater near Kalispell. It was a folksy blue grass band

and while that wasn't necessarily her favorite, it was okay. The scenery more than made up for the lack luster music. There was a storm gathering to the west and the sunset was incredible.

When Dr. Nichols asked her out again at the door of her cabin, she put him off with the promise to see if the Langstons needed her on the night in question and the assurance that she'd call and let him know. In a way, she was half hoping they would. Greg was all right, but there was nothing there romantically for her. She sighed as she patted Pilgrim's head, let herself in and slipped off her shoes that were wet from the storm that had finally hit on the drive home. Somehow she knew there was nothing there with Greg because there was already too much that she felt for a certain cousin of Fo's. A cousin who was still very much allergic to her. She really missed that easy friendship the three of them had enjoyed for the first few months of the summer.

Her thoughts about her and Luke's friendship, or the lack thereof, were brought up short as she went to walk into her bedroom. Her bare feet on the wooden floor planks noticed the moisture on the very first step. She stepped back and flipped on the light and found exactly what she had worried she would. Large, wet footprints went from her front door toward the bedroom door of her cabin. Without hesitating for a second, she grabbed the heels she had just stepped out of and went back out the door and toward the bunkhouse.

In bare feet and in the rain and dark, she had to go more slowly than she wanted to, but she still arrived there out of breath, probably more from fear than from exertion. When she realized Fo still wasn't back, she waffled about whether to bother Luke and then settled for waiting in a chair there on the porch in the dark. Fo shouldn't be too long. It was after eleven and he had to work the next day.

If she saw or heard anything questionable in the mean time, she would barge in on Luke anyway.

It was a longer wait than she thought and by the time Fo showed up after midnight, she was shivering from the cold. He got out of his SUV and came up on the porch and stopped short when he saw her there. "Charlie, what's going on? What are you doing up this late and hanging out in the rain?" He draped an arm around her shoulders as she stiffly got out of the chair. "Holy, Charlie, you're an iceberg! Come inside. What's going on?"

She gladly followed him inside where he automatically pulled a heavy jacket off of the coat hooks and wrapped it around her and then asked again in a whisper so they didn't wake Luke, "What's going on, Chuck?"

Wondering what to tell him, she finally asked, "Could you come up to my house for a second? There's something I'd like to ask your opinion on."

He looked at her closely in the low light and then said, "Sure. Let's go." He grabbed a jacket as well and they headed back out in the rain. At her cabin, the footsteps were still obvious, although now there was a set that came back out of the bedroom and out the door again. Fo swore quietly under his breath. "Had you locked the door?" She nodded and he went on, "Grab some sweats. You can't stay here tonight, even with your gun. Tomorrow we'll have the locks changed and arrange for some kind of security. And we need to file another police report."

Grabbing the recommended sweats, she grabbed the little black gun case as well and followed him back out the door without even bothering to lock it. Tyree obviously had a key. At the bunkhouse, Fo locked the door behind them for the second time and she went into their bathroom to change out of her damp clothes. Fo seemed to understand that she wasn't up to sleeping just then and he dug a package of Oreos out of the cupboard and then cups and milk.

They sat at the little wooden table in silence and dunked their cookies until he finally asked, "How did your date go anyway? What'd you guys end up doing?"

"A blue grass concert at this magnificent outdoor amphitheater where the sunset was better than the music. It was incredible! How about you two?"

Fo gave her a mellow smile. "We talked for hours over fries and shakes at McDonald's. It was incredible too, although I have no idea if the sun even set."

Charlie laughed softly. "Sounds too romantical for me."

"Actually, you'd be surprised. Dipping a French fry into someone else's shake is very intimate."

"I guess I don't have to ask if you're still head over heels."

"Nope. How was the Dr.? You mentioned the sunset, but not the company."

She sighed. "The sunset was unreal. The company was okay."

He laughed. "He would be so disappointed to hear that. Ever since he met you, he asks about you. You must have made quite an impression."

"That's what I'm afraid of." She picked up their cups and the cookies and carried them to the sink. "It's late and you have to work. We should call it a night."

Watching her, he asked, "Do you think you can sleep yet?"

"Probably not, but that's no reason that you shouldn't. I'll lay there and ponder the deep meanings of the universe. At least I feel safe here."

"You're safe." He ruffled her damp curls. "Night, Chuck."

"Thanks for rescuing me."

"Anytime."

Chapter 11

Luke was up and showered and headed out the door when he spotted her tousled curls on the last bunk in the row. He did a double take again when he realized that was a gun case she had stashed next to her pillow and he went back into the bathroom to ask Fo what was going on. Fo shrugged and kept shaving and when it became apparent that he wasn't volunteering much, Luke shut the bathroom door and braced him. "Look, Fo. Is something going on or not? She wouldn't just show up again. Do you know why she's here?" Fo nodded. "Then out with it. This is my home. I run this place. I have the right to know."

"Tyree has a key to her house."

"What!"

"I saw the tracks inside myself and you know she's conscientious about locking it."

"When was this?"

"Last night. I found her shivering on the porch when I got here at a little past midnight."

"Shivering on the porch? Why didn't she just come in? I was here." Fo just glanced at him and kept shaving and Luke said almost to himself, "All right, all right. I haven't been terribly warm and fuzzy lately. I don't blame her. But doesn't she realize that of course I'd welcome her? Especially when her safety is in question?"

Fo answered calmly as he wiped off his face, "Apparently not. She knows darn well you don't want her anywhere near you. She's not stupid."

Almost snapping, Luke replied, "Of course she's not stupid. And you and I both know it's exactly the opposite of not wanting her near me."

"Look, don't get ornery with me, Luke. You're the one who's trained this monkey. You can't be all offended when she's done just what you wanted her to do. Stay away. She only waited for me because she knows beyond anything else in the world that I have her back. That's the way I've trained the monkey. And why are you asking me all this? She's right out there. Go ask her."

Luke looked toward the ceiling and put up a hand to rub the back of his neck and Fo looked at him in disgust. "Don't tell me that you consider saving your heart more important than her safety."

This time Luke snapped in earnest, "Of course not! I just don't know how to untrain the monkey, so back off! Where did she get the gun?"

Fo snapped right back, "She bought it the other day when she got a restraining order against him after he took some of her jewelry."

"Oh and was anyone going to mention this to me?"

Fo looked at him blandly. "I recommended she tell you and I believe her exact words were: I can't. We're not speaking. And I have no idea why."

Luke made a sound of complete disgust deep in his throat. "And you let her get away with that? Fo!"

Shaking his head, Fo said, "Look man. That was just after you had said you weren't willing to even approach her about staying. Exactly what am I supposed to do here? I'll watch over her, Luke, if you're truly not willing to deal with her. I've been doing it for about twenty years now and I'll take her back to Utah in a couple of weeks as well, if you honestly can't see she's worth fighting for. But I have to tell you. You're being a bone head. She's a one in a billion and you're a fool. And you'd better lower your voice or you're going to wake her up."

From the other side of the bathroom door they heard her drowsy voice. "She's already awake. What are you two arguing about in there?"

Fo looked at him wordlessly and then opened the bathroom door and said, "We're not arguing. At least not anymore. Luke just has some monkey issues. How did you sleep?"

She looked from Fo to Luke hesitantly and said, "Fine, thanks." Turning around, she said over her shoulder, "Thanks for the sleep over. I need to go get busy."

Fo glanced at Luke, but Luke ignored him and walked out of the bathroom to stop her at her made bunk as she picked up her heels and gun case. "Oh, no you don't." He put a hand on her arm. "You and I need to talk. I want to know what's going on that you showed up here last night and didn't even come in and wake me when you knew there was someone in your house."

Still obviously tired, she looked up at Fo and then down at Luke's hand on her arm. Shrugging it off, she said, "Fo handled it, thanks. Everything's fine. I've got to go start breakfast."

"No, Charlie. They can eat cold cereal." He stopped her again. "I'm having a locksmith come today to change out your locks. How many times has Tyree been back here?"

"Twice in my house that I know of."

He met her striking blue eyes, unbelievably sad that he'd made her feel as if her safety was of no concern to him. Softly, he asked, "Why didn't you tell me? Didn't you know I'd want to know so I could help take care of you?"

Several emotions he couldn't quite place flitted across her face, ending with hurt as she finally said, "I'm fine, Luke. In three weeks I'll be gone anyway. I'll be fine until then."

Fo came past them on his way out the door. "Gotta go. One of you two call me, would you?" He ruffled Charlie's wild hair as he went by. "Watch him, Charlie. He's a tad irritable this morning. I don't think he realized how out of control his monkeys had gotten. You might need to help him get a handle on them." He smiled at her. "Metaphorically speaking of course. Good luck." This last was directed to Luke who sighed. He was going to need it.

With Fo gone, Luke took Charlie's hand and led her back to the couch as she asked, "What monkeys have gone over board this morning? What's he talking about?"

Deciding to take the bull by the horns, he looked at her and said, "You, Charlie. He's inferring that you didn't tell me about Tyree because you thought I wouldn't want to know. Or wouldn't care or something. Please forgive me for giving you that impression. I'm sorry. Have a seat, would you?"

"Sure." Looking slightly wary, she sat on the edge of the couch and ran a hand through her hair. "It's okay, Luke. Everything's under control. With new locks, I'll be fine. I'll pay for everything, by the way. There's no reason for your family to have to foot the bill for my troubles."

"Charlie, do you really think a stalker at our home isn't our problem? C'mon, girl. And I know I've been more distant, but don't construe that as unconcerned about your safety."

She looked at him quietly again and he could see the little cogs turning in her brain before she said nonchalantly, "I'm perfectly safe, Luke. And I really do need to go get busy. The kids are going to be up and into things." She'd pulled away from him almost visibly and he knew he truly had been the one to train the monkey, but just now it made him ashamed. In the long run it was probably best, but it still ripped his heart out.

After considering for a moment, he said, "Okay, I'll let you go on one condition. That you tell me if you even wonder if there might be a problem in the future."

She dropped her eyes to her hands in her lap and then looked up at him again. "I'm sorry, Luke, but I'm not going to promise that. Under the circumstances I shouldn't. But it doesn't matter anyway. I'll be fine. And then I'll be gone. Everything is okay."

Geez, everything is not okay. His whole world was sitting here in front of him, refusing to let him even be involved and it was his own doing and he knew it. Protecting their hearts was one thing. Her physical safety was another. He'd never forgive himself if something else happened to her here, especially if she didn't level with him.

He watched her, trying to figure out what his options were. He wanted to demand that she keep him informed, but he knew he didn't have the right and had to sadly admit defeat, "All right, Charlie. I deserved that. But I wish you'd tell me. I truly do want you to be absolutely safe and I'd like to help. Know that at least. Maybe you could think about changing your mind." She nodded and got up to go. "Will you at least let me take you to your house and check it out this morning?"

"Sure. I'd love that. Thank you."

"Let's go then."

They walked side by side to her house in silence, and when they got there, he went inside while she stood on the porch with her bare feet.

There was no one in her house, but as he checked her bedroom, he found a note sitting on her pillow that said, "Charlie, I love to watch you. You're beautiful when you sleep." It made the blood rush to his heart. The instant anger made his swear. What was wrong with this guy?

While he was still standing there, wondering how to deal with this, she came inside. After taking one look at his face, she looked around. Seeing the note, her face blanched and she backed up until she was clear back to the doorway. He looked at the abject fear on her face and walked across to wrap her into a hug. There was no way he could let her just stand there afraid like that.

She nearly melted against him, but in only another moment, she pushed him away, took a deep breath and walked back into her room to open a drawer in the dresser. Still standing in her doorway, he said, "I'll wait here while you dress and then I'll walk you up to the house."

Shaking her head, she said, "No. I'll be fine. And with new locks, he won't be able to do anything. He never comes around in the day time. Go get your work done."

Looking at her stubborn face that still held fear and a hint of hurt, he knew that he'd indeed trained his monkey well. And she wasn't going to let him untrain her here this morning. Not by a long shot. Maybe that was best in the end anyway, although he hated this. All of it.

Letting out an inaudible sigh, he said, "I'll call that locksmith and then I'll arrange for some live security from here on out. And don't touch anything. You need to call the police and report this. I'm sure they'll come and check for fingerprints." He stood in front of her and looked into her face. "I'm sorry all of this is happening, Charlie. I'm so sorry you have to deal with something like this."

She only shrugged. "We'll manage, Luke. Thanks for checking for me. I appreciate it."

"You're honestly welcome, Charlie. I'll be around if you need anything."

"I'll keep that in mind, thanks."

She went into her bathroom and he let himself out of her house. *Yeah, you'll keep it in mind, but you won't ask.* So much for untraining the monkeys. And he'd thought watching her go out with Dr. Nichols was hard.

****

When Fo got home from work that evening, Luke didn't know what to say when he came in and studied him for several seconds without saying anything. He finally had to laugh when Fo said, "Bad monkeys! Bad, bad monkeys. No monkey chow tonight!" He took off his sport coat and hung it up and added, "Maybe what you need Luke, is a new monkey trainer. I'm sure there are a number of men who would volunteer. I could ask Dr. Nichols for you."

Luke glowered and Fo laughed. "Gee, thanks, Fo. I'm sure that would solve everything. Phone him right up, would you?"

"Actually, Charlie described her date the other night as the sunset was spectacular and the company was okay. So you're probably safe as far as Dr. Nichols is concerned. It's that shooting instructor you need to worry about."

"The other one was a shooting instructor? Gees, that's all I need for competition. That's nearly as bad as an attorney."

"Nah. I'd lots rather be shot than sued. And I thought you had taken yourself out of the competition, my self sacrificing friend."

"I have. Thanks for reminding me. I forget every time I see her."

"This is insane. You do know that, don't you? You're going to regret this for eternities."

"I know. But it's the only thing that's fair to Charlie."

"You don't know Charlie."

"I know Charlie far too well. That's the problem. If I'd never met her, I'd be fine."

"You'd have missed out on the greatest woman you'll ever meet in your life, Luke. I wish you'd get honest with yourself instead of trying to be all selfless. She doesn't want to go to law school. I'm telling you. If you asked her to stay, I'll bet she would."

"Maybe, Fo. But would that be fair to her?"

"Fairer than smashing her heart."

"Oh, as if I'm smashing her heart." This time Fo didn't have a come back and Luke looked over at him, but he was studiously hanging up his clothes. It made Luke wonder what Fo wasn't saying so loudly.

****

He thought about that again, later that night when he and Charlie passed on the bunkhouse porch in the dark. Where they had made a habit of hanging out late together, now they politely excused each other when one or the other was hanging out with Fo. Even Fo had begun to get antsy as they did it. As Charlie came and settled into a chair and Luke went inside, he wanted to swear, but instead just said, "Good night, guys. Be sure to see her home safe, Fo." Fo couldn't be right. She acted fine without him.

Before he went to bed, he called the security guard that he'd hired to double check that they were watching out there tonight.

The next day as he was mentioning that Richard had gotten tickets to the Kalispell Symphony for everyone, she was so cool and poised that he thought he must have been mistaken after all about her caring for him. Either that or she had gotten over him incredibly fast. She looked at him and nodded and then went back to grilling cheese sandwiches for lunch and acting like she hadn't a care in the world.

And then the night of the symphony, as they all dressed up and went into town to the concert, she was absolutely stoic even though she looked liked a million bucks in her little black dress and matching heels. She had each of the little girls by the hand as they went in and he was actually glad for the distraction of carrying Jamie when he found his eyes following her every move in the sleek outfit. Fo had come with and brought Amy and even when Charlie was greeting them, her mask of serenity was flawless as she moved into the auditorium and found her seat. He sat down beside her determined to enjoy the symphony in spite of the emotion, or lack of it that arced between them. No, she definitely wasn't heart broken that he could see.

****

They were well into the third cutting of hay and the grain was ready to be cut as well and the busiest time of year found him with little time to even dread how soon she would be leaving. On top of the haying and combining, he had several hands come down with some nasty stomach bug and he found himself working twenty hour days to try to get the grain cut before a storm blew in that next week end. He dragged in to eat dinner about three days into this grueling pace and then was headed back out when Charlie stopped him as she was clearing the table. "Are you okay, Luke? You don't look so good."

Fo came in just then and Luke tried to grin at them as he answered, "Thanks, a lot, Charlie. And yeah, I'm fine as long as being a zombie qualifies."

Fo joined in. "What's going on? You haven't been to bed that I've seen in three days."

Luke tried to explain and was surprised when Charlie volunteered, "Is driving a tractor all that much more difficult than regular driving? Fo and I could pitch in." She nudged Fo with her elbow and smiled at him as she said, "Fo's not that great of a driver, but I have a perfect record if you don't count stalls."

"No, driving a tractor is pretty straight forward, but we'll be okay without you. Another couple of days and the others should be feeling better."

"But what about the storm? I thought your dad said if a storm hit with the grain this heavy it would ruin it."

"It will. I'll just keep going as long as I can and we'll get through as well as possible."

At this, Charlie turned on him. "Look, Luke. I know you don't want to deal with me right now, but don't let it cost you part of your crop. Put your aversions on hold. Take the help. You can go back to keeping away from me when the others are back at it. All you have to do is deal with me long enough to show me how to start up a tractor. You can handle that."

"Charlie..." Luke was too tired to either argue or set her straight. She didn't answer him, just looked at him and finally he said tiredly, "Okay. Go get a jacket and your gardening gloves."

Luke looked at Fo and Fo said, "Hey, I'll help buddy, but you know I can't handle one of those monsters."

Charlie rolled her eyes. "He's just scared, Luke. Get a tractor ready for him too and I'll give him a pep talk on the way out. He'll be fine. It'll do him good to get his office hands out into nature for once." She turned to Fo. "Come on, big guy. Your cousin is in the mire. You can do this. I know you can." Luke left them to their pep talking and went to prep the requisite tractors, knowing that Fo wouldn't have had a chance against her even if he'd been serious about not going.

Forty minutes later, Luke had gotten Fo started and was pulling into the field on a four wheeler with Charlie on the back behind him doing her best not to touch him as they'd bounced over the chuck holes in the gravel road to get there. He pulled up and parked the bike next to where the huge combine was parked and continued to explain what he needed from her as a combine driver here.

Together they climbed up into the cab of the behemoth machine and he was grateful to see that she didn't seem too intimidated by the sheer size of the thing. He made a lap around and showed her how to keep it in alignment and then dump the grain out of the hopper into the huge grain truck that would come pick it up. "If you have any questions at all, call me. Otherwise there should be enough here to keep you going until you're too tired and need to come in. Just park it and ride with whoever is driving the truck and I'll come back out."

She nodded her head. "Okay. I think I've got it. Just keep the wheels in the last row. Okay. Go home and go to bed. We'll be fine."

Luke looked at her. She was unreal. He'd never known anyone who could take stuff in stride the way this girl could. He couldn't help himself and reached up and caressed her cheek with his hand. "I've never known anyone like you, Charlie Evans. Be careful out here. And call if you need to."

A shadow crossed her eyes as she nodded wordlessly and he got out of the cab. How was he ever going to forget her?

He was really thinking that the next morning at dawn when he found her there at the edge of the field with her head bent over the steering wheel of the tractor, dead to the world. He never dreamed she'd drive for more than twelve hours straight while he slept. He surveyed how much she had gotten done and he could hardly even believe she'd been able to do that on her first time driving a combine.

He also couldn't believe the neat loop the loop that she'd made on her last pass through the long straight part of the field. Leave it to Charlie to doodle with a ten ton combine. He shook his head and laughed as he put a hand on her shoulder to gently wake her up. "Come on sleepy head. Let's get you home to bed. You did a wonderful job, by the way. I can't believe you could do this the first time."

She sleepily followed him down to the truck he'd brought, saying, "I just kept the wheel in the last row, like you said."

"I can see that." Luke laughed and she looked up and then smiled tiredly. "Oh, that. I was actually going to cut over it before anyone saw it but, I ran out of gas in the combine. Randy is bringing me some right now."

"Randy is home in bed, which is where you're headed too. Someone else will cut over your curly Q."

She looked at her watch and shook her head. "I can't go to bed. The kids are going to be up in less than two hours and I'll never be able to get back up if I lie down now. I'll just stay up."

"Angela is home. She can watch her own kids for once. Go back to your house and crash. Fo came in at midnight and I thought you'd do about the same. You've been a machine." She didn't answer and he looked over to see that she had gone back to sleep. He reached and pulled her against his shoulder as a pillow as they drove back to the ranch yard. He'd never known anyone like Charlie Evans, and he doubted he ever would again. Fo had told him that first day that they'd never be the same and he'd been right. She had a way of completely reshaping the world around her wherever she was.

After seven hours of rest, she was right back out there that afternoon and put in an even longer night this time. As the last truck full of grain rolled out of the big field and the wind kicked up, he hauled both of their tired bodies home again, more grateful than he could express for her help those two days. He'd have never gotten all that grain cut without her help. And he'd never have seen a curly Q cut into a wheat field for that matter either. Talk about your beat of a different drummer.

It was four o'clock in the morning and he left her at her house and went on to the bunkhouse and literally lay over his bunk fully clothed he was so tired.

When he was finally rested enough to want to take off his boots and jeans, he was surprised to realize she was in the last bunk again with the dog Pilgrim asleep beside the bed. *Now, what the heck?* He went in and changed into pajama bottoms and a t-shirt, wondering what had gone on this round that he hadn't realized at the time.

Both she and Fo were gone when he next regained consciousness and he tiredly got up and phoned Fo to find out what was up. When Fo didn't answer, he dressed and went in search of Charlie. She might not think he'd want to know, but he was going to push for answers anyway.

He found her in the garden with the children and he joined them picking beans and squash for a few minutes while he tried to figure out the best way to ask her what had happened at her house last night. He hadn't gotten around to saying anything yet, and at first he didn't understand when she said to him off handedly, "He brought the earring back."

Picking a few more beans so that their conversation wasn't obvious to the little ones, he asked, "Who brought what earring back?"

She gave him the look. "The guy who took it in the first place."

"Oh. The earring. I see. To the porch?"

"Nope. To the jewelry box."

Luke stood up, no longer even trying to act nonchalant. "Even after the locksmith? And the full time security?"

Charlie nodded and gave him a slight grimace and glanced pointedly to the children, but Luke asked anyway, "Do you have any idea what time?"

"I would guess, sometime between dusk and just after four when we got in."

"Have you talked to security?"

"They saw nothing."

"I'm moving you into the house. This place is too big to guard decently."

Charlie rolled her eyes. "No."

"No?"

"No. There are things there that are far more valuable than earrings."

"As if there aren't in your house. Then you're coming to the bunkhouse."

"No."

"Charlie."

She turned to whisper to him, "It's bad enough that I've been there those nights already. Think if Tuckett would see me. Or these guys."

At that he took her hand and pulled her out of the garden and around the corner of the house where he backed her up against the wall and asked bluntly, "Do you realize we could be talking about your life here?"

She put both hands on her hips. "What do you think, Luke?"

"I'm sorry." He looked down, sorry he had been offensive and feeling guilty because really he just wanted to back her right up against this wall and kiss away the frustration that flared between them. "If you won't do anything I recommend, what do you have in mind? Can I ask?"

She hesitated and then admitted, "I haven't gotten that far. The best I can come up with is to simply go home ten days early."

He met her eyes, miserably torn at the idea of her leaving and wondering if he should voice the fact that Tyree would very possibly follow her right to Utah. If he was crazy enough to do what he was already doing, it wouldn't be a stretch.

"I know." She said it out of the blue and he had no idea what she was talking about.

"You know what?"

"That he'll probably follow me to Utah. That's what you were thinking, wasn't it?"

He sighed and admitted, "Charlie, you've got me so mixed up that I have no idea what I was thinking. Yes, he could follow you. We'll deal with that later. What are we going to do tonight?"

She blew her breath out in a huge sigh and he was completely non-plussed when her eyes filled with tears and she started to cry. She turned and went to walk away and he put out an arm to block her and then pulled her close into a hug as she whispered, "I don't know."

"Don't cry." He rubbed her back as she only cried harder. "We'll figure it out. In the mean time, I'll call and have the kind of dead bolts put on that can't be opened from the outside once they're locked and we'll double security and start clearing your house before you go inside. And we'd better bring the police back in. Maybe they can find something and pick him back up. Do you know how to use that new gun?" She nodded. "Do you want some more practice?" This time she shrugged.

He continued to hold her as he said, "I can't believe this is happening here. We never even locked a door before this."

"I'm sorry. I should leave. It would make everyone here safer."

"Shh. Honestly, you're the only one who seems to be at risk here, Charlie. He has very discriminating taste." She pulled back and looked up at him and he smiled at her. "Well, he does."

At that, she smiled through her tears and pulled away. "I need to get back. Jamie will have harvested every last minute squash because they're so cute."

He just looked at her for a long moment and then pulled her close again in spite of himself. "Hang in there, Charlie. We're going to get rid of this guy and you'll feel safe again. I promise."

That made her start to cry again and she spoke so softly he almost couldn't hear her, "I hope so, Luke. I hope so."

She went back to the children and Luke went straight into the office and began making calls to beef up her locks and security. Richard was in there and Luke brought him up to speed on what had been going on and then said, "And don't be surprised if she comes in and says she's leaving sooner than she'd planned. I could see it in her eyes."

Richard paused at what he was doing and asked him, "And what then, Luke? What are you going to do when she climbs into her ugly little car and drives away?"

Luke shook his head. "Swear. Hit someone. Cry? I don't know, Dad. It's a good thing I'm not a drinking man. It's going to be awful."

"I know. How are we ever going to survive around here? Can't you talk her into staying?"

"She has the right to make her own decisions in life."

"Doesn't she have the right to know all of her options as well, before she makes those decisions?"

Luke was quiet for a minute while he considered that. Finally, he asked, "Do you really think she doesn't know her options?"

Richard looked at him steadily. "You tell me, Luke."

****

When Fo got home from work that evening, the first thing he did was go in search of Charlie. He found her on her cabin porch, staring out over the valley to the south, her mind obviously a million miles from the Langston cattle ranch.

He dropped into a chair beside her and pushed it gently with his foot. After several minutes, she was still looking out when she quietly said, "I'm not going to go to law school, Fo. I can't do it. I called and left a message on my parents' machine." She was trying to joke past the sadness when she added, "We can probably expect a team of Navy Seals or the FBI as a result." Just when he was going to ask her if she was going to stay in Montana, she continued, "I guess I'll go back to Utah with you and find a job. Would that be all right?"

"Of course." He rocked for a while again and then asked, "When I'm done with school and come back here, what then?"

She shrugged. "Maybe I'll have gotten a contract to teach and will have to stay. If not, who knows? Would Amy hate me if I came back and found an apartment in Kalispell? Other than what a fool I've been, I really love Montana. Although, someday I'm going to have to stay away from you. Maybe now is the time to just do it. A wife will hate a close friend that's a girl."

"You know she'd be thrilled if you came back with me. She understands us. She wants to set you up with her brother, remember? Marry him. That would be perfect."

Silhouetted against the western sky, she shook her head. "No brothers. Not right now. I'm too tired." After a few more moments she reached up and brushed at a stray tear that trickled down her cheek. For the first time in almost two decades, Fo had no idea how to deal with her. He'd never seen her spunky spirit this quiet before, and he didn't have a clue how to shore up her broken heart.

Finally, he simply said, "Charlie. I'm sorry this summer has been so hard for you. I'm sorry I talked you into coming. I thought it would be best, but I was wrong. I'm sorry."

She reached over and took his hand. "No, Fo. This too shall pass and I'll be stronger for it. It just hurts right now going through it. That will dull, in time. In some ways, this was the best time of my life. At least it was at first. Before."

He didn't ask if she meant before being assaulted and stalked or before falling in love with Luke because he knew they had both affected her more deeply than anything else ever had since he'd known her. He rocked and cussed himself for throwing her and Luke together. He'd honestly thought they'd found each other for a while there. He honestly had. It made him feel guilty for being so happy with Amy that he wanted to laugh and dance and do the Toyota jump, when Charlie was so obviously devastated right now.

It was almost as if she could read his mind as she turned to him and in a voice so bright and cheerful that it sounded brittle, she asked, "How was your day with Amy today anyway? Are we still thinking forever?"

"Do I dare tell you yes, when you're this blue?"

More sincerely, she said, "Yes. I'm so happy for you I'll cheer right up. Be sure and let her know she's welcome to come stay with me in Utah anytime she needs to come and visit you. Heck, I'll rent an extra bedroom just for her.

Something tells me that you two aren't going to be able to stay apart all that well this next thirteen weeks."

Fo groaned. "I'm already dreading being apart. It's funny, but I never thought I'd feel this way about a girl. I've surprised myself."

Charlie laughed a real laugh. "I knew you had it in you all along, buddy. I was simply waiting for you to figure it out. It took you long enough."

"Slow learner, I guess. At least when I figured it out, I got it right the first time. That's a miracle."

"That's true, but you've always been the steady one." After a moment she went on, "I wish I'd been so smart." The tears were back in her voice and he was trying to figure out what to say when she volunteered, "I'm going to leave day after tomorrow. I know I was going to stay and come with you, but I need to go. I'm worried that Tyree is going to hurt someone if I stay here. I'm going to tell Richard in the morning."

"He'll understand."

"I know." The tears flooded her eyes in earnest. "It's the kids that I'm worried about. How am I ever going to tell them goodbye?"

At this he got up and helped her up and switched over to the porch swing where he could sit next to her as she cried her heart out against his shoulder. He had no answers. He just hoped she could take some comfort from his unconditional friendship. That was the best he had to offer, but it had always seen her through. Until now. Now he didn't know how to comfort the hurt she was feeling, compounded by the fear.

As they sat there like that, the sun went down. Night fell and still she leaned on him and cried. She hadn't even begun to wind down when Luke quietly came around the corner and stopped dead in his tracks when he realized what was going on. He met Fo's eyes, and Fo gave a minimal shake of his head. After standing there for a minute, watching, Luke turned and went back the way he'd come without ever saying a word. As sad as Fo was because Charlie was heartbroken, maybe it was a good thing for Luke to see how she was struggling. Maybe he'd finally get a grip and stop her before she was gone. He could hope at least.

****

When Luke rounded the corner to understand that Charlie was sobbing like her heart had broken into a million pieces, he knew that his wasn't far behind. Without having to be told, he knew she was leaving and the gaping hole that left in his chest was physically painful. He couldn't even breathe as he turned and went back to the bunkhouse. How had he ever believed he could make it through the days without her? And what would be the point anyway?

Once in the bunkhouse, he dropped to his knees beside his bunk and tried to listen for an answer from the only one he knew who could fix this tangled mess he'd made. For the first time in his life, he was going to move away from here of his own free will. The only solution he could see was to follow her to Utah and see if she would be willing to let him into her life along with her law school. It would mean giving up this home he had loved and lived and breathed from the day he'd been born, but that was nothing compared to facing the rest of his life without her.

He prayed until he worried about falling asleep and then slowly got up and got ready for bed. With that done, he walked over to the door of the bunkhouse and went out onto the porch, wondering how she was doing over there on hers. Was she still crying? Or had she been able to let some of it go and find a measure of peace? It was all he could do not to go back to check on her. Bitterly, he thought, she wouldn't even want that from him the way he had pushed her away these last weeks.

Keeping his distance had seemed the wise thing to do at the time. He just hadn't realized there was no way he could actually keep her at arms length from his heart. But he'd had to learn that the hard way. He was still learning it the hard way.

Dropping into a porch rocker, he leaned his head back and looked up at the numberless stars in the big Montana sky. He'd always tried to make wise decisions. And he'd always tried to do his best. He'd always treated women with respect and deference and he'd always hoped that someday he would find a girl he would want to spend the rest of his life with. Now that he'd found her and messed it up so thoroughly, it hurt so much he almost wished he'd was still wondering if she was out there somewhere. Then at least there'd been hope.

He was still sitting there, wondering if Charlie was okay when the sound of a dog growling reached his ears. He was so caught up with his thoughts it took a minute to clue in to what he was hearing. For some reason that sound made the hair on the back of his neck stand up and he stepped inside the door and took a deer rifle off the wall before he went to investigate. Whatever one of the dogs had pinned down was either an animal that wasn't supposed to be here in the ranch yard, or a human who wasn't, and he wasn't taking any bets on which.

Following the sound to the far side of some machinery sheds, he was attempting to walk quietly through the gravel when whatever it was broke and ran with the dog in pursuit. He knew exactly when the dog caught whatever it was that it was chasing and the expletives that suddenly broke the quiet of the night ended all speculation about whether it was man or beast. Luke had nearly reached the snarling, snapping, fighting dog, when there was the sound of ripping cloth and running footsteps and then only the whine of an injured dog.

Luke continued on around the shed until he found the dog, a shredded piece of plaid cloth still hanging from his teeth. "What are you up to, Pilgrim? Did you get a mouthful of stinking rotten Homo Sapien?" He leaned down to see if he could tell how badly the dog was hurt in the dark. "What'd he do to you, old buddy? Where are you hurt? Huh?"

Fo spoke out of the darkness, "You okay, Luke?"

"I'm fine. Pilgrim is a little the worse for wear. Is Charlie with you?"

"Yeah."

"Well, bring her to the bunkhouse, even if you have to pack her. I'm sure that was him again."

When Luke and Pilgrim found their way to where Fo and Charlie were, her eyes were huge and fearful even in the near coal blackness. Luke went up to her and said gently, "Please don't argue, Charlie. Come up to the bunkhouse with us where we can make sure you're safe. Please."

She nodded. "Okay. Can I go back to my house and grab some sweats?"

"And your gun. We'll come with you."

Even as dead tired as he knew the three of them to be, sleep was almost a non issue there for awhile. They had locked the doors and windows, pulled the blinds and put in a movie, but the tension in the room was still palpable. Fo and Luke made an effort to appear to be watching, but Charlie just went to bed and laid there with big, haunted eyes in the dark as Luke watched her. She eventually got back out and came and sat between the two of them and finally fell asleep and her head slid to Luke's shoulder.

Chapter 12

Working in the office early the next morning, Luke's head came up sharply when he heard Charlie and his dad in earnest conversation next door in the kitchen. His heart plummeted into his stomach as he heard her tell him she was going to leave first thing the next day to go back to Utah so she could protect their family from Tyree. He wanted to jump right up and go in and reassure her and beg her to stay, but he knew he couldn't. Hearing her start to cry as they talked made him want to interrupt even more. He sat at his desk, struggling to make it through this and was surprised to hear his dad say. "I'll double whatever we're paying you, Charlie, if you'll stay." She must have shaken her head without saying anything, because then he heard his dad say, "I'll triple it. C'mon Charlie. We can't live without you. What if you stayed now and I offered to pay for law school later if you still insist on going."

Luke didn't realize he was holding his breath until he was starved for air as he waited to hear her reply. He could hear the tears in her voice as she finally said, "I've decided I'm not going to go to law school, Richard. My heart is so not in it. I'm just going to go back to Utah and get a job and then come back to Kalispell when Fo comes back to marry Amy. I've learned to really love Montana. And I'd love to stay and work for you, Richard, but you haven't talked to Luke about this, have you? He would be upset if he knew what you're offering. I have to go away from here. Luke can't stand me and your family isn't safe as long as Tyree is around."

Once the shock of her answer wore off, Luke stood and moved around the desk to the door as his dad started to reply. Richard got as far as, "You're wrong, Charlie. Luke..."

They both looked up in surprise as Luke stepped into the doorway and advanced into the kitchen, took Charlie by the hand and almost dragged her into the pantry and shut the door behind them.

Flipping on the light in the tight quarters, he could see she was all but afraid of him as she looked up at him warily. For a second he only searched her eyes, wondering if she meant what she had been saying. Finally, he asked, "You're not going to law school? You're truly not? You love Montana?"

She looked down at her hand still tightly held in his and started to pull it away as she shook her head and answered with a sigh, "I can't do it, Luke. I can't make myself go to law school right now. I just can't."

"But, you're going to come back to Montana? Next winter, with Fo?"

Her eyes filled with tears again at his question. "Would I bother you even if I was clear in Kalispell? You'd never even have to see me, I promise."

He shook his head in frustration at her misunderstanding. How could he make her see how he felt about her? And it was no wonder she was so mixed up. He himself didn't even know what to think and how to feel just now. He reached down and took her other hand as well and then changed his mind and put both hands up to gently touch her face. "No. Charlie, no. The only thing that will bother me is that you'll be so far away in Kalispell. And do you absolutely have to go back with Fo? Couldn't you stay here? Please? We'll deal with Tyree, I promise. I'll hire twenty security guards if I have to. Just stay. Please."

She involuntarily stepped back and her eyes narrowed as she tried to figure him out. "What?" She stood looking at him as if he'd grown purple hair and then shook her head and said it again. "What?"

"Please stay, Charlie. We'll pay you quadruple what you're making. And I'll make Chase stay completely out of your way. I so can stand you, Charlie. It's having you go away that I can't stand.

She raised her eyebrows at that and stared at him with big eyes and then reached up to feel his forehead. "Luke, are you okay? You're not having a stroke or something, are you?"

He groaned out loud and ran a hand through his hair. "Help me out here, Charlie. You've just given me a whole new sense of hope in my life. Don't assume I'm losing it. I lost it weeks ago when I knew you were going to get in your taco rocket and leave me. Hearing you aren't going to law school after all and that there is a possibility you'd come back..." He paused and then wrapped his arms all the way around her tightly. "I need you to stay with me, Charlie. I need you ten times more than the children do. I don't want to manipulate you, but please tell me you don't have to leave."

She stilled in his arms and he pulled back to look at her. With confusion etched into her expression, she asked warily, her voice low, "What's going on, Luke? Why are you acting like this?"

He shook his head and laughed softly. "Ah, Charlie, why is the sky suddenly bluer and the sun brighter?" He pulled her close again and asked quietly, "Last night I decided I would come to Utah to live too, so I could still see you. Be with you. It's not that I don't like you, Charlie. I love you. I just didn't know how to deal with losing you. I thought if I stayed away from you that telling you goodbye would be easier. Then I realized I couldn't tell you goodbye at all. That I'd have to follow you. If you'd have let me. I know I've been a complete idiot, but..." He let her go for a second and put his hands on her shoulders. "I'm so sorry for jerking you around. I wasn't trying to. What I was trying to do was not pressure you to do what I wanted. I felt you had enough of that from your family." He sighed. "But, oh, I've wanted to. I wanted to get down on my knees and beg you to stay."

She just kept staring at him in shock and he caressed her cheek with one hand and smiled. "I would still get down on my knees if there was room in here. Please say something. You're looking at me as if I've lost my mind."

She nodded almost woodenly. "I think you have, Luke. I don't know what to even think, let alone say."

He gently tipped her chin up so she had to look into his eyes and then he whispered, "Say you'll stay." He leaned down and kissed her gently, for a long moment and then whispered it again, "Just say that you'll stay."

He was looking into her eyes, literally trying to will her into agreeing when the pantry door opened and three different little dark heads peeked inside. Luke rolled his eyes and looked around at the children in frustration, but for the first time, Charlie started to smile. Jamie was sucking on a link sausage and he pulled it out of his mouth, looked back into the kitchen and asked, "Daddy, why is Lukey huggin' in the pantry wif Charlie?"

From behind the door they heard Richard chuckle and answer, "I'm not sure, Jamie, but maybe you'd better shut the pantry door and let them finish. Come in and sit down."

As the door slowly swung shut, all three little heads traveled along with it until Luke reached out and firmly shut the door and turned back to Charlie. "Sorry. Where were we? You were just getting ready to tell me that you'd love to stay in Montana. Remember?"

Charlie gave him an honest smile, but then she shook her head and sobered. "Even if I didn't believe this is temporary insanity on your part, there's still Tyree. I have to go to keep your family safe."

"This is not temporary insanity, Charlie. This isn't temporary anything. You've had my heart since that very first day when you busted me in only my jeans. If my feelings were temporary they would have been gone a long time ago. I'm afraid I've got it bad for you for forever."

She tipped her head to the side and gave him another hint of the smile he'd grown to love over these last months. "Somehow, Luke, I never thought you'd wax eloquent in the pantry like this. This is a whole new side of you for me."

He began to nuzzle her temple with his lips and murmured, "Tell me you'll stay and see what whole new side of me you find. I know Fo will be gone for a while, but he'll be back before you know it. And maybe I could watch over you while he's gone. Come on, Charlie." He put his fingers up into her hair and gently pulled her head against his throat. "Please say yes."

He felt her sigh against him and turn her face right into him as she said, "Luke, this is too sudden. This is like a hundred and eighty degrees from the way you've been treating me. What's going on? Why are you suddenly so different?"

"Charlie, I've wanted to be different the whole time. I just didn't think I had the right to ask you to give up law school and I know I work ridiculously long days. I knew I couldn't ask. But if you want to come back anyway and aren't going to become an attorney right now, maybe it wouldn't be pressuring you too much to ask you to stay here in Montana with me forever."

Her eyes flew to look up at him. "Forever! Luke! What are you saying?"

He looked steadily down into her gaze. "I'm saying that I love you, Charlie. And I want to be with you forever. Stay in Montana and marry me and we'll live happily ever after."

"Luke!" He realized he'd gone too far when she got a look of all out panic.

She began to pull away and he backpedalled, "Okay. Okay, Charlie. I won't talk about forever this morning, but don't leave. At least tell me you're not going to leave in the morning. Give us at least one more day to think things through. Maybe we can come up with some ideas. Would you agree to that?"

She nodded, but at the same time she said, "You're forgetting Tyree again. I need to get away from here, remember?"

"We'll figure it out, Charlie. Just one more day."

Her hesitation was starting to ebb and he knew it. He bent to kiss her one more time and her eyes watched him all the way until he touched his mouth to hers. As he kissed her, her eyelids slowly flickered closed and then he felt her melt against him. He finally dared to hope that someday she would be a permanent part of his future.

His lips left her mouth and he kissed her temple as gently as he could, and he whispered, "Thank you, Charlie. You won't regret it. I promise."

In a voice that was slightly breathy, she said, "I didn't really agree to stay, Luke."

He went back to her mouth and kissed her again, long and slowly. "Yeah, I think you did. At least your body did. I felt it when you made the decision."

She gave a small sigh. "Once I get a little way away from you, you're going to have to give me a minute to make my mind get on board as well. I'm having a hard time making any brain waves function with you this close, this close." She nodded at the loaded pantry shelves that surrounded them and Luke had to smile.

"At the time it seemed like the closest privacy. Sorry. But I had to talk to you. For months I've struggled with you going back and feeling like I couldn't ask you to stay. I love you, but I didn't want to try to force you like your family always does. You utterly changed my whole outlook with what you said to my dad. How did your parents take your announcement, by the way?"

She sighed and reached up to resecure the clip that was supposed to be holding her hair up. "Actually, all I did was leave a message. That's another reason why I need to leave immediately. I figure I have about forty eight hours until the Federales show up to escort me either directly to law school or ground me to my room. I should be gone from here when that happens. It won't be pretty."

"No, Charlie. I'd face a fire breathing dragon rather than have to watch you drive away. We'll deal with whatever together. You may not believe this, but I really am stronger than your mother."

Shaking her head without smiling, she said, "I don't doubt that, Luke, but what if she sends Elroy? I'd hate to get you sued over my issues. And you know how attorneys are. They think they're untouchable for that exact reason. No one wants to cross them."

"No one's suing anyone, Charlie. You're twenty three years old. You can do what you want and marry who you choose and it's not damaging anybody. Now if you left, then you'd be damaging somebody. My heart would never survive it."

"You just said you were stronger than my mother."

"My will, not my heart. Right now my heart has had all it can take." He pulled her back into his arms again. "Leaving would kill me for sure." He leaned in to kiss her one more time, grateful that if she wasn't exactly mauling him back, at least she wasn't pushing him away. Just when he knew he should back off before he scared her again, the door to the pantry came open and they heard Madge gasp and then close it again quickly.

Pulling back, he gave her a grin. "Come on, Charlie. We're going to have the whole house on its ear before breakfast. Much as I hate the idea, I guess we'd better come out of the pantry." He glanced around again. "Somehow, I've come to really like this little storage room, though. This is a great pantry." He laughed and kissed her again and then took her hand and went to open the door.

Before he could even turn the knob, it opened again, this time to reveal Chase and Tuckett. Tuckett laughed when he saw them and Chase looked disgusted as he said, "I wondered why Madge looked like she'd seen a ghost. What do you think you're doing in there, Luke? Get your grubby hand off of her."

Luke kept hold of her hand as he pulled her past his brothers. "Oh, lighten up, Romeo. Can't a guy even have a minute with a girl in a pantry once in a while? What's the problem?"

Luke seated Charlie at the dining table with Richard and the little kids as Chase returned. "She doesn't like guys to touch her, ya know. Haven't you figured that out by now?"

Coming around to his own seat between Tuckett and Madge, Luke glanced at Charlie with a smile. "I wasn't aware of that, no. I'll keep that in mind the next time I steal Charlie away to the pantry." He turned to Madge. "Are you okay, Madge? We didn't mean to scare you. I just had some very important things to talk to Charlie about this morning."

Madge patted his hand. "I'm fine, Luken. A trifle surprised. I went in for syrup and got more than I bargained for. Is that what you call that? Talking?"

Luke grinned at her. "Well, it started out as talking." He turned to address the rest of the table, "Speaking of kissing, would all of you other Langstons please help me talk Charlie into staying here with us instead of moving back to Utah? I did my best to convince her, but I'm sure all of the rest of you begging would help. Except you, Chase. You leave her alone. She doesn't like guys touching her, remember?"

Chase glowered as the other adults grinned and Evie asked, "What did he mean, Daddy, about speaking of kissing?"

At that, Charlie blushed and Richard opened his mouth, but hesitated over what to say and Luke rescued him at Charlie's expense. "I just meant that someday I'd really love to kiss Charlie in the pantry, sis. Who's going to say the prayer this morning, Dad?"

Before Richard could answer, Chase stood up and turned to Luke in outrage. "You kissed her? You kissed her? You... You..."

Calmly, Richard said, "I'll say it. Fold your arms, Jamie." When everyone bowed their heads, Chase finally closed his mouth and sat down as Richard began to pray. Luke glanced over at Charlie who was still blushing and winked and then bowed his own head.

When the prayer was over, the little kids dug in as if nothing was out of the ordinary and Madge beamed at Richard and said, "It's been too long since we've had kanoodling in the kitchen. Don't you agree, Richard?"

With a watchful eye on his two oldest sons, Richard hesitated again. "I'm not exactly sure, Madge. I'm not sure what to think of this whole morning."

Chase was still glaring at Luke who made a point of ignoring him, while Tuckett was grinning like he was in a comedy theater and finally, Charlie said, "Tuck, do you think you could stop smiling long enough to pass the syrup?"

With another gasp, Madge stood up with her hand to her chest. "Good heavens! What with all the kanoodling, I completely forgot to go after the syrup again!" She headed back into the kitchen and Richard shook his head and began to laugh and the little kids joined in.

Evie laughed for a minute and then turned with a perplexed look on her face. "Daddy, what's kanoodling? Is it a dessert? Do we get dessert after breakfast today?"

At that, Richard gave Luke a pointed look and shook his head again. "No, honey. Kanoodling is like snuggling between adults who love each other. Well, I guess you could call that dessert, couldn't you? If I let you have dessert after breakfast, will you ask Luke the next tricky question?"

"Sure, Dad. I want a banana popsicle." Then Evie turned to Luke and asked, "So if you were snuggling in the pantry with Charlie, does that mean that you love each other?"

Charlie blushed crimson this time, Tuckett totally cracked up and Richard murmured, "You deserved that one, Luke."

Luke smiled at Evie and then looked at Charlie as he said, "I'm not sure if Charlie loves me, Evie, but I know that I really love her. That's why I want her to stay so I can talk her into marrying me someday."

Evie's eyes got only marginally bigger than Charlie's huge ones and the whole table got quiet for a minute as everyone looked at Luke and Charlie looking back at each other. Finally, Chase got up and stomped out in disgust and Jamie broke the tension when he asked lustily, "Would everyone quit looking at all of us and can I have anudder teeny hock dog? I love deez teeny hock dogs."

Charlie absently picked up the platter of pancakes and handed them to Jamie, who burst out, "Charlie! That's not hock dogs. I want the teeny hock dogs. I don't want anymore pancakes."

She was still staring at Luke. "Sorry, Jamie. Here."

She put the pancakes down and handed him the butter at which point, he put both greasy little hands to his cheeks and said, "Oh, great! Daddy, I think Charlie is still kinda tired. Could you give me a teeny hock dog, please?"

Charlie finally realized what she was doing and handed the plate of sausages to Jamie. "Sorry, buddy. I must be tired. Would you like some more milk?"

With a sausage in each fist, Jamie gave an exuberant, "Yes!"

Charlie reached over and poured orange juice into his almost empty milk at which Jamie's whole countenance crumpled and he started to cry as he said, "Charlie, why did you do that for? I don't like orange juice wif mioke."

She picked up his cup and looked into it. "Oh, Jamie. I'm so sorry. Don't cry. I'll get you another cup." She got up and went into the kitchen and reappeared with another cup and then sat back down. She looked at her plate for a few seconds before getting back up and saying, "Excuse me please." Taking her plate and utensils, she went into the kitchen where Luke found her a minute later, absently staring out the window with the water running and a plate in one hand.

Turning off the water, he took the plate and asked, "Are you okay?"

She turned to look at him. "I'm fine. Fine. And you?"

"You don't look fine." She raised her eyebrows at him. "Honestly, you look a little dazed. Are you in there?"

She answered him, "Yes." But it took about three seconds to pronounce the word and then she followed it with a tentative. "'I think so. I'm just so surprised by you this morning. I have no idea how to take you. You shouldn't tease about important things so."

Putting the plate down into the dishwasher, he straightened and looked at her. "Is that what you think? That I'm teasing?" When she nodded, he came closer to her. "I'm not teasing, Charlie. Maybe it is sudden because of your revelation this morning, but I'm absolutely sincere. I do love you. I do want you to stay here and let me talk you into marrying me. I do want to talk to you in the pantry. And stuff." He looked pointedly at her mouth and she turned away and began to load the dishes again.

When he didn't move out of her way, she looked up at him and said, "Be serious, Luke. This isn't really a joking matter."

He reached for both of her hands. "Charlie, look at me." When she did, he said quietly, "I do love you, Charlie Evans. And I do want to be with you forever." She dropped her eyes and he asked, "What? Do I have to write in on the silo in John Deere green or cut it into a field or what? Why would I be joking? You've been here long enough to know when I'm joking. Haven't you?"

She nodded and then said, "But Luke, how do I reconcile this morning with this last few weeks?"

"I tried to tell you why, Charlie. All I can do is ask you to believe me and try to make up for it. Isn't that all I can do? And keep on telling you and showing you?"

"Yes, I suppose so. But can you give me some time to get used to you like this?"

"Sure, Charlie. I can do whatever you need me to. Always." He put a hand under her chin and she looked up first at his mouth and then into his eyes as he continued, "Because I truly do love you."

"I love you, too, Luke. But I'm still kind of afraid of you."

He smiled sadly, "I know. We're going to work on that. But be prepared. Not fighting for you didn't work too well. From here on out, I'm going to do everything I can to make you want to be with me." He leaned down and kissed her gently. "I have to go. Have a good day, okay?"

She nodded. "Okay."

Chapter 13

Charlie was having a good day. All day long she'd been catching herself day dreaming about Luke kissing her. She still couldn't believe the way he'd acted in the pantry. Or that kissing could be that incredibly intoxicating. Luke's mouth was... Oh, My. There she went again, staring out at nothing and remembering how good his lips had felt against hers. She had to stop this. At least Madge hadn't caught her this time and given her that knowing smile like she had been doing all afternoon.

And Luke had helped it along by dropping in every so often to give her that long, deep look before giving her that long, sweet kiss that made her forget her own name. The last time, he'd even brought a bouquet of wildflowers to go along with the kissing. She hadn't gotten much done, what with all the day dreaming, but... She felt herself sigh and almost felt a little ridiculous. Luke was a really wonderful kisser.

Yeah, she was having a good day. A great day!

Right up until she saw a black Hummer pull up in front of the main house that evening as the sun went down while she was working in the garden. She knew as soon as she saw it she was in trouble. She hadn't thought her parents would send someone this soon, but it was entirely fitting that they show up in an armored military vehicle.

As not only her mother, but her father as well got out, followed by Elroy, she glanced down at her cut offs and t-shirt and bare feet and was eternally grateful they hadn't seen her there among the tomatoes.

When they were welcomed inside, she snuck out the back of the garden and made a bee line for her house, hurriedly changed her clothes and then headed for the bunkhouse.

Fo and Luke looked up as she came in and both of them knew instantly something was wrong. Luke stood up and came to her. "Is it Tyree again? In the daylight?"

She was slightly out of breath, but tried to joke anyway. "Worse. Elroy and both all-powerfuls. Up at your dad's house."

Luke was relieved. "Oh, good. I thought he'd gotten into your house again."

"Good? You think this is good?"

"Well, it's better than Tyree. What did they say?"

She shook her head. "I haven't talked to them yet. I was in the garden in cut offs and bare feet. My mother would have had an infarction if she'd seen me like that. I ran home and changed."

Luke took her hand and led her to the cowhide couch. "Calm down Charlie. It's going to be okay. Stop and think about what you're going to say to them. And remember that you're twenty-three years old and smart and competent and especially beautiful."

Fo laughed and Charlie rolled her eyes. "Oh, that'll help."

"He just doesn't know them, Charlie. Cut him some slack." Fo turned to Luke. "It honestly probably isn't going to be especially beautiful when they see her. They really do think they can force her to obey."

"They really don't know how much I want her to stay here and marry me."

Fo turned to look at Luke as if he'd spoken in tongues and Charlie actually laughed before she said, "Luke, I'd have to be married and expecting our second child before they'd let this go."

Luke got up and went over to his bunk, opened a box on a shelf and dug through it and came back. "Well, I can't really go that far. I mean I intend to eventually, but... Charlie, would you marry me? Here, put this on. It was my mother's."

She looked up at him in confusion. "Oh, sure I'll marry you. We'll have a lovely June wedding. This is the perfect time for a marriage proposal. Luke! Stop messing around! This isn't a joke!"

"Honey, I'm not joking a bit, and they are on the porch. Will you marry me? Give me your hand." He put the ring on. When she looked up at him to tell him he was crazy, he hauled her into his arms and proceeded to kiss her like she'd never been kissed in her life. At first, she was surprised and then a little mad and then blissfully oblivious until she heard her mother gasp and Elroy swear. Still, it took her a minute to pull herself together enough to face them after that.

When Luke pulled back, he must have known she'd need his support to stand, because he left his hand around her waist as they turned to greet her parents. And Charlie didn't have to feign surprise. She was still in complete shock from Luke and his ring and kiss. She swallowed and said, "Mom, Dad, Elroy. We weren't expecting you."

Her mother pulled herself so upright that she did, indeed, look like a tough old bird with her neck stretched like that. "Obviously! I knew we'd have to talk some sense into you, but I didn't realize we'd have to pry you out of some cowboy's arms to do it!"

Biting back the venomous retort she wanted to let fly, Charlie simply smiled as well as she could and said calmly, "I'm marrying this particular cowboy, Mother. I'm sure you remember him. Luken Langston. Luke, you remember my parents, Norma and Dr. Evans. And their trusty sidekick, Elroy."

Charlie was absolutely proud of Luke when he smiled confidently as well and stepped forward to shake their hands. "Doctor and Mrs. Evans. It's so good of you to drop by. And Elroy. Good of you to come and celebrate our engagement. I respect that. Welcome to Montana."

Covering her near strangulation from his greeting with a cough, Charlie said sweetly, "Uh, darling. I hadn't actually mentioned to them that I was engaged. They must have heard it from Fo and decided to come and celebrate." She turned back to her parents. "That was so kind of you guys. I actually thought that you'd be a little mad. Can you stay here at the ranch with us or are you getting a hotel in town?"

Her mother may have decided to have an infarction anyway. The veins began to stick out on her elongated neck and her face turned a fiery red. Thankfully, her husband put a soothing hand on her arm and said, "Norma, calm down. We need to talk this out." He turned to Charlie, "We don't expect the Langstons to put us up, Charlie. We have rooms in town. We can talk about things there over a late dinner. Come along."

When he went to take Charlie's arm, Luke neatly pulled her against him and said, "I'm sorry Dr. Evans, but Charlie and I have a prior engagement this evening. We won't be able to come into town tonight. Would tomorrow work? Say lunch at eleven thirty or so? It'll be my treat."

Her dad didn't skip a beat. "No. We have a plane to catch at ten in the morning. We'll talk to Charlie tonight after your prior engagement." He turned to Charlie. "Elroy will bring you when you're ready."

With that, the three of them turned and headed for the bunkhouse door, only pausing as Elroy turned around and said, "We'll see you later then. It was good to see you again, Fo and Logan. Take care now."

As the door shut behind them, Charlie sighed and Luke smiled as Fo mimicked, "Take care now, Logan."

Charlie began to pace the length of the bunkhouse as Luke sprawled onto the couch. Fo brought Oreos and milk but even that didn't get Charlie to stop fuming at the all-powerfuls.

Finally, she threw herself onto the couch beside Luke and Fo with a laugh. "I'm sorry. I know I'm acting crazy, because I truly am fit to be tied, but you were so dang funny, Luke! How could you even keep a straight face when you thanked Elroy for coming to celebrate our engagement? I had no idea you were such a great actor. You should be in Hollywood! And prior engagement?"

Luke dipped another Oreo and said blandly, "I wasn't acting. You mean he didn't come to celebrate with us? But he was so enthusiastic about it all. And we had the most literal prior engagement on the planet. You said yes, by the way. I'm holding you to that. And I must say, you are an excellent kisser!"

Charlie shook her head and laughed until her eyes started to tear. She reached for an Oreo. "If this wasn't so dang awful, it'd be hysterical." She only made it through half an Oreo before she got up to pace again. Finally, she said, "I gotta go. I'm going to go for a run to get my head together before I have to go talk to them."

"Charlie, no!" Luke lunged off the couch to catch her. "We'll go with you. You can't go running alone in the dark until Tyree is put away. Remember?"

Fo choked on his Oreo and then said something to Luke that neither of the others could understand through his mouthful. Finally, he swallowed and said, "Are you crazy? We can't run with her. We'd die! She's not a jogger, Luke. She's a machine. A long distance machine. A fast, long distance machine. You might be able to keep up with her, but I'd lie down and kick the bucket in half a mile."

Luke grinned at Charlie. "Really? You're a fast, long distance machine?"

"No, but I have run him under the table the couple of times he's come with me. Never mind. I'd forgotten all about Tyree. I'll just go meet them now and get it over with. Otherwise, I'll only worry until I do."

Luke shook his head. "Charlie, Charlie, Charlie. You're not going to go meet them now. *You're* not going to go meet them at all. We are going to go meet them. And we're not going to go do it for about another four and a half hours. That'll make it what? One-thirty Montana time. Three-thirty Connecticut time. I'll honor your parents' demands to a point, but we're not going to play their all powerful games. And I know I'm being domineering to say this, but we're not going at all unless you give me your word that if it gets out of hand, we're walking out."

Fo whistled and said, "It's about time you started fighting for her, big guy. Way to be possessive finally!"

Charlie sighed. "Do you truly think this is going to work, Luke? It might be awful."

He came to her and put his arms around her. "Of course it's going to work. Losing you isn't even an option. Do you truly question me? Would you honestly be willing to have someone force you to go somewhere you don't want to go and be with someone you don't choose to be with?"

"No." She shook her head. "You're right. But they're tough. They're really tough."

"Charlie, it's our future they want to take. They have no right to force anyone. God himself wouldn't force someone, even if it was for their good." He smiled. "I'm going to force you to try to remember that, okay?"

She gave him a tenuous smile and nodded. "Okay."

Nudging her chin up so he could look into her eyes, he said, "Good. Because on a serious note, I can't live without you." He gave her that long look again and leaned down and kissed her gently. Fo cleared his throat.

"So, hey, what am I missing? Last night, she was sobbing her eyes out and moving in the morning and you were bitter and depressed and downright surly. What in the heck is going on here tonight?"

Charlie looked at Luke. "You didn't tell him about the pantry?"

"No. Didn't you?"

"I didn't tell him."

"Neither did I." Luke came close to her, smiled and kissed her. "Should we tell him?"

Charlie laughed and kissed him back. "I don't know, what d'you think?"

"Maybe in a minute." At that, Luke proceeded to kiss her in earnest and it almost scared her. It was fun to tease Fo, but facing reality after their charade was going to be tricky.

Fo made a sound of complete disgust and said, "All right, you two. I wanted you to get together, but do you have to do this here?"

Luke pulled away and laughed. "He's right. We should go to the pantry again."

He took her hand and headed for the door, but Fo called after them, "Oh, no you don't. Don't you two dare leave until you tell me why you're so much happier tonight. I have a right to know, you know. I'm the one who has had to listen to both of you blubber. Out with it."

Charlie laughed as they turned around and said, "In all honesty, Fo, I haven't a clue what happened. One minute, I was tearfully telling Richard that I had to go and the next, I was stranded high and dry in the pantry with your cousin here and he was absolutely out of his head. He's still that way. I just hope he stays this way long enough to get rid of my parents."

"Yeah." Luke sat down on the couch and pulled her down beside him. "I've been out of my head since about four months ago when this strikingly beautiful blonde surprised me just out of the shower right over there. Fo knows what a mess I've been, so he isn't going to be surprised. But he could have told me that you had decided you didn't want to go to law school."

Fo put up both hands defensively. "Hey. Just like I told both of you already. This relationship was far too important for me to get in the middle of and screw up. I told you both that. I was caught in the meat grinder between you. So what happened in the pantry?"

Luke pulled Charlie against his side and smiled at Fo. "We can't tell you. A true gentleman- or true gentlewoman- true gentle people never kiss and tell. So we can't tell."

"Well, I figured that, Valentino. Why were you kissing was the question?"

Luke looked down at Charlie and gave her a look that made her stomach go into instant butterflies before he glanced at Fo with a grin and said, "Because it's really fun?"

"Gee, that was informative."

Charlie smacked Luke. "Quit hassling him. I don't know about you, but he truly has gone far beyond the call of duty with me. Just tell him what you told me. Maybe I'll understand it better this time as well."

"I only told her that trying not to pressure her to forego law school and stay here was killing me by degrees.

When I heard her tell my dad she'd decided she wasn't going to go to law school after all and that she loved Montana and was going to come back, I couldn't help myself. I had to haul her into the pantry and fall onto my knees and beg her to accept my hand in marriage and live happily ever after."

Fo turned to her. "Please tell me he's joking."

"Well, yes and no. The pantry is too small for any form of kneeage, but the rest is pretty accurate."

"Holy peanut butter! What did you do?"

Dryly, Luke answered for her. "Felt my forehead and asked me if I was having a stroke. It was very deflating actually."

Fo shook his head and laughed. "Somehow, I don't truly have to ask if you're being serious. I can just see her doing that."

Charlie chipped in, "He failed to mention the other six, yes, six people who were involved in the pantry scene. The only one who didn't try to come in with us was Richard. He just stood outside and chuckled at us."

Mimicking Charlie's response from a few nights before, Fo said, "Sounds too romantical for me."

Charlie chuckled. "Yeah, buddy."

"So did you get yourselves all ironed out so you truly can live happily ever after?"

Both of them hesitated and then Charlie said, "Sort of."

Luke added, "We're working on it."

Fo looked dubiously from one to the other. "So then what's the problem?"

They looked at each other for a second, and then Luke smiled and said, "Charlie's a chicken."

"Huh!" She nudged him with her elbow. "He asked me to marry him like thirteen seconds after he'd been shunning me for forever! What did he expect?"

Fo spun to look at Charlie in disgusted amazement. "You turned him down? You've been blubbering for weeks and you turned him down?" Fo got up and came toward Charlie and she screamed as Fo said, "That is it! You are getting a swirly!"

Charlie latched onto Luke's shirt with a death grip and buried herself into his side. "Luke, no, save me! I had to do it, Fo! Luke! Help me!"

Luke obviously had no idea what to do here. He finally put his arm around Charlie and Fo backed off as Luke asked, "What, may I ask is a swirly?"

Shaking her head, Charlie said, "Oh. You don't even want to know. He never actually does it, but he almost does and it's awful!"

Fo rolled his eyes. "Yeah, please! I've threatened like twice and she's absolutely as strong as me and almost kicked the stuffins out of me the last time. I only have to resort to that when she does something one hundred percent brain dead!" This last he directed loudly at Charlie. "Like turning him down! Man, Charlie. I thought I'd raised you better than this! This is your all time dumbest stunt ever!"

Charlie giggled. "No, it's not. Remember that time when we were in Mrs. Michaelis' class and we were learning to sew together and I accidentally sewed my pant leg to yours and then stood up?"

Fo began to laugh uncontrollably and then collapsed into a heap on the couch beside them again. "Oho, yes I do."

He laughed so hard he fell right off and kept on laughing and finally Luke asked, "Did what I think you're saying, happen?"

Fo tried to catch his breath. "Not only did she pull her pants nearly off in front of our whole third grade class, but she ripped them as well. I remember it clearly. She was wearing polka dot underwear."

"Forest Eldridge! He did not need to know that! You're probably making it up anyway."

"True story. I remember thinking I was so glad boys didn't have to wear stupid looking derwear like that. I had absolutely no sense of adventure then."

"Keep it up, buddy and you'll get a sense of adventure." She turned to Luke. "So, if we're not leaving for another four hours, what are we going to do to keep me from stewing the whole time?"

Luke gave her a wicked grin. "We could go back to the pantry."

"Luke."

"Okay, never mind. We can kiss right here too."

Fo laughed, but then he said, "No, you can't. True gentle people never kiss on the same couch as their roommate. How about a cut throat game of Monopoly. I should be just about whipping up on bof of y'all at about one-thirty."

"In your dreams, Fo." Charlie got up to go get the box out of the trunk in the corner and put it on the coffee table in front of the couch. "You always end up in jail while he and I snap up all the properties."

"Well, then you fall asleep and he always wins you anyway."

"You have a point there. I want to be the hat. What do you want to be, Luke?"

"I still want to be the guy in the pantry."

"Pantry. Now is that by Park Place? Here, be the boot."

"See that, Fo? Just goes to show you can't trust a woman in a top hat. We've only been engaged forty minutes and she just gave me the boot."

"Hey, that was a pretty good one, cuz." Fo and Luke touched fists like a high five.

Charlie handed Fo the box to choose his game piece. "It could have been worse. I could have given you the thimble or the iron. Heck, I could have killed you with the lead pipe in the conservatory. Count your blessings."

"Yeah, I guess getting the boot is better than being killed with a pipe. Do we dare trust Fo to be the banker?"

"Oh, heavens yes. Just make sure you keep him in an office. It's that manual labor you have to worry about with him."

"Look whose talking, Miss Loop the Loop in a hundred and fifty thousand dollar combine."

Charlie was shocked. "Dang, that thing was worth a hundred and fifty big ones? Holy moly, Luke. You trusted me with something that valuable?"

"Ah, honey. I've trusted you with something even more precious. Mah heart."

Fo and Charlie exchanged looks and then she said, "He's *your* cousin."

"Yeah, well he's *your* fiancé'."

"This might be a really long game."

****

It was a long game, but Charlie didn't know that. She finally fell asleep on the couch beside them while Luke soundly beat Fo.

At one fifteen, Luke woke her up and said, "Charlie, you'd better fix your mascara, honey or Elroy is going to think we've been in the pantry all night."

Groggily, she asked, "Does being proposed to smear your mascara? Or kissing?"

He helped her up off the couch and hugged her to him. "You know, I don't believe I've ever been proposed to while wearing mascara. So, I'm not sure. Do you need anything else?"

She stretched and sighed. "Only you to watch my back tonight, Luke Langston. I'm so glad that you're going to be with me, even if you are suddenly bossy."

"Anytime, Charlie."

****

Once they got on the road, Charlie called her dad and asked where they were staying and didn't even feel guilty when he sounded dead tired on the other end of the line. He wasn't very happy to realize Luke truly was accompanying her and that she wouldn't let Elroy come and get her. Then he wanted them to come up to their suite, but Luke had her arrange to meet in the hotel coffee shop instead. Charlie thought it was a good idea. Her mother was less likely to throw a raving fit in public than in private.

At the hotel, Charlie and Luke were seated in the almost empty little restaurant before the others made it down. They chose a large booth near the entrance and Luke had Charlie sit down and then he slid in next to her. When her parents came down with Elroy in their wake, they looked so wasted that Charlie squeezed Luke's hand under the table. This was either going to turn out that they were even grumpier than ever or it would work like a charm. They were all three obviously dead tired.

As soon as they were seated, the waitress came and asked what they wanted to order and Luke ordered a chocolate milkshake. On an impulse, Charlie ordered French Fries and Luke squeezed her hand this time. Fo must have told him about his date the other night as well. Her mother ordered a Diet Coke and the others declined anything. As the server left, Luke said, "What did you need to talk to us about?"

Her father frowned right off the bat. "Honestly, Mr. Langston. We wanted to talk to our daughter alone."

Luke lifted her left hand with its huge flashing solitaire onto the table in front of them and idly began to play with the ring as he replied, "We've chosen to spend the rest of eternity together, Dr. Evans. From here on out we want to make plans for our lives together. What was it that you wanted?"

Leaning forward, her mother answered bluntly, "What we wanted was to talk some sense into our daughter, Luke. She's a brilliant, talented girl and we'll not see her throw her life away with some cowboy at the outer edge of civilization while she teaches school like some commoner. I'm assuming it was you who encouraged her to abandon her plans to continue her education at law school, and while that may benefit you, it certainly won't benefit her. As her loving parents, we must demand that she end this foolish engagement and let us take her back and help her get ready to move on."

Charlie was frankly surprised that she didn't feel intimidation, only deep, seething anger. She stood and beckoned the server and when she came over, she said, "I'm so sorry to inconvenience you, but could we get that milkshake and order of fries to go please. We won't be staying after all."

The waitress left and Charlie sat back down and calmly faced the two suddenly not so all-powerfuls and their pitiful sidekick. "I'll have you know, Mother, Luke didn't know anything about my decision to forego law school until this morning. I will also have you know that I know this is what the Lord has in mind for me and that it's turned out to be the best decision I've made in my life. I'm where I'm supposed to be, with whom I'm supposed to be and if you can't love and accept me as a wife and mother and someday, when my children are grown, as a kindergarten teacher, then you will have to live with your decision. I truly hope that won't be the case, but if it is, I'm still going to choose to live at the outer edge of *heaven* and be a *commoner* married to a wonderful, godly rancher who loves me whether I have a high status career or not."

She stood and leaned on her hands across the table. "Do I make myself perfectly clear?"

Her mother stood as well. "Charlene Marie Evans, I will not be spoken to in this manner!"

Charlie dug in her purse and pulled out a twenty dollar bill. She handed it to the server who was approaching their table. "Thank you so much, for your help, Miss." Luke stood as well as Charlie looked at her mother again. "My name is Charlie, Norma. And soon it's going to be Charlie Langston. I hope you have a lovely flight home." She picked up the paper sack the server had brought and said to Luke, "Come, my dear common cowboy. Let's go home." Without another look at her parents, she turned her back on them, took Luke's hand and they went out of the restaurant and through the lobby to the parking lot.

As he helped her up into the driver's side of his truck, she started to cry and he wrapped an arm around her and pulled her close. "Don't cry, Charlie. You were magnificent. Don't cry."

She sniffled as he handed her a handkerchief. "I'm sorry. I just hate having to treat someone like that. But there was no way I was going to sit there and have her insult you the way she was."

Starting up the truck, he buckled his seat belt and then helped her buckle hers. "It is heartbreaking Charlie, to have to speak to your mother that way, but I honestly don't think she would have listened to you and respected your decision if you hadn't. You kind of had to speak her language. Maybe now that she's accepted that you can make a decision and stick to it against them, they'll back off."

She smiled up at him through her tears. "You're kind, Luke. I doubt it will be that easy, but wouldn't that be wonderful? Thank you so much for helping me through that. I could never have done it without you." She reached and patted his cheek with her sparkling left hand. "You're such a sweetie."

He leaned down and kissed her, once, long and slowly. "You're tired."

"Yes. Way tired."

He kissed her again. "And you're welcome."

"Thanks."

"And you're beautiful."

She gave a single laugh as he kissed her again and she said, "Thank you, Luke, but we should get back. It's after two in the morning."

"But we need to eat those French fries dipped in the shake."

"You drive. I'll dip and share them with you. Have you ever dipped fries before?"

"Never. But I've heard it's very romantical."

When they crossed the bridge, Luke asked, "Where do you want me to take you, Charlie? Can I take you back to the bunkhouse? It's almost two-thirty."

"Would you mind checking through my house for me to make sure no one is inside? I truly shouldn't stay in the bunkhouse. It looks terrible."

"Honey, I'm worried about your safety. Not how it looks."

"I'll be safe inside with the deadbolts locked. But thank you."

"Will you be afraid?"

She didn't want to answer that. "Sometimes. I'm sorry. I try not to be."

"I'll take you to get some of your things, but then let's take you back to the bunkhouse. Or the main house. You pick."

"The bunkhouse. You know, we still didn't seriously finish talking about me moving away to keep your family safe. It has to be done. We might as well face it."

He pulled up in front of her cabin. "Let's face it in the morning, Charlie. I'm too tired to argue with you tonight. Stay here with the doors locked for a second while I check out your house." He got out and then reached under his seat and pulled out a pistol that looked just like hers only about twice as big and then took the key she held out to him. A minute or two later, he came back out and got her and took her in to retrieve her things.

By the time she was settled into the bunkhouse, she honestly was too tired to worry about appearances and went right to sleep.

Chapter 14

She could hear the others stirring the next morning and she sat up and looked over to see Luke headed to the shower with his shaving kit in tow. Fo was dressed and sitting at the little table with a bowl of cold cereal in front of him. She got up and slipped into the jacket to the warm up pants she was wearing with her t-shirt, made her bed and gathered up her things. Running a hand through her hair, she gave Fo a high five as she headed out the door. "Thanks for letting me crash again. Tell Luke I said good morning. I'm going for a run."

Fo finished his bite and then called after her, "You watch yourself, Chuck. Which way are you headed?"

"Just down across the little bridge and through the south meadow along the creek. I'll have the security guys check it on the four wheelers before I go and I'll be in sight the whole time, I promise. I'll be fine. Have a great day."

"You too."

She stretched for a moment on the porch and dug her cell phone out of her pocket to call the security guys. Then she went down along the path, wishing that Fo hadn't mentioned Tyree again, even as tactfully as he had. It made that fear come up in her again like bile in her soul.

She hated feeling this way all the time lately. It all but over shadowed the sweet euphoria she'd been feeling ever since the pantry scene. And it tended to jam any inspiration she was getting from the Spirit. She felt like she was being prompted to be cautious every single moment it seemed and it was wearing on her. Even right now, in the clear light of a beautiful morning, she felt as if it wasn't safe to be out here running in plain sight of everyone.

Glancing around nervously at the scattered trees here beside the stream, she turned her head to listen better. It was hard to tell if what she was hearing was just the riffle of the water, or if there was another sound occasionally that didn't belong amidst the gurgle of the creek. Holy moly it would be nice when Tyree didn't haunt her.

****

Luke got out of the shower, dressed and shaved, then was disappointed when he walked out to find Charlie's bed neatly made and her gone. Fo looked up from his breakfast and said, "She asked me to tell you that she wished you were out here to drop to your knees and beg her for her hand in marriage and to live happily ever after."

"Seriously? She said that?"

Fo laughed. "No. But maybe she was thinking it. She did say to tell you good morning."

"Where'd she go?"

"For a run. South along the creek. She said she'd have security check first and stay in sight. She just left. She's probably still at her house. Maybe you should go up there and drop to your knees and..."

"Yeah. I got it already. Have a good day at work. Tell Amy hello." Luke walked out the door and stood on the porch looking south toward Charlie's house, wondering if she would laugh if he went and dropped to his knees to beg for her hand in marriage and to live happily ever after. He saw her on the trail beyond her cabin, running smoothly, her blonde curls pulled back into a bouncy ponytail.

He turned away and went to step off the porch and at that moment she screamed.

Looking back toward her, he could see her fighting with a man who must have come from somewhere on the stream bank below her. Luke sucked in a breath and turned and ducked back into the bunkhouse and yanked the rifle off the wall again as he yelled at Fo, "Tyree has her down by the creek. Call the police and come help me."

As he leapt off the deck, she miraculously broke free for just a second, but Tyree caught her again and began dragging her, kicking and fighting toward the willows near the creek. Luke threw the rifle to his shoulder and being careful not to aim anywhere near where Charlie was fighting him, he squeezed off a shot. Tyree was startled and Charlie jerked away again and this time got clear free for longer, but once again, Tyree caught her.

Richard and Tuckett and several of the hands appeared in response to the gunshot. When Luke was sure they could see what was happening, he dropped the gun to the deck, ripped open his truck door, grabbed his handgun and headed for Charlie on the run. He stumbled and nearly went to his knees as he charged down the incline beside the road and was immensely grateful when he heard a shot come from the proximity of the main house. His dad was a crack shot and he was sure Tyree knew that. Richard was a bit of a legend in the valley.

A third time, Charlie broke free and this time when Tyree went to lunge for her, a shot from the house either winged him or startled him enough that she was able to slip out of his grasp. She began to run back toward the ranch yard as fast as she could fly. And Fo had been right, this girl could run! Tyree made one more lunge for her. This time there was no doubt he'd been hit as his leg buckled beneath him and he went to the ground in a heap as Charlie ran for all she was worth toward Luke.

Relief burned through Luke like a straight hit of adrenaline and then he was horrified to realize that even though Tyree was down and out of commission, he had produced a pistol and was now shooting at the girl he had just tried to abduct.

Luke skidded to a stop on the path and pulled his gun up as he yelled, "Charlie, drop into the ditch! The ditch!" She understood and made a dive into the dry ditch beside her as Luke drew a bead on Tyree with his pistol. He was still sixty yards or more off, but at least Luke could deter him from aiming for any part of Charlie that was still exposed by the angle of the hillside.

Before Luke could squeeze off the trigger, another shot rang from the house. Tyree jerked again and then tossed his gun aside and raised both hands, one higher than the other. Luke could hear him curse and yell, "Okay! Don't shoot! Okay! Don't shoot! Don't Shoot!"

Several men from the ranch yard advanced with rifles and the security guard came roaring by on an ATV. Disgusted with their failed check of her running route, Luke ran ahead to where Charlie lay flat against the bottom of the ditch. He looked up at Tyree, then back at the advancing riflemen and dropped into the ditch beside her.

She was face down and he put a gentle hand on her back. "Charlie, are you hurt? Can you talk to me? Turn over, honey. You're safe now. The others will keep him until the police come and take him away."

She slowly turned to look at him, her face deathly pale, her eyes huge but tear free. That almost scared him. She appeared to be half in a state of shock. "Are you okay, Charlie? Talk to me. Where are you hurt?" All she did was shake her head and he sat down beside her and gathered her tightly into his arms. "Say something, babe. Are you hurt or just scared?"

"Just... Just scared. At least I think so." She turned her face into his neck. "I knew you'd come, Luke. I knew you would."

"I did. I did come and he's going to be gone for good now. And you're okay. Keep talking to me, tell me if anything hurts. Did he hurt your shoulder again? Did you land okay? When you dove in here?"

"Yeah, I landed okay. My shoulder is a little tender. I knew you'd come. Oh, Luke, knowing that made such a difference."

She finally started to cry and he took a deep breath and held her even tighter. "That's it, let it all go, Charlie. It's over and I came and you're okay. It's finally over."

He rubbed her back and shoulder as she cried and spoke low and softly into her ear and encouraged her to let it all go. They were still sitting there in the ditch when Richard approached and squatted down beside them. Luke looked up and met his eyes and said, "Charlie, my dad is here to check on you." He smoothed her back again and said absolutely reassuringly, "She's okay, Dad. She knew I'd come and she's okay. Tyree's going to finally be taken away permanently and it's over. And she's okay. Aren't you Charlie?"

She nodded against his neck and then looked up at Richard, the tears still streaming down her face. She tried to speak through her tears. "I truly am okay; I don't know why I can't get a handle on these tears. Just give me a... Just give me a minute and I'll be... I'll be fine."

They finally heard sirens coming down the road. Luke pulled her close again and held her, still rubbing her back as his dad headed out into the field. A few minutes later, two police cars came up the lane and pulled right into the field between where Charlie and Luke were sitting and where the others had Tyree spread eagled on his face. Both officers went toward Tyree and a minute later another siren sounded and then an ambulance pulled in as well. The paramedics on board approached Luke and Charlie and when she tearfully refused help, they headed for Tyree.

One of the hands pulled up on a four wheeler and got off and said, "Your dad said to bring this to you. Do you want me to help you lift her?"

"No." Luke shook his head. "She'll be okay in a minute. Leave it there, would you? Thanks." He leaned down close to her ear. "Charlie, they brought us a four-wheeler. Are you up to a short ride? Let's get you out of this field, shall we? I can take you to your house or up to Madge or the bunkhouse. What do you want to do?"

She finally raised her head, tears still in her eyes. "Can I just go back to my house? Would you stay there with me for a while?"

"As long as you want, honey. Let me help you up."

Back at her house, he pulled the quilt off of her bed and wrapped her in it and went and sat in the porch swing with her bundled in it. It was probably seventy degrees out here, but she was still shivering and trying not to cry and he began to worry about her going into shock again. Fo came around the corner of the house and Luke had never been so glad to see someone. He leaned in close to Charlie's ear again and said, "Hey, Fo's here. Do you want to talk to him?" She opened her eyes and smiled at her old friend and just enough of a hint of her old spark showed through to make Luke heave a sigh of relief.

Squatting down beside the swing, Fo ruffled her tangled curls. "It's over, Chuck. This whole mess is finally over. You can move on with your life now. Doesn't that feel awesome?" She blinked away the last of her tears and nodded and Fo went on, "Would you like a blessing? It might really help right now."

She rolled back from Luke's chest and looked up again. "I would love one, thanks. Do you mind?"

"Absolutely not. What do you need right now?"

She looked from one of them to the other and took a shuddering breath. "Strength. Strength to get back up and keep on and not live in this fear anymore. Strength to go forward and deal with my family. And wisdom and judgment. I don't want much, do I?"

Luke hugged her. "Those are pretty reasonable needs right now, Charlie. Your Father in Heaven loves you and will send what you need."

They blessed her and then with Fo on one side of her and wrapped in Luke's arms in her blanket, the emotional storm took its toll and she fell into an exhausted sleep.

****

The police had grilled Luke over and again and finally left after promising to come back and question Charlie. And Fo had gone off to work. Luke was still sitting in the swing holding her when he was surprised to see both of her parents come around the corner of her house. They came up to him and looked down at her sleeping and for a second he wasn't sure how to react. Finally, deciding he was going to treat them as if they would someday have the friendly in-law relationship he'd always hoped for, he said pleasantly, "Dr. and Mrs. Evans, this is a surprise. I thought you'd long be on a plane over the Midwest by now."

Her dad replied tersely, "Elroy left. We decided to stay. Is she sick?"

Surprised that they hadn't heard what had happened, he answered, "Not exactly. She's just not feeling so great right now. I don't think we should wake her up.

Go on in and make yourselves at home. Do you need anything?"

Still not mincing words, her father said, "No, we're fine. We'll go run some errands and be back in a while."

An hour later, she stirred in his arms and after a moment, she looked up at him with those remarkable, clear blue eyes that matched the sky there above the river valley. He smiled down at her, "Welcome back, Sleeping Beauty. Were you able to rest?"

She nodded. "Oh my heck, I can't believe I actually fell asleep. I'm sorry I've made you waste your whole morning."

With a shrug, he said, "There are worse ways to spend a few hours than holding a beautiful girl. Plus, it gave me some time to think. Are you hungry?"

"Starving." She sat up and began to unwrap out of the quilt. "And way warm. I've probably roasted you out. Sorry."

"It's all okay, Charlie. I was happy. In spite of it all. Happy and grateful that you are still here, all in one piece, in my arms."

A shadow flitted across the blue of her eyes and she asked, "Was he okay? Did he make it out of the field?"

Luke sighed and reached for her hand. "Yeah. He made it. He had a pretty busted up leg and a bullet hole through one arm, but he'll live to learn to make license plates until he's much more mature. How are you feeling?"

The tears welled back up into her eyes. "A little stiff. And like you, grateful to still be here in your arms, all in one piece. And unbelievable grateful that they caught him."

"I asked Dad to threaten to sue both the security company and the whole state of Montana for all of it after he'd been arrested and even had a restraining order against him. I doubt they would have ever let him out on bail, but I'm sure they won't now." He hesitated. "Um, you should also know that your parents are here, somewhere. They showed up about an hour ago, without Elroy. I don't think they had even been told what happened here this morning. I didn't offer to wake you and they decided to go run errands."

Charlie groaned. "I pretty much expected that. Although I'm surprised that Elroy wasn't with. Where was he?"

"They said he left."

"That probably means they spent the night checking into your background and found out that you're suitably wealthy. Maybe they've decided to have him bow out gracefully so it won't be so hard to insist I go back to school."

He put an arm around her to pull her gently against him. "Now, Charlie. You're sounding positively bitter. That's not like you."

"I know. I'm sorry. But did you hear the way she said, 'Commoner' last night? I swear, she should have used a British accent. She sounded as if she thought she was the Queen of Buckingham Palace thrice removed. Commoner!"

"She only wants what she thinks is best for her daughter."

"No." Charlie leaned up and turned to look at him. "She may think that, but this is about appearances. And I'm sorry, but I'm not playing her game."

He tugged her back to lean against him again. "I know, honey. And I'm so proud of you. Both for standing up to them so well and for having your priorities right. I don't think you'll ever regret making your career a lower priority than they have. I think your children will feel much differently about their mother than you do about yours."

She got quiet for a minute and then she began to finger the ring he had given her the night before with the big solitaire diamond. Finally, she said, "We need to talk about some things, Luke."

"I know."

"No. I mean." She tipped her head to look up into his face from where she laid against his shoulder. "I do love you, Luke. And I'm truly grateful you gave me this ring when you did. And I think it will work to get rid of my parents eventually, although it may take a little more time. But I can't expect you to honor a proposal made because two tough old birds were pounding on the door like the big bad wolf. Getting roped into being engaged to me to protect me from them is no more fair to you than offering to marry Lindie out of a sense of responsibility because of the baby."

Luke paused for a minute, hoping to say this right and not mess it up. "I knew you were going to say that, Charlie. And I'll agree to taking it back. But only with the understanding that you know I want to give it right back to you over a candlelight dinner and in a more romantic setting. You and I are nothing like the situation with Lindie. And I'm sorry we even have to have this conversation. At the time I talked to her about getting married, it was simply that I felt it had to be done for her and the baby. I do love Lindie, but she's like my little sister."

He looked down at Charlie's mouth and then back up into her eyes as he stroked her fingers with his thumb and said huskily, "What I feel toward you, Charlie, is most definitely not brotherly."

He leaned and kissed her gently, letting his mouth linger and taste her lips as she kissed him back. Finally, he pulled back. "No, definitely not brotherly. I want to be the father of those children of yours that we were talking about."

Her eyes flew open and he had to smile at the mixed expression of panic and need he saw there. He chuckled. "Sorry, but I don't want anymore misunderstandings between us. I'll take the ring back, but I love you and I need you and I can't let you go. It has to be with the understanding that you're getting it back."

She watched him quietly, her face there only inches from his and he could hardly help himself when he found himself kissing her again. He pulled her tightly into his arms and literally tried to breathe her in as she kissed him back for the first time without any of the hesitation he'd felt from her every other time he'd found himself unable to resist that beautiful, sweet mouth.

The feel of her mouth and her scent and this heady emotion filled his brain like a drug. He'd never felt this way about a girl. Never even knew it was possible. It was amazing how much more vital the eternities had become now that he knew he had found her and that they were looking and planning toward the future. So much that had been frustrated hopes of someday had finally distilled into sharp, clear, inspiring focus.

It was a demanding "Huthumm." that brought them screeching back to the present. It nearly made him swear to pull away from her. *Geez, what a frustrating interruption.* It took them a second to look up and face her tough old birds. Charlie kept her composure very well, all things considered. She didn't even bother to sit up straight out of his embrace as she said, "Mom, Dad. Luke told me you were here somewhere. I thought you said you had a plane to catch."

Luke leaned forward as her father said, "We decided it was more important to stay and try to talk some sense into you than go home and deal with a number of vital, pressing responsibilities. Your life is by far more of a priority."

Charlie made a sound of complete, tired frustration. "Dad, did it ever occur to you that my life was *my* life? I'm twenty-three years old. Was it not just glaringly obvious that my life is dandy right now? Don't even start. I'm too tired to argue. As inhospitable as it sounds, if you're only going to start in ramming your ideology down my throat again, frankly, I have better things to do. Go home and operate on someone and let me get on with my own, beautiful, peaceful existence out of your circle of status.

"If whether I have the properly heavy hitting spouse and career is that much of a desperate concern to you, then lie to whomever you're trying to impress at the time. Make up some fairy tale scenario that properly strokes your ego and I'll stay here at the edge of heaven and no one will be the wiser. Just leave me the heck alone."

She looked back up at Luke and then leaned against his shoulder again. "Go home, Mom and Dad. I'm never going to cave this time. I'm through with your social farce. My priorities are poles apart from yours and I'm finally sick of trying to keep you happy. There's too much at stake now. Luke's and my children will *never* go to daycare. Just go home. Maybe you can get Elroy to marry a Nobel Prize winning PhD slash MD slash MBA attorney who owns a university and you could claim both of them and tell people I was killed out in Montana. You can even tell them I died in law school. Just don't expect me to be anything other than an at-home mom for years and years and years. Cause it aint gonna happen."

She emphasized the last part with a marked drawl and a slight raise in volume and Luke was hard put not to crack a grin, in spite of the anger he could feel emanating from her father.

Surprisingly, her mother seemed to visibly wilt. She appeared to age years as the tough old bird in her became a weathered chicken. Luke wasn't sure what caused the change and what to expect, but he caught an inkling as she said, "You're wise beyond your years, Charlie. I wish I'd had the chance at your age to make a choice like that. We'll go. You're right. We have no right to interfere. And it would appear you're perfectly capable of being decisive, finally." She turned to Luke. "Please be good to her, Luke. She's a wonderful girl. But I'm sure you already know that."

Norma Evans turned back towards the Hummer parked in the gravel drive and Charlie's father glowered as he looked at his wife. "Now wait a minute here, Norma. What do you mean, we'll go? You're not just going to let her get away with this, are you?"

"She loves him, Keith. That should be obvious."

"Love isn't the issue here. Don't be ridiculous!"

The tough old bird was back as she faced her husband. "We're not going to lose a daughter over this, Keith. She loves him. Look at her. And she's right. She's old enough to choose and she's obviously finally learned to make decision. She's an intelligent girl. And it is what the prophets counsel, after all. If they can afford it, she should stay with her kids. She'll never wish she'd spent more time with her children the way I do. And we're *not* going to lose a daughter over this."

She turned back and walked to Charlie. "Oh, and we heard a news story as we drove. A local woman was attacked and nearly abducted and killed as she jogged somewhere nearby. I know you like to jog occasionally. Be careful. It appears to be quite lawless out here. Goodbye, honey." She leaned to hug Charlie for a long moment and said, "We truly do love you. Please stay in touch."

With that, she walked to the big military vehicle and let herself into the passenger seat as her husband nearly stomped after her saying, "Norma Jean Evans, don't you dare give up that easily." He got into the Hummer beside her and Luke and Charlie tried not to watch as they had an obviously controversial discussion for several minutes before her father started up the engine and drove out with a little kick of gravel flying off the back wheels.

Charlie and Luke sat in silence for a minute or two before Charlie finally said, "I can hardly even believe it. She respected my will. That's amazing." She shook her head in wonder and then went on softly. "I knew she'd worked to put him through med school, but I never dreamed for all these years she'd had regrets. Who would ever have guessed that?"

"She had to have had, didn't she? She's not stupid. She knew you hated day care. And you yourself said she was a wonderful Christian woman. Maybe all of this hype has only been to rationalize the choices they've regretted all these years. At any rate, I think they honestly are going this time."

Charlie turned and looked up at him earnestly. "You know. I probably truly owe you some huge apologies. Not only did I let you muddle through all of this beside me, but I also said some things to them I didn't have the right to say, since you and I haven't honestly discussed them all that thoroughly. I'm grateful for your help with my parents, but please forgive me for taking advantage of your willingness to convince them."

"What are you talking about, Charlie?"

"Mmm, well, I've said a lot of things to them that I feel strongly about, but in light of our lightning fast engagement, I didn't actually clear any of it with you first. Take for instance insinuating that we truly are going to be married and have a family and have me be an at- home mom for years. That wasn't very fair to say when we've never talked about it."

"You know how I feel about wanting to be married to you. And you know how I feel about children needing to be mothered. If you truly can be happy without an outside career, you know that's in the best interest of our family. None of that's a problem, is it?"

She hesitated. "It's just that I feel I took advantage of your willingness to rescue me at the spur of the moment, Luke. If you recall, it was only early yesterday morning that you were still very allergic to me."

He thought about that for several minutes and then asked, "Charlie, tell me something, honestly. Did you mean what you said about knowing you were where your Heavenly Father wanted you, with who you were supposed to be with?" He looked into her eyes and waited for her to answer.

He could feel the tension build in her and then she looked away and nodded her head. Her voice was low and so quiet, he almost didn't hear her when she finally said, "Yeah. I did."

"And do you believe me when I tell you I'm in love with you and want to be with you forever and ever?" Again she nodded. "Then give me the ring."

Her eyes flew to his as her fingers settled around the ring on her left hand almost defensively. "What?"

He smiled. "We need to settle this once and for all then. Give me the ring."

"What are you saying, Luke?'

He stood up and pulled her to her feet. "I'm saying that I want to be officially engaged without you questioning whether I truly want to be that way. Don't I need to go through this big charade of taking it back, and then planning some incredibly involved and intricate scheme to propose to you to make you know my intentions are honorable and eternal?"

She hesitated again, still watching his eyes and then asked, "Haven't we just gone to great lengths to convince my parents we aren't interested in charades?"

"Yes."

"You're not going to change your mind about me anytime soon are you?"

"Not for eighty or ninety million years, at least. Why?"

She smiled shyly at him. "Well, do you think we could settle for some middle ground and just meet back in the pantry to do this?"

Luke couldn't help himself and laughed and said, "I believe I could handle that. Do we have to wait any certain period of time?"

"No. Definitely not."

"Good." He took her hand and together they set off down the path toward his dad's house.

He had to laugh again when she asked, "Luke, do you think that after we get unequivocally engaged, we could eat some Oreos in the pantry? Because I'm starving."

Nodding with a grin, he said, "Absolutely. After all, they are the fifth food group."

The End

About the Author

Jaclyn M. Hawkes grew up in Utah with 6 sisters, 4 brothers and any number of pets. (It was never boring!) She got a bachelor's degree, had a career and traveled extensively before settling down to her life's work of being the mother of four magnificent and sometimes challenging children. She loves shellfish, the out of doors, the youth, and hearing her children laugh. She and her extremely attractive husband, their family, and their sometimes very large pets, now live in a mountain valley in northern Utah, where it smells like heaven and kids still move sprinkler pipe.

To learn more about Jaclyn, visit, **www.jaclynmhawkes.com**.

Jaclyn loves to hear from her readers. Write to her at jaclynm.hawkes@yahoo.com